TRUE COLOURS
of the CHAMELEON
Manda Benson

TANGENTRINE

www.tangentrine.com

Tangentrine Ltd,
Unit 2, The Old Poultry Houses
Alcombe
Wiltshire

www.tangentrine.com

Second edition published by Tangentrine 2024
First published by Tangentrine 2014

British Library Cataloguing in Publication Data. A catalogue
record for this book is available from the British Library.

ISBN: 978-0-9566080-9-3

The meeting of two personalities is like the contact of two chemical substances: if there is any reaction, both are transformed.

-Carl Jung

1

BLACK SHEEP

I know there are a great many people who think the decisions I made and the things we did were wrong. Had circumstances turned out differently, perhaps I would have had to stand up in court and admit I'd made a mistake, and apologise sincerely to the jury for it. That's what my barrister would likely advise me to do, and with all the evidence against us it would be lunacy to plead Not Guilty. But if I had the chance to live it again, I wouldn't have any of it differently. I'd rather face my guilt with him beside me than suffer a clear conscience alone.

He chose the engagement ring I wear. There's a piece of paper that says we're married, although the names on it aren't ours, and there was never a ceremony and we didn't swear any oath. Depending on each other for our very survival bound us together more strongly than any wedding vow or legal document ever could.

I don't blame myself for what happened in the past any more. To claim I was completely unaccountable for what went on would be unrealistic, but I see now that it would be equally naïve to think it my fault entirely when other people had taken it upon themselves to make things difficult. I don't think any more about what might have been, and I've stopped envying them for having what I haven't. That's just the way the dice fell.

There's a scientific theory to do with quantum

mechanics, that says every time a decision is made, the universe branches into different contingencies. If that's the case, somewhere around in all that abstract metaphysical stuff there's a version of reality in which we didn't fuck up our lives. There's a parallel universe where we're not both dead.

2

FADED TO GREY

A van had just pulled up as I was leaving the Jobcentre. The side of it displayed only the Birmingham City coat of arms with no indication of what division it belonged to, but I guessed from the appearance of the driver and the things he was getting out through the back door that it was pest control. The Chinese takeaway had rats.

A man stood smoking, blocking the pavement between the van and the road. I've worked with several of the compounds in tobacco smoke. You need to sign a health and safety form saying you understand the risks and listing what precautions you'll take before you're allowed to use them. A couple of them, there's even a law that says you're not allowed to work with them at all if you're female, in case you get pregnant and don't realise, and they make the foetus deformed.

"'Allo," he said as I tried to pass him.

I glanced at him quickly and said, "Hi," in return.

"Excuse me," he continued, before I'd made it far enough away to reasonably pretend I hadn't heard. "I've seen you here before. You're the doctor, right?"

I stopped and faced him. I wanted to get back to the car and get home. Today wasn't going well and I didn't want this conversation. Probably the man thought it amusing, but I didn't see my qualifications as a positive thing any more. I'd applied for several jobs paying minimum wage. Employers wouldn't look at me twice. I was overqualified.

"I think you're mistaken."

The man glanced up and down me, like he was appraising my attire for a job interview. He was middle-aged with close-cropped receding black hair, and either very tanned or he had a bit more than just Anglo-Saxon in his DNA. "I don't think so. You're the doctor who comes down the dole office."

"I'm not a medical doctor."

He cocked an eyebrow. "What kind of a doctor are you, then?"

I sighed. "No offence, but what does it matter? I used to have a job and now I haven't. I'm the same as everyone else who comes down here."

The man met my dismissal with a persistent stare. He breathed smoke in a steady stream through his nostrils. "It matters 'cause I could have a lead on a job that might suit you."

I didn't expect he did. The staff in the Jobcentre couldn't find me a job, and this man didn't look like he worked there. Only a nagging suspicion that something wasn't quite right stopped me from walking away, that and desperation...

I needed a job. My savings were gone. Jobseeker's Allowance on top of the mortgage contributions didn't cover the cost of the house, let alone food and other necessities. With summer drawing to a close, it would soon be getting cold again, and there would be nothing to pay the gas bill. If there was even a chance, it might be worth it. "I used to be a research chemist... a scientist who designs medicines."

"Ah."

Something in the man's manner suggested more. Then it occurred to me: perhaps the work was illegal.

"Now, I wondered if you might like to come to my meeting tonight." He shrugged and heaved his eyebrows. "There's a position going that might be right up your street."

"Meeting?"

"There are six of us. We talk about work, and the lack of it, and how we can make some. It's like, self employment, making your own business. It's at eight and we meet up the road in the bridge club if you're interested." He pointed out the direction.

"Thank you." I wasn't sure how to react. "I'll see if I can make it."

The man raised his cigarette and dipped his head at me as I left.

It was a muggy afternoon in late September, the leaves on the trees lining the pavement becoming dusty and worn. A cloud passed over the sun, fading out the shadows of foliage and parked cars. Going over the conversation in my head as I walked back to my car gave me an unnerving feeling, product of having spent my youth being warned of the dangers of strange men, yet that didn't make any sense. Pimps and perverts might prey on kids and drunken undergraduates, but they don't prey on thirty-year-old women who wear sensible shoes.

Perhaps he worked for an employability programme and he wanted a good cross-section of different backgrounds for his meeting. But then, why had he not said so? There would have been forms to fill in and dotted lines to sign if that had been the case. He would have been sitting at a desk wearing a badge, not standing outside. I couldn't rationalise away the only explanation that made any sense: that the man intended to do something illegal and he wanted a scientist to help him because it involved explosives, poisons, or illegal drugs. From his brazen approach, I was to take it he didn't care if I suspected this.

A suffocating wave of hot air escaped the car when I opened the door. I sat in the driver's seat and put the key in the ignition, leaving the door open to let cooler air in. I sighed as I took the SatNav out of my handbag and slotted it into its stand. The easiest and most sensible thing would be to go home and forget this, and hope never to cross paths with the man in the Jobcentre again.

"At the end of the road," said the SatNav in David Attenborough's voice, "turn left."

*

My father crashed his Cavalier when I was nine years old. I'd been sitting behind him, and to this day I still recall the screams and the flying glass. He'd always been a careful driver, not the sort to turn right in front of an oncoming Morris Minor. When the police questioned him, it transpired he'd lost his job a week earlier, but he'd been too ashamed to tell my mother and me. He'd let it gather pressure inside him, carried on going out every morning, almost as though pretending hard enough would make it true. I've no idea where he spent the days.

I watched him fall apart, watched the person he'd been sink into the black waters of a nightmarish lagoon. I hadn't expected to follow in his footsteps. Thinking back, it was probably, subconsciously, one of the reasons I took all those qualifications. Back then, and I suppose still now, university was hyped up as a passport out of the vagaries of the job market.

A letter lay on the mat when I opened my front door. Inside it was an electricity bill, for over a hundred pounds.

I searched all the trade websites for jobs. There was only

one I was qualified to do, and it was working with someone I knew was a professional friend of my old boss. There was little point in applying for it. I would write that I had into the record the Jobcentre insisted I bring in every week. That would keep their requirements satisfied.

I hid the bill under the cushion on the sofa, and put a DVD on. I'd seen it so many times before it had become banal, but it was better than letting the silence get inside me. All the surfaces in the small kitchen were covered with unwashed pots, but I couldn't bring myself to do anything about it. Perhaps tomorrow.

I found myself studying my possessions again, wondering what I could get for them and whether I could manage without. I couldn't really cancel the phone line, as I needed Internet access to apply for jobs. The same went for my laptop. The television itself wouldn't sell for much, but at least I wouldn't have to pay the licence fee. As it didn't need renewing until December, there was no point doing anything yet. I considered some other things, the pans in the kitchen, the shabby furniture I'd bought from a charity shop when I'd moved in, because I'd put down all my savings on the deposit. Nothing else was worth anything.

I was going to have to face up to this and sell my car. Although it had been valuable when it was new, I wouldn't get much for it now. I'd been so proud of that car when I'd bought it. I'd worked so hard to save the money. Now it had been reduced to a white elephant, something that drank ever-more-expensive petrol and ate MOT and tax and insurance bills every year. If I got invited to a job interview I'd have to use public transport or rent a car, and get a loan to buy another if I did eventually get offered a job. I didn't use it much now because I couldn't afford to. I did my weekly shopping by walking to the supermarket dragging a suitcase with wheels on the bottom corner. It would probably take more than an hour to walk to the Jobcentre, but I'd have to manage. I used to be able to walk that far every day to university when I was an undergraduate, but two years ago I'd taken a tiny fragment of glass from a lab explosion in the knee, one that surgeons couldn't easily remove without doing more damage, and these days it was bad enough after doing the shopping once a week.

It would buy a few months at best.

It felt like my ribcage was shrinking around a pressure building up inside, as though something was trying to burst out. We fight so hard for the things we want. When things are good, we don't think the wind will ever change, but it does, and then life turns on us and takes them. I forced myself to inhale, concentrating on an imaginary point deep inside me and pushing the ache back down into that space. I pictured a black hole there inside me, that I could sink my stupid emotions in. Panicking over it would not help.

The smoking man's invitation came back to me. Desperation was the only reason I was even considering taking it up. I didn't need a criminal record on top of all the other things that were stopping me getting a job, but if there was a chance of getting money out of what he was offering, wasn't that worth at least trying to find out more? If it meant I didn't have to sell the car, and could last a bit longer? If it was bombs or poison, I couldn't agree to that. But what if it was drugs? That might be something I could countenance, if it might mean the difference between staying afloat a bit longer or going under. If I didn't go I'd never find out what it was about and confirm or disprove my suspicions. I might regret it tomorrow.

The DVD had finished now, and the machine switched itself off. The house was growing oppressively still once more. I'd never been a very social person, but the idea of meeting some people for once was novel compared to another evening at home, listening to music I didn't even like any more because I'd played it so often. Perhaps I'd have more in common with these people than with my colleagues in my old job, whom I'd never felt I quite fitted in with, whose company I'd only endured for the sake of politics and the wish not to be alone. It would be better than spending the evening alone and letting my mind take the route it invariably did if it wasn't otherwise occupied.

It wouldn't do any harm to at least go to the place and look about. If anything looked dodgy, I could always turn around and go home. Driving to the location put me in no obligation to go to the meeting. I could make that decision when I had more information.

The day had faded into muggy dusk when I went out to the car after a meal of boiled lentils and vegetables that had been reduced in the supermarket because they were about to pass their expiry date. The air carried a smell of barbecue smoke and burnt food. I started the engine and set the SatNav. Headlamps cut through the half-light, illuminating the road ahead as I turned out from the drive.

"Taking the third exit at the roundabout, continue for half a mile," said Robbie Coltrane's voice.

I reached across and pressed one of the buttons on the SatNav. It had been a present from my aunt and uncle, whom I used to drive around. They had lived in a village nearby, but shortly before I got made redundant their house had been burgled, and they had decided to move to New Zealand to be near their son, fearing they would become decrepit and incapable of managing alone in their old age. They said they didn't want to be a burden, that I shouldn't be working all my free time as an unpaid chauffeur to a pair of old farts. They didn't seem to understand that I liked their company, that responsibilities do people good.

A different route for today. "At the roundabout," said Jeremy Clarkson's voice, "take the second exit, avoiding the speed cameras."

The daytime traffic had dwindled by now, and I drove fast down empty lanes towards the city centre. I was going to forget the fuel economy for now; I was going to drive like I did in the old days, and pretend, just for tonight, that there might be a new beginning around the corner. I would think about the realities of losing the car to pay the mortgage a few months longer in the morning.

The lights stopped me on the way into my usual parking area in Birmingham. Flowers long past their best grew in boxes on the railings and suspended from lamp-posts, their scent gone and their petals discoloured from sun-baked dust and exhaust fumes.

I parked the car in the same place I had that morning. The street was deserted, asides from occasional young people on their way to the pubs. I sat with my hands on the wheel and watched them for a bit, thinking of the bank statements and bills in the sofa, and concentrating on that black hole inside my chest. I could start the car again, turn around and go home, worry about the petrol I'd wasted. There's a parallel universe where I did just that, and things went on as they were. Or I could go to this bridge club, to find out if there might be a solution to my problems there.

After a moment I got out. It wasn't as though anyone would see me. I took a golfing umbrella out of the car boot. It would do to hit people with if anything funny did happen.

I put the car keys in my pocket and set off up the street, carrying the umbrella and my handbag. Light shone from the houses and streetlamps, and from open windows drifted the clatter of people clearing up after the evening meal. Here lived the living, in their world. Strange that I walked in it, a marauding ghost, yet it made me feel that bit more alive by being here. On the opposite side of the road a car stood with the bonnet up, and a man and a woman poked at its engine and argued about why it didn't work. They didn't notice me passing by, a stranger in a foreign land.

Up on the main street, aluminium shutters protected the shop fronts. The Jobcentre's windows were covered by blinds, its familiar interior dark. The Chinese takeaway was shut; the health and safety inspectors must have issued a notice on it.

I came to a side-street. This part of the city was made up mostly of old Victorian terraces, three storeys high and with big bay windows facing on to the road. Many of them had been converted into offices for small businesses, private dentists and suchlike. Two unbroken lines of cars stretched bumper-to-bumper down the kerbs.

A wheely bin standing behind the railings in the front yard of one of the houses caught my attention. *Bridge club,* read letters painted in white. I checked behind me and on the opposite pavement to make sure I wasn't watched. Moving closer, cheap Venetian blinds patterned the light coming from the window. A shadow moved past, its form broken by the horizontal lines. I put my hand to the gate, trying to make out what lay inside the room. I could turn back now, if I chose. I wouldn't know who the man was, or what he wanted me for. How many other people might be in there? Enough of the houses in this street were residential. A loud shout would draw attention. Surely there could be no real danger, here in a respectable district of Birmingham... well, as respectable as one can get in Birmingham...

Looking around the dusk-darkened street, it occurred to me that I felt more alive than I had done in a long time. Was a life without purpose and risk really worth giving up for?

Last chance to turn back.

I inhaled deeply. The hinge of the gate hummed faintly as it swung open. The door had a number on it: 182. A small placard behind the glass read 'bridge club'. The door was ajar.

The light was off in the hallway. In the gloom I made out a banister and stairs and a stale sort of odour suggestive of regular use, but not of habitation. My shoes sounded heavy on the floorboards through the thin carpet. A rectangular line of light marked out a door on the ground floor, and it was towards this I moved. Men's voices came, indistinct, and my hand brushed a heavy panelled door, probably original to the house.

My fingers tightened on the handle of the golf umbrella as the door swung back, and I was standing on the threshold of the room facing the man I'd met earlier that day. Five other people sat in there, all of them men, on plastic chairs with metal legs of the sort used in schools. I became aware of a strong odour of sweat.

"Aha!" said my host. "I'm delighted you could make it! Gentlemen," he turned back to those who were seated with a flourish of his hand, "this is Doc."

"Actually, my na—"

The man interrupted me with a raised hand. "We don't mean to offend, Doc, but we'd rather not intrude on your own private business. Just Doc will be more than adequate, and all we need to know."

I stared at the men in the room. The two standing near the window looked like the sort I'd expect to see in CCTV footage, holding up a bank on *Crimewatch*. The three on the other side of the room looked more like ordinary people picked at random, chosen perhaps to fulfil an Equal Opportunities policy. One was elderly, one was young and black and dressed in jeans and a hoodie, and the other was broad framed and somewhat overweight, probably around my age.

The man from outside the dole office continued. "Now, you can call me Genghis. These two are Tweedledum and Tweedledee."

The *Crimewatch* stars both muttered greetings and took their seats.

Genghis turned to point to the lad, who had his fists in his jacket pockets, tilting back his chair on its rear legs into the wall cavity beside the chimney breast. He was a very young man, not past twenty I estimated. "This is Ace."

"Fuck you!" Ace exclaimed. His chair dropped back to all fours and his hand flew up and clapped over his mouth. "I mean, nice to meet you."

Before I could come up with a response to this, Genghis's arm moved to indicate the old man, immaculately dressed and with neatly combed white hair, who watched us through his spectacles, both hands clenched awkwardly on the handle of a walking stick. "Sage."

Genghis pointed to the final man, who sat next to Sage in front of the chimney breast, leaning forward with his elbows on his knees. His eyes met me with a sudden jolt. The man rearranged his expression. He had medium brown hair and a moustache, a pencil balancing behind his ear. His attire consisted of a football shirt and a cheap gold watch, several signet rings, and a chain. He looked like the sort of bloke who drank six pints a night and played darts.

"This is Cam. Please, have a seat."

One seat had been left empty, the one nearest the

door beside Ace. I wondered if Genghis had arranged it anticipating that I might want to run away. It was starting to feel that way again, that outcast undercurrent of not fitting in I used to get when I went to social events with the people I used to work with, of having to sit through a meal I didn't enjoy followed by several rounds of drinks. The smell in the room was becoming oppressive.

Sage held out his hand as I sat down. "Delighted to meet you, Doc." He smiled, his handshake firm and warm despite the knotted mass of swollen joints and ropy tendons that made up his fingers.

Ace tilted his chair. "Raining out?" he asked, motioning to my golf umbrella.

"Uh, no." I put the umbrella on the floor and pushed it up against the skirting board.

The darts player sniffed.

Ace grimaced. "Cam, you fucking stink."

Genghis turned back from closing the door. "Cam, don't you think you're taking it a bit far?"

Cam shrugged and sniffed again, his face twisting in a disagreeable way.

Genghis pulled up his own chair on the opposite side of the room. "I can't imagine you don't have some idea of what we're here for by now."

He paused, and I said nothing. A brief tension passed over his face. He feared I might go to the police. That was why I hadn't been told anyone's name, and why he had interrupted when I'd tried to give mine. That was why we were in some anonymous house, pretending to be a bridge club. He wanted us to agree to mutual discretion.

"Well, Doc." Genghis flashed a nervous grin. "Thing is, I'm an honest criminal. If I'm going to do something, I'm going to do a decent job of it and hire the best. That's why I've got a proposition for you."

So my suspicions were confirmed. I thought of that bill, under the cushion on the sofa in my living room. I swallowed and managed a nod.

"I'm looking to branch out. Into drugs, to put it bluntly. Quality stuff, not street crap that's half cement dust and glass. I don't know if you're aware of it, but there's a loophole in the law. If, say, you were to synthesise E and make a few chemical modifications to it so it wasn't technically E exactly, it's not really legal, but it's neither the kind of thing they can put you away for years for."

I knew of this sort of chemical modification, not specifically though, because I'd only ever worked with legal drugs, but I was pretty sure I could transfer my knowledge to that sort of framework. The man was right. He did have a job I could do.

"So you want me to synthesise Ecstasy derivatives for you?"

"Derivatives, huh? Fancy terminology from the lady." Genghis gestured to the other people in the room. "There'll be good money in it for you, and you don't have to make a decision tonight. All I want for the moment is to explain the work and introduce you to the others who'll be assisting you."

I hesitated. Dealing in drugs was a jail sentence. I had no idea what the penalty for making them was. Quite possibly the man was also naïve, and assumed that chemistry was all about Bunsen burners and smelly things in antiquated glass apparatus. "I don't mean to be patronising, but I'm not sure if you realise what equipment is involved. I can work out how to synthesise any drugs that already exist and various substances that are similar and will have the same effect, but to actually make them I'm going to need reagent-grade chemicals, and an accurate balance, and probably some other equipment."

Genghis stared back at me, and then he flashed his odd grin again. "That's not a problem. We can furnish you with a start-up grant. Is that what they call them, in academia?"

"Yes." I frowned. "But the kind of chemicals I'll need are controlled substances. You need to order them from specialist companies, and they won't sell them to just anyone. You have to be employed by a recognised company."

One of the *Crimewatch* stars spoke. "Then we fake a recognised company."

"Cam's your man." Genghis pointed to the darts player, who throughout the conversation had been sniffing every thirty seconds or so. "And probably we'll need Ace for some stuff to do with the order. You work out what you need first and discuss it with them."

I looked from Cam to Ace, and wondered how someone who was barely more than a boy and this shabby, working-class man who sniffed and smelt unwholesome could know anything at all about ordering specialist chemicals.

"I tell you what," said Genghis. "Why don't you walk the lady back to whatever transport she uses, and you can arrange when to meet up?" This remark seemed to be directed at Cam.

"Please don't trouble yourself, it's not a problem," I said, feeling I'd rather go back to the car alone and mull things over.

"You can't be too careful," said Genghis. "There are all sorts of thieves hanging around here." He glanced about the room to a general murmur of amusement. He produced a wad of cash from his back pocket. "Consider this your travel expenses for your job interview." He flashed his odd brief grin again, and handed me the money. "If you change your mind, you needn't see us again, and we won't think anything of it."

Cam put his hands on his knees and heaved himself to his feet. A waft of BO hit me in the face as I stuffed the money into my handbag. It looked to be all twenties, and there must have been a few hundred pounds there at least.

That would pay the bill, and cover the mortgage for a month, maybe two.

"I need to talk to you two about the cocktail umbrellas for the party," Genghis said to the two *Crimewatch* stars as I moved to the door. *Cocktail umbrellas* was probably slang for knives or something of the sort, I supposed, and the party was probably an armed robbery.

Cam led me out onto the street and I pulled the front door to behind me. "I parked over there," I told him, gesturing.

Cam belched loudly into the still night air and started whistling a tune as we set off. He walked with a shambling gait, his big shoulders collapsed and his hands shoved in his trouser pockets.

"Is Monday morning, 10'o'clock-ish, all right for you?" He had a strong Birmingham accent.

"I think so," I said.

"Gives you enough time to decide what... wotnots you want for your order?"

"The weekend should be enough."

"Monday's probably best then. You know where the Lloyds Bank is on the main street round the corner?"

"I think so."

"I'll meet you outside of that. I've gorra go there anyway to get some banking done."

We walked on in silence for a few minutes, and then Cam said, "If you decide you don't wanna come, you know, we won't mind."

I shuffled my handbag under my arm. "Okay."

We were approaching the car now. I fumbled in my pocket for the keys, and the indicators flashed as I pressed the central locking button.

"03 Audi TT," he identified it, and let off a low whistle. "Nice car, Doc."

"Oh, thanks," I said. "You know, once upon a time, money wasn't a problem. Seems a long time ago now." I forced a laugh.

"What is it, the 1.8 turbo?"

"It's the 3.2 VR6."

Cam crouched to examine it. "You like your cars? It's in good nick considering its age." He shook my hand rather enthusiastically. "Well, it was nice to meet you, Miss Doctor, and I'll see you again on Monday."

I waited until he had turned back and headed off before discreetly wiping my palm down the leg of my jeans. I got into the car and watched his figure shambling into the dark, hands in pockets, with a swell of relief at finally being alone in the privacy of the car. I wondered what on Earth I thought I was doing. Perhaps it was the onset of an unusually early mid-life crisis.

I put the keys in the ignition, and then I realised I'd left that bloody golfing umbrella lying on the floor in the bridge club.

3

OUT OF THE BLUE

The money Genghis had given me came to six hundred and twenty pounds. I paid the bill at the post office directly. Afterwards, I went to the bank and paid enough into my account to clear the overdraft and make it up to next month's mortgage payment. Then I filled the car's petrol tank to the max and bought food from the supermarket, including meat: economy chicken and imported, unethically reared bacon, because they were cheap.

Twice in the past few weeks I'd eaten roadkill, a pigeon and a rabbit I'd found by the side of the road while walking home on separate occasions. I'd known they were fresh because I'd not seen them when I'd passed earlier in the other direction.

I know how to clean game animals because years ago my friend Paul and I had been into adventurous eating and being ethical and knowing where our food came from, and we'd been shooting a few times. Paul probably was my best friend, as we had known each other since University, but he moved to Germany with his work and we drifted apart and lost contact. Ironically, before I accepted my last job, I was offered a post in Germany too, but I took the one in Birmingham because I thought it was a more secure option. Perhaps things would have worked out better if I'd chosen differently.

The pigeon had tasted bad. The only real substance it had was in the breast meat, and it was bruised and embedded with fragments of the bird's breastbone from the impact with somebody's front grille. The rabbit had been stringy and not great either. Reflecting on it as I ate my proper meal, money in my wallet, a disbelieving horror came upon me.

I'd lain in bed the night after the bridge club, turning over what had been discussed in my head and wondering if there was anything on that umbrella that could trace it back to me, and trying to come up with a convincing alibi for how it got there. There'd certainly be fingerprints on it, and probably DNA as well from where the catch had bitten my thumb.

I woke the next morning and I felt well, and after breakfast I did what I did every morning: switched on my computer and checked all the sites I knew where jobs in my field are advertised. There wasn't anything new, so instead I looked up the chemical structure of Ecstasy and how the law stood on derivatives of it. Soon, I was sketching synthetic routes on the back of an envelope, and it was almost like I was back at work. From what information I could find, the legal situation on the matter of inventing new recreational drugs was unclear. If I did this and I got caught, it was not at all apparent if I'd be prosecuted or not. I had no idea what the risk of getting caught might be at any rate. Possibly crime, perhaps even quite serious crime, goes on all the time without being noticed, and people live off it, but the only crime the public hears about is what ends up on the news, what gets detected. If criminals are getting away with it, they're not exactly going to want to publicise how well they're doing.

Someone had been murdered streets away from where I lived last year, and the culprits had never been found. Where had the police been when my aunt and uncle had been burgled? They'd said it had probably not been professionals.

They'd found fingerprints on things, and marks on the floor from shoes, but they'd not been able to find those thieves who'd left their evidence strewn everywhere. Those disorganised, opportunistic, and presumably uneducated thieves. Those same people who would probably be the end consumer of any drugs I synthesised for Genghis. If I didn't make the drugs, they'd only get them elsewhere. Besides, people like that owed people like my aunt and uncle for taking their sense of security.

Perhaps I would have seen it differently in the past. Perhaps what had happened had changed my perception of right and wrong. It wasn't taking anything from other people, and I needed the money. I wanted to live this way, having enough and not being under constant fear of losing the house. No, now I'd thought about it, my only compunction was it being against the law. But then, the police are never around when you need them. Why should I assume they would be around if it was me who was committing an offence? Perhaps the police left you alone if you didn't stir up shit and they didn't need you to make up the numbers the government wanted from them. The police might be too busy to bother chasing after crimes of this sort.

Besides, it would give me breathing room. It would only be until I found a job and could make a living legally.

So that was how I found myself outside the bank on Monday. I couldn't see Cam outside. I tried to peer surreptitiously through the window, but I couldn't see him inside either.

Banks have security cameras. I didn't want to make it look like I was hanging around waiting for someone, up to something. I went over to the end of the queue to the outside ATM. A thin woman in a trench coat, a man with a young kid, and a tall, portly Sikh gentleman in a blue turban and a beige anorak stood between me and the machine. I glanced about. I hadn't thought what I would do if the queue went down before Cam arrived. I didn't even have an account at Lloyds Bank. I'd have to open my wallet and pretend I'd forgotten my card, and maybe swear and act all annoyed to make it convincing.

The Sikh in front turned sideways and looked at me. "Hello."

"Afternoon," I said, and I pretended to look for something in my handbag so I wouldn't have to engage in conversation with him.

"Hi."

I looked up at the odd grin on his broad, bearded face, and I realised he was holding my golf umbrella. "Bloody hell," I said, lowering my voice and checking to see we weren't watched. "Cam?"

"You forgot this." He glanced down at the umbrella, before raising his eyes to my face. "I thought you might like it back." His accent had changed — I don't know much about accents of the world, but I assumed it originated from some part of India.

I took the handle he proffered. "I have some business to attend to first," he said. "I hope I shall not be keeping you waiting long."

I moved away from the queue and towards a shop window, where I tried to feign interest in the ugly china ornaments on display. I didn't dare look about to check whether or not any CCTV might be directed at me, focusing instead on a repulsive effigy of a swan being molested by fairies with a price tag of £299.99. My mother used to like things like that, horrible cluttery things that collected dust and threatened to get knocked and break every time someone went near them. They filled her room in the nursing home, and she lay in her bed there like a pharaoh's mummy surrounded by his worldly goods and the elaborate trappings of the life he once lived.

Cam came over from the bank a few moments later. "Ready?" he said, and we set off together down the street. Cam walked in a quick, lively manner, using short strides, back held straight and chin high, very much different to the shambling figure he'd been the evening of the previous week.

I didn't say anything to him on the main street, partly because I wasn't entirely sure what to say, but mainly because there were too many people who might overhear anything I did say. As we walked, he folded something in half — it looked like a handful of white envelopes — and tucked it into the inside pocket of his mac.

"This way," said Cam with a jovial manner, turning towards a side street.

I looked all ways to make sure no-one was in earshot. "Why are you dressed up as a Sikh?" I hissed.

Cam shrugged, almost as though he was offended by the question. "Have you worked out why they call me Cam yet? It's short for something."

"*What?*"

Abruptly, he turned his head and shot me a grin as we walked. "*Chameleon.*"

Perhaps I was getting slow as a result of unemployment, or encroaching middle age. Back when I'd been an undergraduate, I'd always been the first one to get riddles and read hidden allusions.

Cam sidestepped to avoid walking into a concrete bollard, and nodded discreetly without looking at me. "Genghis came up with it." He still spoke in the same accent, and I wondered which was the disguise: the man from the bridge club, or this one. Then it clicked into place. He'd come in disguise because there was a risk I might not have turned up, that I might have tipped off the police.

"And what are you really called?"

He glanced at me, and a slight, almost playful smile caught the corners of his mouth. "I've been called a million different names."

"I'm sure that's an exaggeration," I said. "You can't possibly have been called as many as a million. There's probably only ten thousand or so days that you've been alive and able to understand that you have a name."

Cam let out a sudden laugh, deep throated with a rich exotic timbre. "Probably. You're going to fit right in to our little club."

"Where are we going?"

"We're going to Ace's flat. He's got something for you."

"His flat?" That didn't match up with Cam turning up in disguise, or the anonymous meeting at the bridge club. I might tell the police where Ace lived, for all Cam knew.

He shrugged. "Ace has several flats. He does not rent properties under his own name. It is in the nature of the work he does."

We arrived in a street where narrow Victorian terraced houses had been converted into shops. I followed Cam through an alley to the back of a locksmith's. In the yard, steps led down to a basement flat. A black binliner full of rubbish had been thrown at the foot of a battered door. Cam muttered to himself and kicked it out the way. The door was on the latch and opened up to a dingy stairway.

"Ace!" Cam shouted, his voice echoing in the unfurnished hall.

I followed him inside. Identical DVD boxes were piled up on the edges of the stairs. Pirate DVDs, I realised. An old beige telephone sat on the bottom step, wires trailing from the plug up the stairs and to the flat above.

"Mind you do not trip over." Cam gestured to the clutter as he went up. "Curse that boy!"

At the top of the stairs were three doors. One of them led to a bathroom and another was bolted and padlocked. Cam went into the third.

Sunlight streamed through the south-facing bay window. Ace waved at us, from his position lying on his stomach on the bed. The room looked as though he had played Tetris with the furniture, and lost. There were two desks, an electric oven shoved up against the wall, various cupboards, and a bedside table with the drawers hanging open, overflowing with clothes. More clothes lay on the floor, and a bin with empty Pot Noodle containers stood under a sink containing two mugs and an assortment of plastic spoons. A laptop computer with cables hanging from the back lay on the bed in front of Ace, and at least two desktops occupied the tables along with partially dismantled computers and mounds of components. A heap of white envelopes was caught underneath them. It took me a moment to realise they were DepositPoint envelopes, of the sort one puts cash and cheques inside with a paying-in form and posts through a slot in the bank out of hours or simply if the queue is too long. Odd that Ace should take them out of the bank. A continuous whirring sound came from one of the computers, and the light on its optical drive flashed steadily. The room smelt of sun-burned dust.

"You might at least have tidied up your flat, if you were knowing you were to have visitors." Cam glanced around the room as he spoke, and his voice maintained its accent.

Ace twitched, a motion that ran over his face and down his shoulder across one arm. The whirring from the computer died away, and the drive bay snapped open and the DVD drawer shot out. "Get that, would you, Cam?" He held a Biro between his teeth that jerked languidly up and down when he spoke.

Cam took the disc out of the drive and set it down on a stack of identical ones. He replaced it with another disc from a second stack, and pushed the drawer closed.

"And press OK." Ace's fingers clattered over the keyboard of his laptop.

"What did your last slave die of?" Cam leaned over the computer to reach the mouse.

"The RSPCA took it away," Ace grinned behind his waggling pen and raised his eyebrows at me as though to share the joke.

Cam turned his eyes upwards in an exaggerated expression of grudging tolerance. "Do you not have something to give to Doc?"

"Ya." Ace rolled his eyes and his pen fell on the duvet. "Cam, you're eclipsing my monitor! There's all gravitational lensing and stuff going on round the edges!"

Cam stepped out of the way. "I'm going to go to the lavatory now," he said, still keeping up his accent. "Unless that in some way is going to be inconveniencing you?"

"Nah. Just make sure you don't sit on it too hard and break it, and don't use all the bog roll." Ace leaned over and reached under the bed as Cam left the room. He pulled out a mobile phone. "Here you go, Doc. This is your business phone, one of the perqs of the job. It's already got all our numbers programmed into it, but we'd all appreciate it if you stick with using it for business purposes and didn't make private calls from it."

"Thanks." I put the phone in my coat pocket.

"We'll sort out these things you need to order when Cam finishes stinking out the place."

"You're not very nice to Cam," I said.

Ace let off an abrupt snigger, like a lecherous schoolboy. "You fancy Cam, don't you?"

There could be no countering juvenile remarks of that sort, so I decided to try to wind Ace up in response. "Where did you learn about stuff like gravitational lensing? Is that what they teach you at school these days?"

"Nah, I learnt them things off BBC4. They don't teach us nuffink in school these days."

I smiled. "I see. Grammar being one of *them things* they don't teach you?"

Ace laughed.

These people might be criminals, but somehow they didn't make me feel so uncomfortable as the people I used to work with, around whom I had to constantly guard what I said lest it be used against me later.

One of the monitors on the table showed camera footage of the street outside, and I traced it to a number of webcams perched on the windowsill. "So why are you called Ace then? Is it because you're good with computers?"

"Sort of," said Ace. "It's a double entendre. Or even a treble entendre if there's one of them. Genghis called me Ace because *I is black*, like the Ace of Spades, and because I come from Dudley in the Black Countraaay."

"His full name is Ace Hole," said Cam, coming back into the room.

Ace roared with laughter. "Fuck off, towelhead!"

Cam widened his eyes. "Racist!"

I looked for a clear surface to put down the catalogues and lists I'd brought and didn't find one, so I emptied the bag on the seat of a chair. "You can have these catalogues. Don't order everything from the same supplier. They have protocols in place to spot when someone orders certain combinations of chemicals that are common precursors to banned substances."

Cam examined the folded spreadsheet printout.

"I've written the reagents I need on there. I put in some decoy stuff to make it look less suspicious." Cam turned the page to look at the other sheet, and I added, "That's equipment I'm going to need. I'll probably need a fridge-freezer as well, but it can be an ordinary one from wherever. I've tried to keep it to a minimum but I don't know if it's any good. It's going to cost about four grand altogether."

Cam folded the pages back together. "It sounds reasonable."

I raised my eyebrows at him. Even in my old job, spending four grand of funding money on startup material for a project would not have been taken lightly. Then again, a professional research group would already have a lab with basic equipment like balances and heaters. "Genghis has four grand to spend on chemicals and balances and rotary evaporators?"

"He's got contacts with dealers and he expects it to recoup the money quickly. He might even be able to shake up some long-term demand."

Long term. Even though it didn't make it any less illegal, hearing that came as a relief. It wasn't like this was going to solve all my problems, but if I could get money regularly out of this, it would mean no more worrying about bills and mortgage payments and having decent food to eat. Exchanging that worry for the ever-present fear of the police behind me over involvement in some nebulous low-grade crime was starting to look like a reasonable deal.

I said, "With these suppliers, everything's handled online, but they'll check the details you enter against their database."

"I'm sure Ace can just about manage that, within his *limited capacity*," said Cam.

"Fuck you, Cam." Ace murmured without taking his eyes off the screen, "I's in 'u'r internets, editin' 'u'r databases."

I stared at him. "You're hacking Sigma-Aldrich?"

"Ya," said Ace. "And just to be safe, I'm using some berk's unsecured wireless LAN to hack it with. So they can't trace my IP address."

Cam leaned on the edge of a desk. "We set up a fake company and insert a bogus entry into their system. That way, they don't ask for the documentation they usually would if we ordered from them the first time."

"But what if they notice the error? Then you've left a trail to whatever address you've had it sent to, and they can identify you."

"That's simple." Ace laughed. "You don't send it to your own address, and then they can't."

I thought through this, but it didn't make any more sense. "How are you going to get the things you ordered in that case? You're going to break in and steal them from the genuine occupier of the address you use?"

"I put a delivery address of a disused unit on an industrial estate." Ace motioned to Cam. "Where's Sage say to use?"

"Here." Cam tore a page off a notepad and handed it to

him. "Call it Stivichall Pharmaceuticals."

It didn't make sense to me. "That's still no good. If there's no-one in the premises to sign for it, they won't deliver it."

Ace sighed. "Cam, you explain it to her. I'm busy."

I turned to Cam. His beard must have been fake, because when last I'd seen him he'd only had a moustache, but despite knowing this I could discern nothing to identify it as such.

"What you do is you stick a note on the door of this disused unit, saying there's a fault and you've recently moved in, and that people attempting to make deliveries should call a telephone number. And the number's the same as the one on the delivery. Then you hide around the back in a van, and when they turn up and ring the number, you answer it and say you'll send a porter to fetch the delivery. And you wear a security uniform and take a bogie out to the front, and it looks all official and you sign and take the goods away, and that's how you do that." He maintained his accent throughout the explanation, and his voice got faster and faster until he finished slightly out of breath. He placed his palms together and dipped his head curtly.

"By the way," said Ace, "I don't need any more from you two. You can both fuck off now. And tell Sage Mumm-Ra won't be big enough. We need to use Zordrak for this shit."

I had no idea what Zordrak and Mumm-Ra meant. Probably it was best not to ask.

Cam opened the door to the landing for me. "You are such a charming young man. Your mother would be very proud of you, if only you could find out who she was."

Ace didn't look up, but he raised a v-sign over the lid of his laptop.

"I need to go through some things with you," Cam said to me as soon as we were back outside in the yard at the back of the shop.

In a weird sort of way, this was becoming interesting. I'd not expected Ace and Cam to be so well organised. What might these people have set up to serve as a lab? I thought of doing chemical synthesis again with an odd nostalgic anticipation. To work, and to be paid for it, was that too much to want? It was beginning to feel less and less like crime. "Okay. So what happens next?"

"You fancy an evening out? I have some business to attend to in Coventry. Meet me at Canal Basin, on the steps, and I'll buy you dinner."

We parted on the street, and I didn't glance back as I walked away. I was concentrating fiercely on not looking like I was up to no good, checking everywhere for police.

*

I wasn't familiar with Coventry, but the SatNav took care of getting there. After parking the car, I inspected the meeting place from a distance to check it was safe. It wasn't the most picturesque of liaison points. The Luftwaffe blew up Coventry during the Second World War and it seemed they had put it back together on the cheap and in a hurry. There was an awkwardly situated pub on the corner, and a footbridge crossing the ringroad. On the other side were a squat Royal Mail building and a DIY shop.

I didn't want to be seen hanging around the steps, in case anyone was watching for either me or Cam, so I crossed the road to a grassed area and seated myself in such a way that a tree slightly obscured my position from the view of anyone on the steps.

After I'd sat there a few minutes, a large man approached the steps. He turned and leaned against the wall, revealing himself to be clean shaven, with thick wavy black hair, dressed in a deep green shirt and smart-casual jacket and chinos.

I remained still and watched. It might not be him; I wasn't sure. No — I remembered Cam had a mole on his right cheek, above the line of his facial hair, one of those raised ones that would still show under thick make-up. I could just make it out at this distance.

He looked nervous, or maybe that was just my imagination. I watched as he pulled a wad of white envelopes from his inside jacket pocket, shuffled them, and put them back. Odd to recall I'd felt so uncomfortable at the bridge club. Now I felt slightly anxious. Even if this was illegal, it was sure to be more fulfilling than sitting at home looking for legal jobs.

I got to my feet and moved towards him. He spotted me when I reached the far kerb, and smiled and raised a hand.

"I know a nice Italian restaurant a little farther along the canal, if that suits you?" His accent had changed again. This time it was Irish.

I couldn't think of anything appropriate to say as we walked up the steps and along the canal path, towards a place ahead where ornate metal chairs and tables had been set out. The late afternoon air was oppressively warm, gravid with the pressure of a building storm.

Cam threw a glance at the sky. "You didn't bring that umbrella? Pity. You might need it!"

I faked a laugh, trying to keep the conversation up. *I'm making a total pig's ear of this.* I'd never been much good at social outings with work, and I'd not been out socially for over a year. Admittedly, I'd never much enjoyed them, and lack of money resulting from lack of employment had been as much an excuse as it had a reason.

Cam signalled a waiter as we reached the edge of the restaurant's seating area. The young man ushered us to a table. He handed us each a menu as we took our seats. "Drinks?"

I realised he was looking at me, expecting my order first. "Water, please."

"Dry white," Cam added.

I quickly picked a pizza from the menu and memorised it.

Cam opened his napkin on the table and spilled onto it a handful of loose change containing a few tattered five-pound notes, a crumpled scrap of paper, and a red paperclip.

"Where did you get that?" I said.

He shrugged. "Out the waiter's pocket."

"You just stole that?"

Cam raised his face to me. "As he was bending over to give us the menus."

"But what if he needs it to live off?"

Cam chuckled in a way that unnerved me slightly, and yet something in his manner was flirtatious, almost sexy. His new accent and his groomed appearance were working for me in ways his other guises hadn't. "It's his tips for one night. They're meant to hand in their tips at the till so they can split them evenly at the end of the day, but he's been pocketing them. And I expect come May he'll conveniently forget to tell the HMRC about it."

I considered this for a moment. "So you're saying it's justifiable to rob the robbers?"

"Oh, no. I'd never claim anything I've done can be justified. I'm afraid you'll just have to learn to live with it, as I have to live with myself every morning I wake up."

Under the table, I clasped my handbag down against my thighs, glad I'd not brought any ID or valuables that he might feel inclined to filch, only the phone Ace had given my and some of Genghis's cash. The impulse came with a conflicting unease of another sort. It being wrong to steal had no meaning when there were bills to pay and no money to pay them, when it was reduced to a choice between me or somebody else.

Cam uncrumpled the slip of paper that had been mixed in with the coins, revealing a phone number. "The lad probably can live without his tips, but I wouldn't want to deprive him of his contact, perhaps a young lady, or a young gentleman — let's not jump to conclusions." He folded the paper neatly and attached the red paperclip. "I'll give him those back when he brings the drinks."

We stopped speaking as the waiter returned with our drinks. I watched Cam carefully, and spotted his hand sneaking back into the man's pocket as he was taking my order.

"How do you do it?" I asked after the waiter had gone. "Without him noticing?"

It's a sleight of hand. Same deception and logic as a magician's trick." Cam rolled the napkin into a funnel and used it to tip the change into his outside jacket pocket. He shifted in his seat and withdrew a pack of cards from the pocket on the other side.

He flipped them out of their box and held out the pack in both hands, thumbs down, and expertly extended it into a wide, evenly spaced fan. "Pick one."

I chose one from right at the edge, wondering if the trick was set up to psychologically make me pick one from the middle. I covered it with both hands as I tilted it to examine the face: the five of diamonds.

"Now put it back. Wherever you like."

After I had returned it to the same position, Cam furled the cards back into a stack and passed them to me across the table. "Now you shuffle them, however you like. Have a good look if you want."

I'd never really got the hang of shuffling cards. I did it carefully, trying not to throw them all over the floor. The pack looked to be in order so far as I could tell.

He took it back, put it back in its box, and returned it to his pocket.

"Aren't you going to tell me which one I chose?"

He shrugged. "In time."

I studied the dynamic surface of the canal's muddy waters for a moment, the names of the ornately painted boats moored along the towpath's length. Soon, the waiter returned with our orders. I hoped he wouldn't think to put his hand in his pocket until after we'd left.

"So, how did you get into this line of business?" I set to sawing a piece off my pizza.

He leaned forward in his chair, setting his elbows on the edge of the table and becoming solemn for a moment. "How do you think I did?" His solemnity evaporated again. "You can have three guesses."

I regarded him for a moment, taking in his grey eyes, sharp nose, and shapely lips. How had I got into this business?

"You couldn't get anything else?" I offered.

"Got it in one." He smiled in a self-deprecating way.

"What did you do before?"

"It's not important." He made eye contact briefly, and looked down at his fingers where they twiddled the stem of his glass. "It's not interesting. That's the best thing about Genghis. He doesn't ask questions. He doesn't dig."

"He must have done some sort of background check. Even if you weren't aware of it. He must have had something on me, before he invited me to the meeting."

Cam raised his eyebrows. "You could also have background-checked him. If he doesn't, it gives you less motive to do it. Don't interfere with us, and we won't interfere with you. It's a gentleman's agreement. It means if any one of us does get caught, we can't reveal the identities of the others."

"Isn't Genghis at all concerned? I could have been dismissed dishonourably from my last job for doing something terrible, for all he knows."

"Doesn't matter if you were. We've all made mistakes."

I thought of the time after I lost my job, when I'd blamed all of it on myself, how I'd agonised over every mistake I'd made, and I thought of the times after that when I'd turned my anger instead on the people I used to work with, bitter when I saw my old employer's website that they were still there, living their lives, when mine had become a ruin.

"How do you live with your mistakes?" I said.

Cam pinched the stem of his glass between his thumb and fingertips, and rotated it back and forth. The skin under his nails blanched with the pressure of his grip. "You build a wall. You turn and you put one foot in front of the other, and you don't look back. And you hope that if that wall crumbles and whatever you built it to contain gets out, you're too far away for what it's grown into to find you."

I turned this around in the privacy of my head for a few seconds. "So I suppose you telling me your name is out of the question?"

"Quite." He looked at me, a slight, secretive smile forming on his face, and raised his glass to his lips. "My name's Cam. Good a name as any."

After the connection I'd sensed with him earlier in the conversation, it felt like a rejection. Perhaps I'd imagined that. He was right, and it was none of my business. Maybe I was acting desperate because I didn't have any friends left. I wondered if there were people at home who knew his name, if he went to the dole office and what name they called him by there. Perhaps he had a wife and kids, an entire life he was keeping separate.

I watched him eating, suppressing an urge to see things that might not be there. "What are the true colours of a chameleon?"

"It doesn't have any. That's what defines it. There's no truth. If there was, it wouldn't be a chameleon."

"Then what would it be?"

He paused to swallow before answering. "Just a bog-eyed lizard."

We continued eating, and neither of us said anything for a few minutes. "So how does Genghis... and... and his *crew* make their money?"

"Mainly confidence tricks. Mail redirection scams as well, Ace's hacking, fraud, things like that. The Tweedles are the heavies. We've got most fronts covered. Or we did, until Genghis decided he wanted to branch out into a market he didn't have a share in." He took a sip from his glass.

"So what happens next with that?"

"Should be sorted out by the end of the week." Cam put down his fork and took a pen out from the inside of his jacket. He wrote an address on his napkin and flipped it across the table to me. "Monday, one o'clock, meet you outside?"

I looked at it before folding it and putting it in my handbag.

"It's not our house, it's... it's something Ace has arranged, so mind you don't just walk in if there's no-one there."

"Okay."

He offered me his wine bottle. "No thanks," I said. "I'm driving home."

"Well," he said, setting down his knife and fork and pushing his empty plate aside. "It's been lovely to meet you, properly this time."

"Thanks, and you." I pushed my chair back and stood, finding my attention drawn by the way his collar crumpled around the soft flesh of his jaw, and the loose lock of hair over his forehead. He might have been trying to suggest something, or not. I knew from my old job that it was best not to get involved, best not to give ammunition to people in positions to use it. *Walk away.*

The sun must have set by now, behind the clouds shrouding the sky. Darkness had begun to close in, and the awakening street lights glowed ruddy. The first fine rain prickled my face and disturbed the canal waters. Time to return to my house and face being alone. This was the way of things, and the money was what was important here. *I'm too old to be fancying people.*

A chair scraped on the floor, and I heard his voice behind me. "Wait, you forgot..."

His hand gripped mine and I pivoted to face him. Before I really became conscious of what he was doing, his mouth pressed against mine, a hint of stubble rasping my chin. He pulled away precipitously, before I'd been able to take stock of it.

"Drive safely."

Now he was walking away. I tasted the wine he'd been drinking on my lips. If all the experience I had said this was wrong, why did it feel so right? I looked down at the hand he'd just clasped — the rose from the vase on our table, its thorns insulated by a napkin wrapped around the stem. And inside the napkin, rolled up and slightly soggy, there was something else, a card, the five of diamonds.

I looked to him and he glanced over his shoulder, without stopping, and smiled broadly. The first sounding of thunder rolled through the sky above the city roofs. The car was streets away, and it was going to rain hard.

And it didn't matter.

4

GREENHORN

I dusted the chemical smell off my hands onto my trousers as I emerged from the outbuilding and stepped onto the lawn. Ace was kneeling with his back to me, on the grass by the border, a trowel in one hand and a heap of weeds beside him. Sage looked up from his seat on a wooden bench. He clasped a glass bong awkwardly in his crooked hands. Smoke trickled from the mouthpiece.

"Where's Cam gone?" I said.

"Off-licence." Ace didn't turn when he spoke.

On my arrival, a man in biker leathers and a heavy metal T-shirt who had turned out to be Cam had met me in the street outside, from where he'd led me around the side of the house and into the garden. He'd showed me to the building they had adapted for use as a lab, where the equipment and reagents I'd asked for had already been stored. He hadn't said much before he'd left, but he had asked if I would give him a lift home later, to which I'd agreed.

Right now I had no idea what to expect might happen then. I'd spent the past week anticipating this day, wondering what might happen when I got to see him again. I wasn't at all sure the connection I'd started to feel to him during the meal we'd shared was real, or whether he'd put it all on and kissed me as part of the particular act he'd been playing that night. Maybe his obsession with pretending to be people he wasn't should have hinted at some sort of mental health condition. Then again, it could be me, playing the cynic, thinking this is another red herring I shouldn't get myself worked up over. It wasn't that I didn't like him; I just didn't know what it was I liked, or even if it could exist in someone as unpredictable as the weather. It was foolish to think about it so much just because of the way he'd left me feeling when we parted at the canal. Letting an emotional reaction to something colour one's perception of it is swimming blind into a dangerous current. Perhaps he was an expert on psychology and he'd deliberately played a part designed to have that effect on me that night. On the other hand, perhaps I only felt this way because of the thrill of a hunt, in pursuit of a truth that might turn out to be a lie.

Perhaps I don't know what I want any more.

The afternoon had turned out unseasonably warm, and a cloudless sky stretched from horizon to horizon. Beyond the fence of the tidy garden lay a small paddock, and beyond that, some allotments.

I wandered over to see what Ace was doing. "Is this your garden?"

"No, it belongs to the old lady." Ace plucked single green blades from the soil, gathering them into his palm.

I knelt down, feeling the dampness of the earth under the grass, and began to pull up the weeds and deposit them on the pile beside him. "Old lady?"

"She lives in the house." Ace turned his head briefly in the direction of the gate leading to the path to the house. "She's nearly blind. I come round here and do her gardening for her."

I looked uneasily to the back of the house, the bricks of its east-facing wall sinking into afternoon shadow. "Does she know we're here and using her outbuilding as a drugs factory?"

Ace twitched and let off a brief, barking cough. "She's not using it. I pay her electric for her so we're not stealing it. I don't expect the police are seriously gunna think it's hers if they find it here."

Cam appeared at the gate and shouldered his way past a bush. He carried a bag full of clinking glass bottles, which he set down on the flagstones at the foot of the deck chair beside the buddleja bush. He took off his jacket and hung it on the back of the chair.

Ace cringed and shielded his eyes. "Don't take your shirt off Cam, you fat bastard!"

"I'm not taking my shirt off, fool!" Cam sat on the chair and reached a bottle of beer out of the bag.

Sage regarded him from the bench. "Don't you have to drive home?"

Cam glanced at me. "Doc's giving me a lift. In her flash motor."

Sage looked at me, a faint smile deepening the lines around his eyes. There was something penetrating about his gaze that suggested he saw more than what was simply in front of him. Or, it might have been merely an effect of the marijuana.

Ace chopped at clods of dried soil with the side of his trowel. He rubbed the flat of the blade carefully over the dirt to smooth it, before gathering up his weeds and standing. A man in the allotment glanced up at us from doing something behind a row of faded sunflowers.

I waved to him.

The man smiled and showed a mud-ingrained palm.

"All right, mate!" Ace called, and he suddenly raised

his hand in a v-sign at the man. The man's expression fell. "Sorry mate, I didn't mean to do that!" Ace shouted.

Laughing, Cam improvised a bottle opener from his elbow and the arm of the plastic chair.

"Shut up, Cam!" said Ace. "And gimme one of them beers!"

Cam grabbed another bottle and bent into an overarm posture as though he meant to throw it at Ace. "Say please!"

"Please, then."

Cam handed him the bottle.

"That's no good. How am I s'posed to get the lid off that?"

Cam shrugged. "You're supposed to invent your own way. Like one of those team-building initiative things you have to go on if you have a job."

"I wouldn't know, I never 'ad no job." Ace began picking up his gardening tools and holding them up to the bottle for comparison. "Doc, do you think a hoe kind of looks like a bottle opener?"

"I suppose it does really."

"Perhaps that's how it got invented. Or the other way round." Ace coughed twice, in a strangely deliberate way. He put the tools down and jammed the bottle against the fence to open it, and took a swig. "Want to see my pot-plants Doc?"

"No, she doesn't," said Cam. He raised his beer bottle and winked at me.

"Shurrup Cam! You're not gunna let him tell you what to do, are you?"

"Certainly not." I made a face at Cam to humour Ace. "Where are these plants, then?"

Ace led me down the path that went behind the outbuilding. The place was crowded with overgrown shrubs, but behind the leaves hid algae-greened glass, and a brick step covered with moss. Peering in through the greenhouse door, I saw it was well hidden, with the only light coming through the roof. Rectangular pots contained splayed leafy fronds with serrated edges. An overwhelming odour filled the air.

"Oh, I see. Your *pot* plants."

Ace grinned. "These aren't to sell or nothing. I just grow 'em to give away and for Sage. It helps his hands." Ace held up a crabbed hand, imitating Sage's condition.

As we returned to the main garden, Cam held up a small rectangle. "What's this?"

Ace stared at it, and recognition dawned on his face. "You picked my pocket, you big shit!"

Cam examined it, sniggering. "Ace Hacking. All your *dubois* IT needs catered for?"

"It's like a sample business card I was gunna show Genghis for a con I had an idea for. I just wrote any old shit on it." Ace was starting to look embarrassed.

"You've spelt 'dubious' wrong!"

"Fuck you!"

Cam fanned the air idly with the card. "I can cut a hole in this and step through it."

Ace elbowed me. "Cam does magic tricks. Watch."

Cam folded the card in half lengthways. Using Ace's garden secateurs, he made slots in one side of it, like a comb. He turned it around and made more slots in the other side, interlocking the first ones. Ace laughed as he opened it out and cut through the crease, and pulled it out like a concertina. Cam put his feet through the middle of the herringbone string of paper and levered himself up from the arms of the chair. "Here we go, then!" He managed to pull it up over his backside, after which point it seemed to become more complicated. "Well, I used to be able to do this." The paper string snapped, and Ace roared with laughter, turning about on the lawn and bending over with his hand on his diaphragm.

"Afternoon, chaps," someone said, and behind Cam Genghis walked through the gate. He looked at Cam and Ace, and the empty beer bottles on the floor.

"Wher've you been?" said Sage.

Genghis cocked an eyebrow. "That's for me to know and you to worry about."

Cam gave me a sly look. "I bet he's been off looking for a job. He's planning on going straight and deserting us all."

"Me, get a job?" Genghis grinned. "I'm not paying tax, so politicians can waste it on houses for ducks, and eco-slums in the greenbelt, and paying the dole to the likes of you, and crap schools like the one Ace went to, and the European Union!"

"Fucktards," said Ace.

"Foreign fucktards," said Sage.

"Now, Doc." Genghis glanced at me. "How's our little operation coming along?"

I showed Genghis to the outbuilding, where I'd spread out the white fluffy crystals on an old melamine tray we'd washed.

"Very nice." He cast a cursory glance over the lab and its new fittings. "I see they found you your fridge."

"Sage found it in a tip," said Ace from the doorway. "It

fucking stinks."

"It'll fucking stink even worse now it's full of fucking, stinky chemicals," I said.

"So," Genghis probed the crystals with his fingernail. "What exactly is this?"

"Well." I indicated a reaction scheme on the wall. "This compound here is Ecstasy, or 3,4-methylenedioxymethamphetamine as its proper name is. Because it's illegal, I decided to make the version with the ethyl group instead of the methyl one."

"Er," said Genghis, "you might want to run through that again in Stupid."

"Okay." I took a moment to compose a simplified explanation. "See this picture here, where the N is?"

Genghis stepped forward to look at the reaction scheme. He put his hands in his pockets and frowned.

"The one in Ecstasy has a carbon and three hydrogens on it. The one I've made has two carbons and five hydrogens on it."

"Ah." Revelation overcame Genghis's face. "So it's like you're playing with Meccano and you added some extra bits on? But the bits aren't in the way of the moving parts?"

"Yes, it's exactly like that."

"Oh good." He stepped back to look at the stuff on the tray. "Is it *cooked* yet?"

"Yes, it should be ready by now."

"Good work, Doc." Genghis made a thumbs-up sign at me. "Now we just need to get it made up into pills so I can transfer them to Tweedledum and Tweedledee. How much of it is there?"

"There's about 200 grams wet. You'll need accurate dry

weights if you're going to calculate dosage."

"Ace, come in here! You're good at maths!"

Ace came to the doorway. He had put his hoodie on, with the hood pulled up and the zip undone, sleeves pulled down over his knuckles. It occurred to me that he looked like a hooligan, strangely transformed by this one item of clothing from the young man I vaguely knew.

"You need to work this out." Genghis showed Ace a piece of paper. For every 250 milligrams of this E thing, you need?"

"No, wait," I interrupted. "The molecular mass of this is higher than E. You need to divide the 250 milligrams by this number," I pointed to the one on the scheme, "and then multiply it by the number of the compound to find out the correct mass, otherwise the dose will be wrong."

Ace flopped his arms about in the doorway. "Is that avocado numbers or something?"

"Avogadro numbers."

"We did them in school."

"Oh. Do you remember anything else about them?"

Ace shrugged, stretching his sleeves. "Nah. I swore at the teacher and got sent out."

"Well, you do this maths like Doc said, and then mix up the E with the pill stuff and the water like it says on the list." Genghis pointed to a plastic bag full of blue powder on the bench.

"Let's do the calculation together, Ace," I said hurriedly. We were going to sell this stuff and people were going to use it. I dreaded to think of them overdosing because we'd made an error. Even if they might be the ones who burgled my aunt and uncle's house.

Ace looked at me. "Are you impugning my maths?" he said, and grinned. "Come on then, Doc, I'll do my maths and you can mark it for me!"

I helped Ace do the calculation. He was good at maths, like Genghis had said, and I was more concerned that he wouldn't understand the scale-up.

While he mixed the reagents in a plastic bowl with a cooking spatula, I went to the doorway, where Cam and Genghis stood talking.

"Hmm," went Genghis through his nose. "Can you borrow a dog off someone?"

"Don't think so. I could look up a shelter place and try to take one for a walk, but I can hardly take it all day."

They abruptly went silent when they saw me. "Cam," said Genghis. "Go and help Ace make pills in that machine."

Cam shrugged and rolled his eyes at me. "I'm just the general dogsbody round here."

"There's not been anything needed forging, or any snooping around in disguises today, and you've sat on your arse and demolished..." Genghis waved his hand in an arc, palm up, to indicate the beer bottles, "who knows how much booze, and I need to pay Doc for her fine services today."

Cam's eyes met me, and he squeezed past me into the outbuilding, his hand brushing against my arm. The smell of him and the feel of his body washed over me like an instant of madness.

By the buddleia bush, Genghis handed me another wad of cash. "Well, Doc, it seems you like the deep end, and you can swim all right."

"Well, thank you," I said, not entirely sure how to respond. I stuffed the money into my handbag.

"I just hope I made the right call back at the dole office. I hope you're trustworthy, because by the looks of things we're going to be seeing a lot more of each other."

"You should have asked for references before you took me on." *Not that my last employer, the only one I could call upon for a reference, would have anything nice to say about me.*

Genghis laughed, and looked at his watch. "I'm off to the off-licence before it shuts." He glanced at my handbag. "Don't let those two see that cash. They're a pair of crooks!"

As he left the garden, I headed over to Sage's bench and sat beside him.

He acknowledged me briefly, and continued gazing at the buddleja bush and the butterflies on it, his expression suggesting he found everything that went on in some way privately amusing.

"So what is it you do round here?"

Sage smiled, lines deepening on his face. "I do the books m'dear; manage the finances and all that. Then there are my mail redirection scams."

"You enjoy working for Genghis, then?"

"Oh, yes." He turned his head and regarded me in his slow meticulous way. "I used to have a job I loved, but I got too old, and they stopped me from doing it. Here, it doesn't matter." He closed his eyes, leaned back on the bench, and inhaled deeply. "I love this time of year."

His manner struck me as a Zen-like equanimity, as though he lived entirely for the present with no sentimentality for the past nor care about what the future might bring. For a moment I almost envied him for it. "How about the other two, Tweedledum and Tweedledee?" I hadn't seen either of them today.

"Oh, they won't come here. Nasty pieces of work, the

pair of them."

"Pardon?"

"They're the blunt end of the outfit."

I paused before replying. Perhaps Sage was just stoned. "Then why do you work with them?"

"We need them as much as we need people like Ace and yourself. We supply speciality goods, as it were, and so long as we do that we're tolerated by the harder criminals of this city. But things are changing. It used to be the Johnson Crew and the Burger Bar Boys. The police cracked down on them a while back and got the leaders locked up, but all that did was make them split into postcode gangs. They're Ace's age, and they're far more territorial. Some of these lads would kill you for looking at them the wrong way."

"So they're what, racketeers? They protect you from the thugs?"

Sage shook his head. "Oh, Tweedledee's loyal to Genghis all right, and Tweedledum's loyal to whomever Tweedledee's loyal to. Point is, we need someone of his calibre if we're to survive in their world. These people aren't just disorganised rabble. They're a hierarchy, a network with connections to the whole of the country."

"You mean you think they might come after us?"

Sage raised his eyebrows and studied the handle of his walking stick. "No, but they could make it very inconvenient for us to continue our little operation. Even if they did start looking for us, they'd have next to nothing to go on. They don't have any names, because we don't even know each other's names. They'd be searching the whole of Birmingham for an old geezer and a lad who blends in very well with everyone else in his generation. As for Cam, they'd never find him in a month of Mondays." Sage chuckled.

At the mention of his name, I found my attention drawn back to the outbuilding, where Cam had gone with Ace. I wanted to ask, but I didn't know how Sage would interpret it, or if he would tell Cam. At length, I asked carefully, "What do you know about Cam?"

Sage smiled at me. "I *don't* know. Same as I don't know who you are, really."

"Have you ever seen him, when he wasn't in disguise?"

For a few seconds, Sage did not answer. "I don't know if there's such a thing as Cam out of disguise. I suppose, in a way, we all wear disguises. We all put on a face we want the world to see."

I sensed that Sage was running evasive manoeuvres. "You know, I'm here to work with you," I said. "I'm not going to grass you up. Asides from it being beneath my own principles, I'm in too deep now and it would only get me arrested too."

Sage exhaled through his nose. "There really is not much more I can tell you, other than what you already know. Cam is something of an enigma to all of us. Genghis came across him about a year ago. Ace joined us about the same time, and those two do seem to get on rather well together, though I suspect it's because they're both oddballs in different ways and they're prepared to accept each other for that. I don't think there's any genuine confidentiality between them."

"You don't think Ace would know?"

Sage exhaled through his nose. "No," he said at length. He looked up from the path and gazed at the sky. A distant expression came over his face, and he said in a low voice, "It's easy to see with Ace. His wounds are still fresh, but Cam has old scars. Cam is running from something. I don't know what, but some day it's going to catch up with him."

Ace's manic laugh came from inside the outbuilding. After a contemplative moment, Sage looked dejectedly at his feet on the paving. "I think Ace has taken my bong."

I found Cam on his hands and knees on the floor, giggling ridiculously. The pair of them reminded me of PhD students labouring under a lax supervisor, and the stench of cannabis smoke perfumed the room. They had dropped the bag with the pills in it down there, and didn't seem able to find it.

"Gimme that!" I demanded in mock chastisement. "Stealing from a pensioner and smoking in my lab!"

The two of them broke out in hysterical laughter. I returned the bong to Sage.

By the time Genghis had come back and left with the pills, Cam and Ace had both sobered up somewhat.

"What's in the box?" Cam asked.

I looked at the cardboard box with the reagent bottles in. "Oh, those are just the things I added to the order as a decoy, so the stuff we ordered wouldn't be suspicious as being materials for illegal drugs synthesis."

"You want to throw them away?"

I considered. "I wouldn't, because some of them are hazardous. Just hide them somewhere safe."

Cam scooped up the box and wedged it under his arm. "I'll take it home and shove it somewhere. You ready?"

We were the last to leave the garden. I'd been both longing for and dreading this time all week, and a sickly sensation had come into my stomach. I had no idea if I was just giving Cam a lift home, or if he was going to invite me in. I was in a quandary over whether I ought to even be doing this. I used to have a partner, a serious relationship and a man with whom I cohabited. His name was Richard.

We did not part amicably. On the other hand, I used to have a friend, Paul. I liked him, and I think he liked me, but I never pressed for anything more out of fear of spoiling what we had, and we drifted apart, and I will always wonder. I suppose on my death bed I might regret every one of them, regardless of the choices I'd made and how they'd panned out.

"You're going to have to give me directions." I reached the side of the car and pressed the button on my key fob for the central locking. "Or at least a postcode for the SatNav."

"Of course."

A flashback of my driving test rose unbidden to the front of my mind, that same fear, that same clamminess between my hands and the wheel.

Cam provided directions. I couldn't think of anything to say, and the stone cold silence discomforted me as we passed two roundabouts. Then Cam said, "You drive well."

I laughed, relieved that he had at least broken the conversation barrier. "No I don't. You just think I do because you're stoned and drunk."

"Really, you do." Cam became pensive and stared at the dashboard.

"I like to drive," I said, trying to keep the talking going. "It's the closest I've ever felt to flying."

He gave me an ironic look. "Learn to fly."

"Learn to fly? How?"

"Genghis is paying you, isn't he? There's an airfield near Coventry... near that bloody thing." Cam pinched the bridge of his nose just below his eyebrows and grimaced. "That Tollbar End roundabout thing. If you went there and spoke to whoever's in charge, I'm sure they could come to an arrangement for you to pay in cash. Just don't go there during the rush hour. That roundabout's a nightmare."

After a moment, he asked, "You talk to Sage?"

"He said he runs mail redirection scams. What are they?"

"There's a funny story behind it."

"Oh, yes?" I found myself smiling. I liked Sage. My uncle in New Zealand must have been a similar age to him.

"Sage used to have a dog. He took it for a walk in the countryside, and some obnoxious, spoilt horse-girl-woman-thing gave him a mouthful of threats and abuse for trespassing on private property. Sage went home in anger and found the details of the person who owned the property off the Electoral Register. He set up a bogus bank account and sent a cheque to the Royal Mail, pretending to be the owner of the property and requesting the mail be redirected to another address, and he cleaned out her bank accounts and used the details he'd got from the post he received to take out loans, set up private limited companies, obtain passports, and so on.

"What happened to the rude woman?"

"Don't really know. No doubt the family had to prove they were the victims of fraud when the police caught up with all the criminal activities and bankruptcies Sage had pulled off with all those companies. No doubt her credit rating was ruined for life."

I thought this over for a bit. "Do you just pick up details at random, or do you try to stick with doing it to people who've crossed your paths?"

He leaned back against the headrest and shot me a sly look. "We do our best to do over people who deserve it. I mean, there are enough bastards in the world we can rip off, without making people miserable who live their lives in peace and mind their own business. So if anyone ever pisses you off, write down that person's address and give it to Sage."

"I will," I said, immediately thinking of my old boss and a particularly obnoxious colleague I used to have.

"Oh. Here we are. Turn in. Park where you like."

Cam's house had a large overgrown laurel bush up the side, which extended the length of the drive, weeds thrusting up between the paving slabs and up through the gravel. He opened the front door to a hallway with shabby décor and a tiled floor.

I hesitated behind him, not entirely sure if I was invited or not, since he'd never specifically asked me. He indicated to me to come in and shut the door, before pulling off his jacket and throwing it over the banister. His T-shirt clung to him when he bent over to push the box of spare chemicals into the cupboard under the stairs.

Folding my arms so I didn't knock anything over, I wandered into the living room. A coffee table took up the middle of it, and a large leather sofa spanned the length of the back wall. A television occupied the alcove between the chimney breast and the bay window, a stereo in the opposite alcove beside a chair. A few DVDs and CDs strewed the floor, and drab-coloured curtains trailed upon the carpet, having become detached from several of their hooks. The chair nearest the door held a box full of pairs of spectacles, and a mother-and-son lamp stood behind the door near the sofa. There weren't any pictures.

Jammed down the back of the sofa was a holdall with the zip flap hanging open, and inside it were a load of white envelopes — DepositPoint envelopes, the same as the ones I'd seen at Ace's flat. The logos on them showed they were all from different banks.

I averted my eyes from it when he came into the room. "Nice sofa," was all I could come up with. It's *well upholstered, with strong arms*, I thought as I stared at his chest and shoulders.

"Fell off the back of a lorry. Want a drink?"

While he was occupied in the kitchen, I went over to the door on the back wall of the living room. The house was one of those typical bland brick efforts from the 70s, hall and stairs to the front with a turnaround kitchen behind and a dining room and sitting room to one side, and I'd guess upstairs two bedrooms and a loo, and probably a boxroom.

The door to the dining room was ajar, and when I pushed it, I found a table strewn with brushes and pots and smeared with dried paint, rather than one in a state that could be eaten off. Easels stood on both sides of the door, presenting lurid canvasses to the light offered by sliding glass doors that took up most of the outward-facing wall. Beyond them lay a small square of blank and untidy lawn, rather gloomy, surrounded as it was by towering Leylandii that afforded no hint of what might lie without the garden. More canvasses leaned in stacks against the two corners, blank in one and painted in the other. Next to the window, a bookcase overflowed with art books and catalogues.

I was studying the painting on the right, of abstract horses in yellow and blue amidst a fractured background of geometry, when Cam returned. "Coffee or tea?"

"Either." I didn't look away from the picture. "Do you paint?"

He came to stand behind me, so close I felt his breath upon the back of my neck when he let off a forceful exhalation. "Franz Marc paints."

I turned to him, seeing a hint of humour in his expression, and glanced at the other painting, human figures worked into a pyrotechnic explosion of colour. "Ernst Ludwig Kirchner," he explained.

"Forgeries?"

"Ever heard of *entartete Kunst*?" He spoke it in a convincing German accent. "*Degenerate art*?"

I shook my head.

"When Hitler came to power, the Nazi party abhorred modern art, and persecuted its practitioners and put their works on display in a gallery of mockery. Many of them were destroyed, and the artists went into hiding. Because of that, it's rather difficult to guess how many works they produced and how many might have survived. Paint a convincing picture in the same style, fake a gallery stamp and a few sales catalogues to map out a history, and..." His voice trailed off.

I looked at the canvasses in the corner, all in similar styles. "You ever paint anything... by... not by someone else?" I almost said *you*, but I still wasn't sure who *you* might be.

Cam heaved his shoulders. "I did try. Nobody wanted them. No money in it."

"But people buy the same pictures if they think they're authentic?"

"And won't they be pissed off, when they find out." Cam shoved his hands into his pockets.

I found myself laughing. "But the picture's still the same. Nothing changes, but they suddenly don't like it because someone else painted it?" The pretentious hypocrisy of the entire idea somehow drew to a sharp point all the feelings I'd had about getting involved in this, the meaninglessness of right and wrong, of victim and perpetrator, and my jaded view of the worst excesses of a degenerating society to which I no longer felt any belonging. I found the distance between us closing, under the oppressive ranks of the Leylandii beyond the window, and when we touched it was with an urge for something palpable, something real from the physical world that had seemed so far gone. I grasped his hair and neck when we kissed, and I pulled him backwards into the sitting room, towards the sofa. He tried to lower himself cautiously, not to crush me, but I wanted to be engulfed. I wanted to feel alive again. I wrapped my arms around his torso and pulled him close to me, groping for something to hold on to and finding only the fabric of the T-shirt he was wearing, which yielded as the hem pulled out of the waistline of his trousers.

He started so violently I immediately let go, and he got to his feet. I sat up in alarm. What had happened? Cam stood, dishevelled, breathing rapid, apparently unnerved, running one hand through his hair and trying to stuff his shirt hem back into the back of his trousers with the other.

"Sorry," he said. His mouth opened and closed for a moment. "I just realised... I need to be somewhere soon. You ought to go."

I stared at him. I didn't understand. "Okay," I said at length.

I went back into the hall in a state of utter incomprehension. Why yesterday, in Coventry? Why now, if he didn't want it?

I noticed something lying on the bottom step, a white envelope. Cam had thrown his jacket carelessly over the banister, and it must have fallen from the pocket. I picked it up and looked inside. It wasn't sealed, and one of the paying-in forms, unwritten on, had been tucked into it.

I took the envelope back into the living room. "I think you dropped this."

"Thanks." He took it stuffed it into his jeans pocket.

"What is it?"

"Nothing." He closed the door to the painting room.

I stood there, and he stood there, and then I said, "It obviously isn't nothing, because I just saw it with my own eyes."

He faltered when I spoke, but he didn't move. He didn't speak. He looked cornered, hostile, in a way I'd never seen him before, in a way that wasn't an act to do with the character he was playing today.

"They're in a bag in here, behind the sofa. You had them before, when I met you outside the bank, didn't you? And they're in Ace's flat. What are they?"

"I didn't have time to fill in the forms at the bank, so I took them home so I could drop them off in the deposit box later." He spoke too quickly.

"But people don't do that! It's not normal to steal loads of paying-in envelopes from banks!"

"It's not anything. It's just something I'm doing for Genghis." He made eye contact, but only briefly.

"What?" Without thinking about it, I had edged back from him. Perhaps he wasn't the man I'd hoped I was beginning to know. "What thing?"

He faced me. "It doesn't matter. It's not important. It's just something Genghis is planning."

"And I suppose Genghis told you to try it on with me in Coventry, and here today, as well?"

For an instant, something flared in his face. It might have been indignance, or fear. "That's got nothing to do with Genghis."

"Then what's going on? What did you expect?" The

thought occurred to me again that all these disguises, these alter-egoes could be symptoms of mental illness, or a personality disorder perhaps. "Why are you doing this stuff with me one minute and completely the opposite the next? Cam, we're not fifteen!"

His expression changed to something I couldn't decipher at all. His voice came out beastly, like nothing I'd ever heard from any of the personas he'd presented before. "Then you know where you can go."

How could he be so friendly, so considerate and nice one moment, and so callous the next? Was his whole life a masquerade? Had the mask slipped to reveal a glimpse of a monster? Did he get a sadistic kick out of playing games with people? A stab of hate and shame hit me. A memory flashed into my mind, my boss standing, his face forced down into mine way too close to me, his voice sneering, harsh, lines on his forehead, eyes penetrating... Before I became ill and couldn't face going to work any more.

My heart was racing, and a tense pressure pushed from inside my head and face. A panic switch had been flipped, and now a slow collapse was underway, like a long line of dominoes.

"I need the loo," I said, and I went back into the hallway and stumbled up the stairs, found the door to the lavatory on the first attempt. I locked the door and leaned on it, pressing against the surface while the walls of the small room reeled and buckled in my vision.

Cam's voice, distant, probably from the bottom of the stairs: "Now I remember why I stayed out of relationships so long. It's 'cause that's what *women* do."

"What?" I snapped. "Now you don't like women because they have to urinate? Don't be so fucking stupid, using something as pathetic as the sex I was born as a scapegoat for your own faults." I slammed down both toilet lids and sat down hard, putting my elbows on my thighs and pressing both palms hard against the sides of my jaw. Concentrating on breathing steadily and deeply and the act of counting backwards were floodgates, and I must keep them up until the swell of panic came down.

He'd spoken to me like I was some kind of annoying mosquito. What would happen if we'd made a permanent rift? How could we work together if both of us were too proud to back down?

My jaw had seized up. I worked my mouth open and shut, trying to force myself to breathe in. I have to stop thinking this, *NOW*. It's a chain reaction, and I mustn't allow it to run.

I should never have become involved in the first place, never allowed the level to become unprofessional. Fool, to forget who I was and everything that had happened in the past. Who was I kidding, trying to play this game with Cam, succumbing to that old addiction? People-Person: that was one of those buzz words they use on CVs in a workshop the dole office once made me attend. I am not a people-person. I am a computer-and-machines-and-books-person. What was I doing getting myself messed up with stuff that never worked, that had resulted in horrendous fallout with every past attempt? This was not for me. I wished I could fly, I wished I could put five hundred feet between myself and the rest of the human race. The pressure in my head and face were getting worse, I could barely breathe, and a cold, trembling sensation had begun to spread up my arms from my hands, towards my chest. It was building up again; it was going to go over the top and I was going to lose control.

Stop it!

I concentrated on a point inside my chest, near my

heart, and focused on pushing back on the rising pressure. I imagined my chest expanding and the tension falling into itself, like an exploding star collapsing back into a black hole. I clawed my sleeve up and bit down hard on the underneath of my forearm until I tasted blood. The pain was enough to startle me out of the downwards spiral.

I sat, and I breathed, and I thought about toilet siphons, because being in Cam's loo reminded me that the toilet in my house was broken because of the siphon, and I'd been managing by filling a bucket of water from the bath taps and pouring that down it. So I made a plan that I would go out and buy a toilet siphon. Then I would have to turn off the main tap, and drain all the water out of the cistern and dismantle everything and take the cistern off in order to fit the new siphon, and then put it all back together again. And I did this to occupy my mind, because it stopped my thoughts from going down that route and crossing the point of no return.

Cam spoke again from behind the door. "Doc, I've had too much to drink and I've been smoking pot. I'm sorry about what I did."

A pause. I held down that tight knot of pressure, thinking of nothing else.

"I… it's been a long time since I was with anyone. I'm sorry. I shouldn't have spoken to you like that."

The worst of it was when someone apologised. Often it had happened before that I'd managed to get away from people and hang on to control, and I would have been all right if I'd had just a few more minutes alone, and people had kept their distance for the rest of the day, and then the person who'd caused it had come looking for me, and apologised for it, like they could tell what was happening to me, and that somehow vindicated the panic and made it rise up twice as strong.

"Please. Let's forget this happened. Let's try again. I'll explain to you."

From behind the door, he did sound genuinely remorseful. Perhaps the connection I'd imagined with him before had some truth in it. There's no person who is perfect, I reminded myself. No relationship simply functions without work from both parties.

"I'm all right. Please talk about something else," I said. Probably he would think I sounded cold, that I had snubbed his apology. But if I said anything else I didn't think I'd be able to keep my shit together any longer.

"Okay," he said after a moment. "Let's talk about the news. There was some bloke got stopped at the scanners in Heathrow. They thought he had a bomb hidden in his underpants, but it was this thing: it's called a chastity device; a metal handcuff round his balls and his dick that stop him from wanking or something like that."

I laughed a little. It wasn't really all that funny, but the panic level had started to go down. I breathed for a few moments, and then I got to my feet and opened the door. Cam had gone, and I found him in the hall downstairs, waiting.

"What those envelopes mean." Cam sighed and thrust his hands into his trouser pockets. "They're part of something Genghis is planning. We can't go on like this indefinitely. Either the police will get us eventually, or the big boys are going to decide we're a threat they're not going to tolerate any more."

I nodded. Sage had suggested this already.

He stepped around the door and sat on the sofa. I hesitated for a moment before following him and taking the other end. "We're planning a major job. If we pull it off, we're fleeing the country."

I stared at him. Was this was what had been holding him back all this time? "And you were just going to leave without telling me?"

"No... I mean, I don't know. I didn't expect all this to happen. I didn't know it would get so... involved. But when Genghis brought you to the club and I saw you for the first time, and then when I got talking to you at the canal and got to know a bit more about you, I just... " He sighed. "If I'd been sensible, I'd have kept it as strictly business."

I looked away from him, letting my gaze settle on the old broken electric fire sunk into the house's original chimney breast. I wanted to say something in return, but the words wouldn't come. Silence in the still house throbbed in my ears.

"We decided it months ago," Cam continued. "The idea Genghis had with the drugs was just something he came up with to tide us over in the meantime. We didn't expect someone else would be working with us when we started planning."

"So you're still going abroad when this is over?"

"I... I expect so. I won't be able to stay here."

And I wouldn't, either, I realised. The life I'd had was gone. I wasn't the person I used to be. I turned to face him. "What if I wanted to go with you?"

"You barely know me."

That was what my mother would have told me. My mother wasn't here any more. "Well, no. But there'd be nothing to say we would have to stay together if it didn't work out."

"Why would you want to go? You've still got a future

here. There's no reason for you to throw that away!"

"What future? I can't get a job. There's no future. Nothing apart from the same day, every day." I think I'd known this for some time, but it was only at this moment, after saying it to someone else, that I accepted it. That was all that used to matter, having a career, being professional. That was what was real. But now it wasn't. Cam and synthesising Ecstasy derivatives were real, and having a proper job was a fantasy, and denying that wouldn't change it. I was unemployable, and the addition of a criminal record to my CV would make no difference. It was time to stop excusing, stop blaming, stop wallowing, and to start again.

"You've got qualifications!"

I shrugged. "That doesn't make any difference."

"Once this recession blows over, you'll find another job."

"There's no guarantee of anything of the sort. You're just as likely to find a job as I am."

"No, I'm not." He slumped forwards, leaning his elbows on his knees and glaring at the carpet. His voice became low, fearful perhaps. "I've burned too many bridges. We all have. Me, Ace, Genghis. Sage has had his life and he just wants to feel useful before he dies. The Tweedles are going to fuck up their lives whatever they do. You're not like us. You're better than that."

I thought for a moment he might say more, but he didn't, and another oppressive silence descended.

"You say you've burned your bridges," I began. "But you won't tell me what it is you've done. By the same measure, you don't know what bridges I've burned before I ended up as who I am now. So don't presume to understand who I am, or what I'm like, or how my past barricades the future from me, or what I might be better or worse than, because you can't even start to understand."

Cam watched me, for what seemed an interminable time. "You burn this bridge," he said at last, his voice low, "there'll be no going back. Not again."

After a moment he reached across the carpet to his shoes. He set about jamming his feet into them and tightening the laces without looking at me.

"Where are you going?" I said, unsure of whether it was a good idea to challenge him after the outburst he'd had earlier.

"You're coming too. I'm going to show you something."

I'd dug too deep, and he was angry. He might be taking me to some remote place, to get rid of me. A morbid thought of a shallow grave in a dark wood came over me. "I don't want to. It's time I went home. Show me another time." Now my courage waned. I wanted to go back and be that shadow-person I was after I lost my job. I wanted to hide in the private sanctuary of my own house, to pretend in a fantasy of a future of gainful employment and keeping other people at arm's length until I wasted away my life and reached retirement age, too afraid to confront reality, until that sanctuary became a prison. I could walk away from this, make sure there wouldn't be another time.

He finished tying his shoes and looked up at me, a savage vehemence in his face. "You asked. You wanted to know."

"You've been drinking."

He laughed humourlessly. "And if I get caught, that'll be the least of my problems."

Cam's car was a middle-aged grey Rover. Everything

that had happened up to this moment, I had told myself, I could turn around and walk away from at any point. Perhaps I should have made a run for my car and got away from there. They didn't know where I lived, and if I didn't turn up at the next agreed time they wouldn't find me. And Genghis had said there were no obligations. But this was between me and Cam. It might have been bad judgement and wishful thinking, but some intuitive sense made me want to trust him, made me hope the explanation I'd been promised would make everything clear.

He didn't speak as he drove, his eyes moving restlessly, his tongue flicking frequently over his lips. It was as though he repressed something desperate to escape him, as if he fought back an urge to confide something in me.

Soon we arrived at a large complex off the main road. Cam swung the car in a wide arc across the parking area, coming to a halt in one of the marked places. He pulled on the handbrake and switched off the engine.

With the headlamps off, we sat in darkness, looking out on the large, modern building of steel and glass illuminated with gaudy lights, traffic buzzing on the dual carriageway behind it. In the shadows I felt safe. I couldn't see Cam's expression. The world couldn't see into me to know the revolution beginning inside me that would turn me against it.

"Cam, what am I looking at?"

"Whatever happens, whatever you decide, don't let on to Genghis that I brought you here and told you this, right?"

I hesitated for a moment, feeling his eyes upon me. "Right."

"That," Cam rested his hand on the top of the steering wheel and relaxed his weight back into the seat, "is the Blue Moon Casino, the second-largest gambling establishment in England."

I studied his face in the scant light coming from the casino and the lamps of the car park. I couldn't make out much, just the outline of the bridge of his nose, his lips, chin, and forehead, and the occasional reflection of the light in his eyes when he moved his head. I watched his hand tighten rhythmically on the wheel's rim. With an unexpected rush of lust, I wanted him to do something to me in the car then and there, wanted his hands on me and his soft, heavy body pressing against me.

I didn't say anything of this to him.

"We've got the end of the year coming up," Cam began. "All these bankers and big business types who ruined the British economy in the first place are loading up their bank accounts with big Christmas bonuses. If you think they spend them on presents for their spouses and kids and all that crap, you've got another think coming. The twentieth of December has been the night of this casino's biggest takings for the past nine years."

"You're going to rob the casino?" I said.

"The morning of the twenty-first, they'll be handing over the night's earnings to personnel from a security company, who will then transport them via a van to the bank for deposit. We've got until then to get a decent plan nailed."

Robbery. This was serious stuff. This was real crime, I supposed, although it didn't feel like that any more. It felt more like a group of mates planning a trip to London or some other complicated yet ordinary event. If Genghis had come up to me that morning in the dole office and asked me if I'd help him and some blokes rob a casino, I'd have run a mile and then I'd have rung the police, but from where I now stood it was a world away from that. I marvelled at how

I'd transitioned from who I'd been that morning into who I was now, and how at this juncture in time the proposal of robbing a casino seemed reasonable.

Cam continued. "We've studied the casino as much as we can from the outside." He raised his hand to the show of lights in the middle of the car park. "What we haven't got is information on the inside. Genghis needs footage and information on the security features in there. I'd be lying if I said there was no risk. Are you prepared to do that?"

There's a theory that says there are parallel universes out there where things went differently. Probably in a great many of them I'd be sitting at home alone this day, trying to soak up the void in my life with something banal and mindless; staring at the television or rambling without motive on the Internet, because I'd not had the courage to walk into the bridge club that evening in September, because I had turned back and reclaimed my place in the shadows.

And from this point on, where Cam and I are sitting in the car, outside the casino at some great cosmic junction, our universe splits into infinite eventualities. In some of them I turn back and want nothing to do with Genghis's heist, and I probably end up being that same shadow-person inhabiting the void between the living and the dead. In others we try this and we fail, and court and prison beckon, or even worse. But amongst these, surely there are strings of possibility where the dice may yet fall in our favour; surely there must be that probability, even if remote.

Cam's voice cut into my thoughts. "We need a driver as well. Sage said he'll do it, but his hands have got worse since. He can't do it and I know he doesn't want to. Are you in?"

There comes a point where we have to make the choice

between lying down and dying when life kicks us over and over, or taking matters into our own hands and running a risk so we can have a chance to kick life in return and steal back what it has robbed us of.

With the engine off, the heating had shut down and the car was growing cold. I folded my arms, tightening my shoulders to fend off the encroaching chill.

"I'm in."

5

BLUE SKIES

The morning had dawned cold and crisp, very still and clear, and with ever-so-slight traces of the autumn's first frost on the grass that grew in the crevices between the paving slabs of my driveway. As I reached the tailback approaching the Tollbar End roundabout, the sky loomed a brilliant azure, empty of all but a few scant wisps of cloud. I gazed up at it through the windscreen, and this morning it held that bit more significance than it would have had any other morning.

The exit the SatNav directed me to turned into a road that ran along beside a high fence, beyond which an empty expanse of flat land stretched. The morning sun glinted upon the white-and-glass fuselages of static planes as I drove past. At the corner of the airfield, the fencing turned inward to make room for a car park and the low buildings beside the control tower, the one farthest out displaying the red banner of the Coventry Pilot Training Centre.

I parked the car in one of the gravel-surfaced spaces opposite. I got out and fumbled in my handbag for my invitation to a first lesson as I locked up the car.

Behind the entrance door was a foyer with a window looking into a hangar full of historical planes in display condition. Aviation magazines cluttered a table. As I closed the door behind me, I spotted an intercom mounted on the wall close to the frame. I pressed the button and spoke into it. "Hi, my name's Pippa Smith." The made-up name felt awkward and unnatural coming from my lips. "I'm looking for Mr Armitage."

"Hi Pippa," squawked a man's voice in return. "I'll be over to meet you in just a few moments."

I fiddled with the Airfix models standing on the shelf behind the sofa while I waited. I hoped the man was not going to ask me to show him any ID. I had some, of course, but Cam had made it and wasn't sure if I should trust it.

After a few moments an elderly man walked across the hangar and opened the foyer door. "Nice to meet you, Miss Smith," he said, shaking me firmly by the hand. "What a marvellous morning for flying, as it's turned out!"

I followed the man through the hangar and out through another door, across the corner of the airfield where three small training planes were parked on a concourse, and through yet another door that led to a suite of test rooms and offices. The central room had a desk with a telephone and a lounging area with sofas. On the wall behind the desk hung some frames containing photographs of Spitfires and Hurricanes in flight, and Gillespie Magee's *High Flight* poem.

Through the window a slight breeze stirred the windsock in the still air. The training planes with their still propellers shone in the sun.

Armitage sat on one of the sofas and I sat opposite. He showed me a model of a plane with wires connecting the rudder and the elevator and ailerons and explained the principles of the different parts and how the steering bar controlled the ailerons and the elevator, and pedals on the floor controlled the rudder. He also explained something called a trim, that I hadn't known about before, that was a wheel that adjusted the resting position of the elevator fins.

I liked Armitage. He seemed passionate about aeroplanes, and I couldn't detect anything in his manner that was patronising or insincere. He smelled of the same soap my aunt and uncle gone to New Zealand used to use.

After he'd finished showing me the models and explained how we were going to fly, we went back out to where the training planes were parked.

"This is a Piper Cherokee." Armitage pointed to the plane standing outward from the others. A material resembling felt roofing covered the inner edge of the wing below the entrance hatch, and a 'do not step forward' mark had been painted on. "If you'd like to get in first."

I stared at the narrow fuselage of the plane perched upon its nimble wings and landing gear as I approached it. It was hard to imagine that this small thing went up into the sky and flew, reliably every time. Treading upon the patch at the back of the wing and taking hold of the metal rail above the door did not feel at all modern, and the inside of the aircraft was all upholstered in aging leather, which caused it to resemble a vintage car more than the commercial aircrafts I'd seen the insides of before.

I clambered across the controls between the front seats to take my position on the other side. Armitage got in after I'd sat down. He carried two pairs of heavy, padded headphones, one of which he handed to me. While he shut the door, I connected the jacks on the end to the ports on the aeroplane's dashboard and put on my seatbelt.

"Now, if you put those on, we can listen to the radio and talk to each other while we run the preflight checks," he explained.

The headphones sealed out the sounds of the real world. When their muffling weight rested on my head and pressed around my ears, they submerged me in some sort of weather reading, a lot like the shipping forecast early in the mornings on the radio. Armitage started the engine with a set of keys lying on the top of the plane's instrument panel. With a shudder that jolted through the fuselage, the propeller beyond the nose portion visible through the front window whirred into motion.

Armitage's voice came loud and clear through the headphones, over the stifled rattle of the engine. "Before we take off, we need to do a visual check of the controls I showed you inside. So, I want you to test the rudder, the elevator, and the ailerons to see they work."

I put my feet out to the rudder pedals and gripped the steering yoke with both hands. Turning my head to look out the window to my left, I eased the yoke anticlockwise and clockwise. The aileron at the back edge of the wing rose and fell. I repeated this watching the other wing, before moving the yoke back and forth to check the elevator flaps on the tail rose and fell correctly, and pushing the rudder pedals with my feet to see the vertical slat of the rudder move in and out.

Armitage gave a nod of approval. "That's fine."

He pressed the button in the centre of his steering yoke and held it down. "Coventry Ground, this is Lima Papa Uniform, request taxi, two POB, over."

The voice of Coventry Ground came back over the background sounds of the weather forecast. "Lima Papa Uniform, taxi holding point Bravo runway three, over."

Armitage said, "We're going to start moving out now. Remember what I told you about the rudder pedals? Once we start moving, I want you to press down the pedals to turn right, towards the main runway."

He pushed the lever at the bottom of the instrument panel, in between the seats, slightly forward. The engine pitch increased and the plane began to move forwards to the runway. I pushed down my right foot gently and felt the left plate budge slightly. The pedals were much stiffer than I'd imagined, not like the ones in a car. The view through the window began to turn, the plane following the yellow line painted on the tarmac to delineate the turn.

"Is that okay?"

"Super!"

The turn in the road began to level out. I eased my feet off the rudder pedals and almost instinctively twisted the steering yoke. "With your feet!" Armitage reminded me, taking hold of his own yoke to stop me turning it.

"Oh, I'm sorry!" I said. "I'm so used to driving cars!"

The plane had now turned level and the runway stretched ahead. Armitage dropped the speed until the plane came to a stop, then he put on the brakes and turned the engine up all the way. Fumes from the engine whipped back over the cabin in the current the propeller generated.

After he dropped the engine back down to its idle speed and took off the brakes, Armitage pressed the button on his yoke again. "Lima Papa Uniform, ready for departure."

"Lima Papa Uniform, cleared for takeoff."

Armitage pushed the throttle forwards. The plane began to move, turning to approach the runway as he adjusted the rudder pedals.

The pitch of the engine grew louder, despite the headphones clamped over my ears. Grass rushed by and the runway raced ahead of the little plane's nose, and now the ground was falling, falling away from me, and the tarmac had gone from beneath the wheels below. Gillespie Magee's first line flew to the front of my mind on a hurricane of adrenaline.

Slipped the surly bonds of Earth...

The perimeter fence disappeared from the bottom of the window as the plane began to climb. My legs were rigid, holding the pedals in position with my feet, but when I looked to the side it was already a long way down under the Piper Cherokee's wings, and there was a road with some great articulated lorry tearing down it, and it looked more like a Matchbox toy. I was inside this tiny unsteady capsule, smaller than the inside of a car, suspended in the planet's troposphere by nothing more than forward momentum and the shape of its wings.

I was flying. And the reality of it brought moisture to my eyes, an unbidden grin cramping the muscles of my jaw.

The landscape that spread beneath basked in the sun of an autumn morning as the plane climbed towards the wisps of cloud above.

"All right, Pippa. You have control of the plane now. If you'd like to try using the yoke, gently, to give yourself a feel for the controls."

Oh yes, Pippa. That was my name today.

Gingerly, I eased the steering yoke to turn the plane right. The right side of the plane began to drop, gravity shifting. The fields and roads and swathes of golden-and-russet-leaved trees rotated below the tip of the left wing.

"Now level out." Armitage guided me as I returned the plane to normal flight. I banked left, feeling the slight unsteadiness all the time of air currents rocking the plane.

"Now fly up through that hole in the cloud." Armitage pointed. "Remember to look where you're going before you start changing course."

After checking, I eased the yoke back so the plane gradually tilted upwards, the horizon sinking below the bottom of the window. Armitage showed me how to use the trim, a knurled wheel set back between the seats that adjusted the resting position of the elevator on the plane's tail. Fingers of mist parted before the propeller as the plane rose into the cloud layer, vaporous haze obscuring the scenery below. After a few minutes of climbing, Armitage instructed me to level out and reduce the engine speed, and the horizon once more levelled up with the plane's nose.

The land below was more distant now, less distinct. Much of the bright autumn foliage had gone, replaced with tessellated shades of muddy man-made grey and blocky buildings, joined by the dark seams of roads and railways. Some distance away a thick grey snake knotted into a great coil, buzzing with multicoloured dots of traffic.

"Is that Spaghetti Junction down there?" I asked.

"Indeed it is."

"I didn't realise we'd come that far!"

Armitage smiled, not taking his eyes from the horizon. "It doesn't feel like it up here, but we're travelling over a hundred miles an hour!"

So we flew on, turning in a circuit to return to the airfield, and though it seemed an eternity I was up there with the bright sun and the clear sky, and the world just a picturesque mirage below with its bad memories so insignificant from this perspective, it was over all too soon, and I was turning the plane back in towards the rectangle of runway and dropping the flaps that would brake our descent, and Armitage was taking back control, and the ground was coming up to meet us.

Cam stood waiting for me in the car park. I could tell it was him because he wore the same anorak he'd had on when he'd been disguised as a Sikh, and a dark blue jersey over a plain shirt and beige corduroy trousers. With his frameless spectacles and floppy blond quiff, he looked like a youthful member of that dying breed of old-school academics that British universities are doing their best to make extinct these days.

"Did you enjoy it?"

I looked back up at the clear sky, conscious of the fathomless heights above in a way I'd never been before. In my imagination, I was still up there. The experience had left me with almost a singing sensation, a vibration just below the threshold of hearing, as though I'd entered into harmonic resonance with the rest of the universe. Perhaps this was what religious fanatics felt when they worshipped. For a time, I'd become something greater than flesh and blood and ignorance crawling about on a two-dimensional plane of dirt and rock, and worrying about my own conceited affairs.

I made eye contact with him again and hurriedly answered, "Yes, thanks." He must have thought I'd been smoking weed in the plane.

I certainly felt as though I had.

"What did Genghis say?"

"He said I could let you in on it and see what you can come up with. I don't think he's committed to splitting the spoils with you quite yet, but he says he'll pay you."

Well, that was good, I supposed. Up until this point I'd been worrying that Genghis would refuse. Genghis agreeing opened a whole new can of worms I would now have to worry about. "So, where are we going?"

"You'll see." Cam rapped on the bodywork of a Landrover Freelander that was parked there. "Meet Nogbad the Bad."

As he drove, I took out my SatNav and followed his course on the maps. He looked to be making for Wyre

Forest. I thought of dead bodies buried in dank woods, those who had got on the wrong side of the criminal underworld. The forest came into view like the frontline of a dark army advancing across the countryside. Trees closed their ranks on either side of the road when the car entered. I needed to say something to allay this fear, to break the thread of tension running through my diaphragm to my chest.

"Nogbad the Bad?"

Cam had been staring at the road ahead, and my interruption of the silence it seemed served to relax him as well as me. "It started as a joke. Sage got hold of one of those manky old Bedford Rascal things as our van at the beginning. It was shit, so it became a joke that he bought it second hand from Tutankhamun, and then we started calling it Mumm-Ra, and since then we started giving all our vehicles code names after classic cartoon baddies."

He spoke with alacrity and at a slightly higher pitch than I'd noticed him use before, taking his hands off the wheel and his eyes off the road to reinforce his words with vigorous gestures and nervous glances.

"We need a place where the road bends to the left, and there's a ditch next to it."

I watched the road ahead and compared it to the SatNav's image. "Do you remember anything more about where it was?"

"It's not a place I've seen. It's a hypothetical place we need to find an equivalent of. The idea is that if you're being followed, you would be able to throw something from your vehicle in a particular place without whoever was following you from seeing it happen."

I knew not to ask. If it became necessary for me to know more, then he'd tell me. This was a trial, on a need-to-know basis. If I showed I was worthy, then I'd be allowed deeper into the circle.

After a moment I suggested, "There may be something that fits that description up about a mile ahead."

Cam pulled over into the layby and switched off the engine. I took off my seatbelt.

I opened the door and stepped out onto a surface mushy with wet leaves. The high branches breathed incessantly in the wind. Cam went to the back of the vehicle. He rummaged through the things lying on the boot floor until he found a large case, from which he removed an expensive-looking SLR camera. He hung it round his neck by the strap and slammed the boot door.

Without speaking, he pointed into the dark spaces between the trees.

The fresh autumn air carried the scent of soil and mould, of living things. The wind towed a constant stream of yellow and red leaves from the upper parts of the trees, but down in the wood we were sheltered.

At the side of the road the ground ran down a steep muddy incline to a ditch choked with fallen leaves. Cam held my arm awkwardly as I slithered down. While I waited for him to follow, I looked about at the trunks of the trees, the cones and needles littering the floor, and the patches of azure sky the fraying foliage bordered above my head.

Cam straddled the ditch that divided the road from the forest and heaved himself up on the other side. We began to walk among the trees, and for some minutes neither of us spoke. If I'd met this ebullient man striding beside me two years earlier, I'd probably have thought him exactly my type. I slid my hand through his elbow and breathed a deep draught. The soft earth underfoot flexed against my tread. A car passed on the road behind us, but it was as though the road had already become part of another universe, more dream than reality.

Cam dug a small book out of the pocket of his anorak and paused by a large rotting branch lying on the ground. He turned the pages carefully.

"What's the matter?" I asked. The book turned out to be a field guide to mushrooms. It looked a bit dog-eared and had fluorescent Post-It stickers poking out from between the pages with notes in black ink and meticulous hand.

I glanced away and caught sight of a movement some distance away in the trees, the unnatural black and orange pattern of someone's coat. He must be acting, to look inconspicuous.

Cam indicated a black, rubbery, wrinkled shape protruding from the disintegrating bark.

"I think it's called a Jew's ear," I said. I at least remembered that from when I'd once gone on a fungus foray with my friend Paul. Paul had spent most of it making rude jokes about stinkhorns. A pang of regret came with the thought, sorrow that Paul no longer shared his crass sense of humour and his company with me.

Cam frowned. "Says in here it's called a jelly ear, or a *Auricularia auricula-judae*."

I shrugged. "Maybe the political correctness brigade got at it."

Cam chuckled, lowering his head and raising his eyes to me. When he looked at me like that, a sensation somewhere between recognition and panic surged up inside me. He looked a different man than yesterday. Nothing was static about this person, even from day to day. His eyes were a watery blue colour, but I had an unnerving sense that they hadn't been before. And yet I was beginning to recognise subtle constants. That raised mole on his right cheek, for example. No matter what cologne or smell he'd put on himself or his clothes, I'd learned to recognise a familiar note beneath it.

As he put the mushroom book back into his pocket his arm brushed my elbow. I stared up at the restless branches and inhaled deeply, until dizziness broke through and made my vision falter.

Last year the four seasons had passed unheeded, and I had been too consumed by myself. Even when I had tried hard to appreciate the world around me, I had been unable to, as though watching from behind thick glass. Had I walked here a year ago, it would have been as a corpse decomposing, turning into the environment, not a living thing walking within it. But now it was different. Something of what had been was coming back to me.

Paul had been a true friend, although I never really realised it until it was over. So often we rarely know the best days of our life until they are passed. We waste today yearning for the future, blinded by ambition or small inconveniences: or we stand faltering, bogged down in the past and what we have lost.

Cam was flipping through his fungus book again. "What's the most poisonous mushroom there is?"

I thrust both hands into my pockets. "Probably the Death Cap."

"And where might I find that, should I decide my life's not worth living any more?" He let out a macabre sort of chuckle.

I had already switched off, engaged my scientific sub-mind. "If you wanted to kill yourself, assuming you wanted it to be painless and swift, I wouldn't use fungi to do it. The poisons in them destroy the liver, so it takes several days for them to kill you, and if you were to change your mind about killing yourself in that time there's nothing that can be done to save your life."

Cam considered for a moment. "So, if you had to kill yourself, what would you say was the best way to go about it?"

I looked away from his eyes. My mouth groped for words.

If only he knew.

It had been Christmas last year. The house was cold because abstaining from using the heating meant saving precious money that might make other essentials last longer, and it got dark at half past three in the afternoon. Cheerful programmes about families and bright futures and festive cheer played incessantly on the television, and I had sat there, freezing, trying to lose myself in the mindlessness of it all; trying to stop my thoughts from returning to what they inevitably must. And I had turned it off, and I'd sat there and done a grim calculation with a pen on the back of a piece of junk mail: the mass of a particular drug it would take to be effective upon a person of my weight, and how much it would cost.

Seeing it in black ink, the final sum, suffused me with a coldness deeper than my unheated house. This was the last disillusionment. I could see myself weighing it out as accurately as I would have done in my old job; I could have stopped thinking, stopped fearing, lain on the floor until I grew as cold as the surroundings, and most likely no-one would have noticed until a bad smell intruded on the neighbours the following spring. I didn't do it because I'm a coward. There's a parallel universe where I had courage and I died that day.

"Are you all right?" Cam nudged my elbow. I realised I'd loosed his hand and a gap had grown between us as we'd been walking. "Sorry, that was a stupid, morbid thing to say. It's the kind of thing Ace would say."

"No, it's all right. I was just thinking about the answer," I said. "It's nitrogen gas suffocation."

"Nitrogen gas?"

"The air around us is mainly nitrogen. If we breathe nitrogen without enough oxygen in it, we don't feel anything. We just lose consciousness without ever knowing it's happening."

A nervous look had come over him. Perhaps it was because of me; perhaps it was just part of his incognito persona. He glanced up at the sky and the procession of coloured leaves streaming from the trees in the ceaseless wind, and he touched his hand to mine, timidly.

I pushed back down on the pressure inside me, refusing to acknowledge or analyse it in any way, forcing it back into the imaginary black hole in my chest. I barely knew him, and what I did know was liable to change or disappear. I had to work with this man, and I'd already had an altercation with him. I was a fool to gamble on this.

And yet... I might live to regret it if I never chased opportunity this time, if I let it recede into the past, as I had with Paul. The past is another country, and there might never be any future.

"We didn't just come here to look for a bend in the road," he said, his voice low, deadly serious.

I didn't answer, and from this he interpreted that I assented to continue. "We need to get into the casino to get some inside information."

A break-in? I wouldn't be much good at that. I waited for him to explain.

"Sage has arranged us invites to a dinner party

being held there Friday night. Ace has some surveillance equipment, but it'll be easier to hide on a woman's clothing than a man's. I'll be able to come with you, and I'll keep you safe as best I can, but you'll be the one wearing the camera and taking the risk."

We had been walking back alongside the road as we spoke, and the bend brought it to us once more. Cam set his feet carefully and scrambled up the bank to stand and look back the way we'd come. "There. You can't see the car from here."

He reached down and helped me up. He was right. The trees hid the car's position from anyone who might be following it.

Neither of us said anything as we walked back on the sodden and leaf-strewn verge. The person I'd been back when I'd had a career and money would never have agreed to this. I wasn't that person any more, and this was the only way I could now make a living and forge any way forward from the stagnation I'd become entrenched in. If there was a risk, perhaps it was worth taking. What might be the worst that could happen if I was caught carrying a camera in a casino? A fine I would be let off paying on account of not having the money? A police warning? Probably it was simply being banned from a casino I had no intention of ever patronising.

The back of Nogbad the Bad had by now come into view in its layby. Cam pressed the button to unlock it on the central locking fob as we drew closer.

Although blue sky roofed the breach in the forest, no sunlight penetrated to touch the road below, almost as if the trees resented the intrusion and conspired and brooded on both sides. The air was growing cold, and the inside of the car was no warmer than out.

"What do I need to do?"

Cam locked eyes with me, studying my expression. Perhaps he was trying to gauge how seriously he could take me, or transmit to me the risk I was exposing myself to. He reached across and yanked open the glove compartment, and dumped an envelope from it in my lap. I could tell without opening it that it contained a wad of bank notes.

"Genghis says to buy something nice, and wear your hair up."

6

SHRINKING VIOLET

I've never really *got* shopping. I used to have a cousin, a sort of stereotype to which *girls* are supposed to conform, who did it for enjoyment. She used to drag me along with her when I was a teenager, goading me to try on things and buy shoes I couldn't walk in and stuff I'd never have the nerve to wear anyway. She got married or lived with someone or whatever it's called now and had kids like *women are supposed* to do, and I lost contact with her because neither of us had anything left in common after that.

What would Cam like? I found myself wondering. A private smile forced itself onto my face as I rifled through the racks of clothes. I couldn't imagine Cam sincerely making a compliment, not unless he was in character. Not because he was inconsiderate or unobservant or anything like that, but because it was my impression he considered them platitudes. I guess I'm not one for compliments either. If someone has the power to hurt you and you let that person know it, you're handing out ammunition in a way. Perhaps making insulting compliments, like Cam often did with Ace, is a shell, to mitigate that harm.

What am I thinking? I asked myself. All this speculation was nonsense. I didn't know anything about Cam, not even his name. Every day he was a different person, and yet I had the feeling of this undercurrent to him, that there was something constant there and that some sort of meaning could be derived from the vagaries of what he said and did.

I gazed upon the assorted garb upon the racks before me. I didn't know what to wear, and this was getting more tedious by the minute. Why wasn't it possible to apply rational analysis to these sorts of things and work out a procedure step by step, the same as I would have done in my old job if I'd had to synthesise a complex molecule?

Or perhaps I could. This was a disguise, so it had to be something that wouldn't make me look like me. When I'd had to go out to meals with work and suchlike before, I'd generally worn smart-casual trousers and a jersey. I don't do dresses, so that would be the obvious place to start if I intended to look unlike myself. On the other hand, it would be a coup if I could pull this off and Cam couldn't recognise me, and the shoe was on the other foot for a change.

What would my cousin have wanted me to buy?

After turning a few hangers I came across something made of green silky material overlaid with black gauze and lace. The heavy mesh of the layers deepened the green of the underlying fabric. I held it up to my shoulder to measure it for length. The hem came down nearly to the floor. It had been styled in a fairly straight, narrow shape, with a boned bodice and no shoulder straps. It looked uncomfortable and impractical. I winced at the price tag. Even though it was Genghis's money and not mine, the idea of spending £200 on a piece of material I would most likely only use once still seemed a flippant waste. My cousin would have been proud.

I found one in the size that had fitted me last time I'd bought clothes. If it didn't fit, I'd have to come back tomorrow. I hated using public changing rooms. They reminded me of being humiliated in PE as a kid.

I found a beaded black lace shawl-cardigan-thing to

complement it. It cost £50, which was silly considering it was made of lace and was thus more holes than actual material. On the way to the till it occurred to me I didn't have any shoes suitable to wear with it; just my old driving trainers and a pair of industrial boots I'd worn at my old job. I headed over to the shoe section of the shop and managed to locate a pair of flat slipper-like things made from black fabric with silver embroidery on them. Probably they didn't match, but hopefully no-one would notice because the hem of the dress came down so low.

*

The woman at the hairdressing shop wore her hair in a fancy bun stabbed through with what looked like chopsticks. She kept asking me questions.

"So, where are you going tonight?" she said.

"To an office Christmas party," I replied. *To rob a casino*, I thought, and wondered what sort of hairstyle she might suggest for this purpose.

"Oh, that's nice. What do you work as?"

"It's my partner's job," I said, which I supposed was true. "I'm going as his guest."

"What kind of look are you aiming for?"

"I'm not sure," I said. "The outfit I have is dark green and black." I tried to think of something very different to anything I'd ever tried before. "What about something like that goth style people used to wear? Are they still called goths now, or are they supposed to be called something else?"

The reflection of the woman who stood behind my back shrugged. She had pulled my hair out of the usual pony-tail that restrained it. She kept poking her fingers into it as she spoke. My hair was originally blonde, and not a romantic golden blonde, but more of a straw-coloured frizz. Within the last few years it had started to grey, and now more resembled old straw that had been lain on by dirty animals. I'd always cut it myself and I suspected the woman could tell. I looked like an old witch with it hanging down on either side of my face, a kink where it had been tied back.

A man in a black shiny shirt, who had been sauntering up and down pushing hair trimmings with the toe of his shoe since I'd arrived, spun a hairdryer at his hip, tossed it in the air, and caught it like a gunslinger playing with a pistol. He pointed the nozzle at the woman, cocked an eyebrow, and grinned. "Emmo," he said.

The woman grimaced and waggled a comb at him. "It's pronounced *eemo*, and that's something else." She resumed combing her fingers through my hair. "If you want to go real goth, you're going to have to go black, and that might not work so well on your hair colour if you just want something you can wash out next morning."

"Is there another colour you could dye it? It doesn't have to be actual goth, just something along those lines that would blend in with it." I felt uneasy about leaving it as it was. The further I looked from my usual self, the better.

The woman and the man discussed this further for a moment. We came to a compromise with the woman dyeing strips of my hair black and styling it into a stripy pompadour with segments of it coiled into rings at the top. The whole thing took half an hour, managing to be simultaneously tedious and awkward and stressful as I sat there worrying that the woman would be in a prime position to recognise me should my face end up on *Crimewatch*, and wondering if she could sense something about me that told her I was lying.

The rest of my disguise was in a bag in the boot of my

car. I drove to Cam's house with my neck held rigid so as not to disturb the elaborate sculpture balancing on my head. Outside the house, I recognised Zordrak pulled up behind Cam's Rover. I slung the bag over my arm and walked up the drive.

Ace answered the door. "You gunna wear that?" he said, mouth full of semi-masticated crisps as he looked me up and down. I brandished the bag at him.

I went into the living room. Food containers and pieces of computer equipment covered the furniture, along with several large heaps of order forms from some catalogues Ace and Sage had made a few months earlier and mailed to a list of names they'd pulled off the electoral register. The catalogue purported to be from a company that delivered champagne and hampers and such things on time as Christmas gifts. Unfortunately, none of the people who'd filled in the order forms enclosed and sent back cheques were going to receive their orders before Christmas. Or indeed, ever.

"I've got summing for you." Ace turned over a burger wrapper and lifted his laptop off the sofa. "If I can find it."

He uncovered a square, dark-green box beneath some cables on the coffee table, which he handed to me. Inside were a pair of large, lumpy earrings, a hair ornament with a plastic comb grip sticking out of the back, and a choker. All were of a matching style, with clusters of different-sized onyx circles mounted on silver stems. The choker had a large pattern at the front with strings of the black beads depending from it.

"It's whatchamacallit. Art Newvow or summing," said Ace.

"Very nice," I said. "Where did you nick it?"

Ace pointed to the hair piece. "Can you tell which one

is the camera?"

I lowered my face to the objects in the box, and when I saw the centre bead in the arrangement closely in the light I noticed it was less convex compared to the others, and that it had a purplish sheen. "Clever."

Ace grinned. "Mint, innit? There's a headset in one of them earrings, so you'll be able to hear me." He levered up the velvet pad the jewellery was fixed to. Underneath was a little black object, about the size of an unshelled peanut. "This is the hard part. You'll need to plant this somewhere inside so we can get something on the timer the safe's on."

"Will the safe be on a timer?" I asked.

"Sure as shit it will."

I put my hand in my pocket and brought out the silver charm bracelet my aunt had given me when she and my uncle left for New Zealand. It was an ugly thing, really, with clunky figures and beads dangling from the chain. The camera had a tiny clip on it, small enough to attach to the bracelet as I'd hoped.

Ace grinned. "Mint."

I got changed in the toilet upstairs, stepping into my clothes so as not to mess up my hair. It took some concentration and care to stick the comb into my fancy hairstyle correctly. The earrings were heavy clip-on affairs.

"Ace, are you receiving me?" I said to the mirror.

"Ya," came back Ace's voice. "Just look at stuff and say things for a bit so I can calibrate the equipment. Oh, and watch what you're doing if you go to see Cam, because he might be nekkid in there and I don't want that shit burning dead pixels in my LCD."

I left the bathroom and approached the bedroom door. It stood ajar and I could hear faint sounds of movement from within. "Cam?"

"Please, come in."

I pushed open the door. Cam stood in front of a desk in there, wearing a kilt made from black tartan with a red pattern, with a formal shirt and jacket and socks that folded over just below the knee. He cleared his throat and spoke with a soft Scottish accent, a charming sort of voice filled with suggestive inflections. "Well, well, good evening. Don't you look delectable?"

"A kilt? Don't you think that's taking it a bit far?"

"Of course not. If I pretend to be someone a little out of the ordinary, it's much harder for people to spot any minor errors. The novelty sorta eclipses them."

I laughed. "Well, are you wearing anything under it?"

Cam rested one hand on his waist and turned to face me. "Why don't you come and find out?"

I tried not to grin too much. It might mess up my makeup. "I might take you up on that, but later. We've got work to do first."

Cam winked at me. "Pick a name for me."

"I dunno. Hamish Macleod?"

"Now that really would be pushing a stereotype too far. Macleod is acceptable, but I'll go with Hector rather than Hamish. Let's practice." He offered me his hand and a lecherous grin. "You look like a nice lady on a cold night. You fancy warming yer hands under my sporran? I'm Hector Macleod. I'm a director working for an independent film production company."

I took hold of his hand awkwardly. "I'm, uh, Jackie... Banks. I, er... does it matter what I do?"

"Well, it would sound better if you were something,

rather than being unemployed or working the graveyard shift at McDonalds."

"I'm a, er, an author... of... children's books?"

He gave his tie a downward tug to tighten it. "That's interesting. Do you draw your own pictures too?"

"Yes." I did my best to hold his gaze and appear honest.

"That's cool. What do you use, watercolours?"

"I... uh, I don't know."

He shrugged and ran his palms over the cummerbund that hid the join between the hem of his shirt and the waistband of his kilt. "Well, I suppose you could pass for someone with amnesia,"

"Cam." I checked through the doorway to make sure Ace wasn't eavesdropping. "I don't think I'm going to be any good at this."

"It's not difficult." Cam adjusted his cufflinks smartly. "It just takes a bit of practice to get the hang of it."

"That's all right for you to say. You're... you can talk to people." I'm not like that. I've never really felt at ease with anyone, apart from my uncle and aunt, and my dad when I was young. *And he took his own life, and the world was broken in pieces.*

Cam put his hand on my arm, just above the elbow. The scaly black lace of the shawl I was wearing chafed between our skin. I might have said more, but then a car horn blared in the street.

"Yo, Bitch," Ace called up the stairs. "Your carriage awaits."

Cam bowed slightly, raised his eyes to me, and gestured to the door.

Ace skulked at the bottom of the stairs, his fists

weighing down the baggy pockets of his hoodie. "Cam, you look like Monsieur Creosote in a skirt."

"Fuck off, Ace!"

Outside, a limo waited in the cool night air. Cam opened the door from me.

"Good evening," said Genghis from the driver's seat. He reached up and touched his cap. "Doc, you look a million quid. And despite the economic climate, that's still more than a million dollars at current exchange rates. Cam, you look like Monsieur Creosote."

Cam slammed the door. "Will people stop telling me I look like Monsieur *fucking* Creosote!" He slapped both hands down on his bare knees. "Besides, where'd you get a limo from? You nick it?"

"Sort of," said Genghis cautiously. "Kind of one of those trees falling in an empty forest philosophy things. If I nick it and put it back before anyone has noticed, does it still count as having been nicked?"

I started. "You stole a limo? What if the police examine it and find our DNA in it?"

Genghis raised his eyebrows. "Can you guess at the kind of things that go on in the backs of limos? I can't imagine your DNA would look anything unusual mixed up with everyone else's samples."

"Urh, thanks Genghis! You would say that after we'd sat on it." Cam squirmed in the seat. As the car swung onto the main road, he glanced around the interior, taking in the upholstery and the mini-bar. "It's kind of gross, isn't it, really? I mean, it's the sort of naff American thing cheap people use when they're trying to look rich for something important."

Genghis said, "Doc, you're into cars. What do you

think?"

I paused, studying the back of Genghis's head. He'd recently clipped his hair and a scar on the scalp was evident through the close-cropped black stubble. "Well, I have a car so I can drive. If I wanted to ride in the back seat, I'd get a taxi."

Cam let off a gruff nasal exhalation. "Touché."

The lights of the Blue Moon Casino stood like a mirage in the concrete sea of the car park. People queued near red rope barriers at the entrance as we pulled up in Genghis's stolen limo.

I stepped out of the car and Cam followed me, throwing his feet out of the door and heaving himself upright in a way that risked exposing himself in the wind the open expanse of the car park drew. He slipped my arm through his and we took our place at the end of the queue.

At the front of the line, a pair of bouncers were inspecting people before they were permitted entry. I rehearsed my fake introduction while Cam fiddled with a large rubber plant in the lobby.

"I'd like to just check inside your bag, Madam," said the officious-looking female bouncer when we reached the head of the queue.

I set the bag down on the table. As I bent over to undo the catch on it, it occurred to me that the camera perching on the top of my head was right under the bouncer's nose. Apart from my wallet, my bag was full of junk accrued from going about my life: pens, tampons, make up, receipts and parking permits. The woman went through them all meticulously.

I wondered who it was we were plotting to rob. Not these people, certainly, nor the young men who waited on the guests with trays of champagne glasses and small chocolate things, dressed in stiff, almost military costumes and who were probably as much there for security as for the provision of blandishments. Beneath all this, did there perhaps exist an individual with whom the buck stopped, a singular owner of the Blue Moon Casino? Or did what profit or loss that might happen here get absorbed through roots and branches of a sprawling tree of shareholders? Could a crime be called victimless if it affected no specific person, but merely a faceless, hydra-headed corporation?

The male bouncer eyed Cam. "And you, Sir. Please open your sporran."

Cam leaned back and tilted his hips towards the man in a vulgar sort of way. "I have nothing to declare."

The man glanced and nodded.

Cam snapped the sporran shut. "Bet you wish you had one like that!" He roared it at a volume that made his Scottish accent raucous and crass. He winked at the people in the queue behind us before following me out of the lobby.

The room beyond was a bewildering confusion of noise and movement. Cam took to it immediately. He seemed to know the names of half the people in the room. I found myself drifting away from him as he stepped into character and began chatting to a gaggle of glitter-covered young women. I wasn't any good at this sort of thing. I'd hated attending conferences with my old job, and networking as they called it. I found a glass of orange juice on a tray standing on a side table — I didn't want my judgment clouded by alcohol in this already difficult situation — and sidled away to a large aquarium taking up one of the walls.

Doc, are you receiving me? Look at your feet if you are.

I inclined my head to glance down at the floor in answer to Ace's request.

Good. Now let's get this survey underway. I'd like you to check the ceiling a moment.

I tried to make it look as though I was simply looking around, and raised my face to the ceiling, holding my glass close to my lips as though I was considering some sort of mural at a stately home. The ceiling was made from a shiny black material that dully reflected the shapes of the people below.

One way glass, Ace said. *So they can see the gambling tables and if anyone is cheating.*

A man with coiffed steel-grey hair and a glass of champagne appeared to have singled me out and was heading in my direction. I turned away from him, trying to look aloof and engrossed in the meanderings of the fish among the corals. Undeterred, the man moved up to stand beside me.

"Splendid, aren't they?" he said, without taking his champagne flute away from his mouth. "That one there," he touched the glass with his index finger, leaving a print, to indicate a rather abstract-shaped fish whose iridescent body was adorned with wild pastel markings, "is called a Picasso's Triggerfish. You can probably guess why."

Who asked that smart-arse over here? Ace's voice in my ear was irate. *Tell him to fuck off!*

"I suppose we have to pick one of these for our first course?" I said, trying to be humorous instead of taking up Ace's suggestion.

The man laughed in a way that was disproportionately generous for the calibre of the joke. He inclined the rim of his glass away from his lips and raised an eyebrow. "So, what do you do for a living?"

"I'm Jackie Banks; I write children's books," I said.

Damn. That probably sounded a little too well rehearsed.

"Oh, really! Yes, I've heard of you." The man grinned effusively. "What publisher is it you're with again? On the tip of my tongue…"

"Uh," I groped with my mouth while my brain flailed for a plausible answer. "Random… house?" That was a publisher, wasn't it? It sounded familiar.

"Ah, yes." Recognition flashed over the man's face. "I'm Julian Roberts. I'm an acquisitions editor with Penguin." As he spoke, he delved into his breast pocket and discreetly passed me a card between his index and middle fingers.

"Oh, look." I hurriedly shoved the card into a side-pocket on my handbag. "Looks like people are taking up their seats." The double doors to the dining area had been opened and the crowd was beginning to mill into the other room. I moved away from the editor who'd just initiated an attempt to gazump another publishing house of a nonexistent author on behalf of his company, trying to find Cam in the crowd. *Shit, what name did he decide to use in the end?* I muttered to myself.

Hector Macleod, Ace reminded me.

I caught sight of a flash of red-and-black tartan between people's legs, and made for Cam's position. I held on to his arm, checking over my shoulder for the whereabouts of the man who had just been talking to me. "You meet anyone interesting?" he asked casually.

Waiters were entering with the starters. "Um," I said, not wanting to alert Julian Roberts, who turned out to be standing behind me. "Do you remember what we ordered?"

He smiled. "No, but I'm sure we'll both remember what sounded interesting to us when they start calling out."

I ended up sitting between Cam and the editor, who

was fast becoming drunk. Across from us sat a woman with an enormous bosom that drooped into her *hors d'oeuvres*.

I rolled and unrolled my napkin on my lap while the staff bustled about with the first course.

"Goats' cheese with toasted pine nuts on a bed of salad?" called someone nearby.

I raised my hand nervously. "Over here. Thanks," I added when the waiter set the plate down in front of me.

Cam waited a bit longer and chose a lobster bisque.

Soon, everyone was eating, apart from a gentleman on the next table who was arguing vociferously with the waiter that he'd ordered lobster bisque and not some crummy vegetarian sunflower seed salad, saying that he was a red-blooded man and 'not a fucking gerbil'.

That looks bloody marvellous, said Ace in my ear. *Wish I could cook.*

I thought it *was* bloody marvellous. Usually I lived off lentils and cheap rice, supplemented by whatever ends of meat and mangy fruit and vegetables I could find in the reduced section of the supermarket in the evening. I might have been able to appreciate it more had Julian Roberts not been persistently trying to initiate a conversation with me.

Okay, when you think it's safe to do so, I want you to look slowly all around the room, paying particular attention to any entrances and exits.

Cam had finished his starter and was now mopping out the bowl with a piece of crusty bread. As he'd been eating, he'd been making comments this way and that across the table, and as he set down his cutlery he girded himself to speak, his back straightening and his chest swelling. He embarked upon a ribald, rambling anecdote that commanded the attention of everyone at the table, apart from the man sitting on the other side of me. It was the perfect opportunity to look around. If anyone did look at me, they would probably think I was trying valiantly to show the editor I wasn't interested whilst maintaining proper decorum.

Okay, said Ace. *Just move your head left a little so I can see that box on the wall. Now hold still and look at the door. They've got some kind of lockdown system on that; must be coordinated by a central computer. It's not on the door to the kitchen, though. That might do for an escape route if we screw up.*

The plates from the starter were being collected. Our fellow guests listened intently while Cam finished his story, his every inflection holding them entranced. At his punchline, they exploded into uproarious laughter. Now the main courses were being brought out. Cam chose roast venison and parsnips; I chose a quail stuffed with shallots and wine.

As we ate, Ace prompted me to glance at various things around the room. Cam got drunk, and Julian Roberts got beyond drunk. People began to laugh a little too loud and speak a little too long.

For dessert, Cam had sticky toffee pudding and I had a raspberry cheesecake.

When all the revellers had finished eating and the plates had been cleared away, a disco started up at the end of the room and the waiters propped open the doors to the gambling hall.

People began pulling the crackers laid out on the table. Inside them were long cylindrical balloons, of the sort one blows up with a straw and releases. The first dancers went to the dance floor, and soon balloons were shrieking and rasping through the air over our heads. Cam was in the middle of the action, at least until one of the balloons swooped up his kilt, and he came back to the table to see if I was okay.

We need to scope out some of the other rooms, Ace told me.

I leaned in close to Cam to make it look as though I was talking to him. "I can't just wander around," I said.

Ya, you can. If anyone asks, pretend you can't find the shitter. Well, I mean, don't call it the shitter to them; call it the bog or whatever it is people of culture *call it.*

"Thanks for those words of wisdom. Cam, I'm going to the loo."

"Okay." He winked at me. "Meet you in the gambling hall."

"Don't waste all your money."

At Ace's instruction, I exited the disco room through a door into a corridor. At one end there was another door marked *Staff Only*.

The safe must be somewhere through there. See if you can get a look in.

I checked behind to make sure no-one would be able to hear me. "I can't just walk in there."

You can open the door. If anyone sees you, pretend you're looking for someone to tell you where the bog is.

"It's right there." I glanced to the pair of doors behind, on the opposite side of the corridor from that I had entered from, marked *Ladies* and *Gentlemen*.

Well, I dunno, perhaps pretend you're foreign?

I sighed and put my palm against the oak panelling of the door, and carefully eased it open. Inside I could see a few leather sofas and the entrance to a large safe built into the wall.

Got it. Good.

I glanced up at the corner in the ceiling above the wall. There was a security camera there, pointed at the safe.

Don't go any further, Ace said. I need you to plant that camera somewhere it won't be found.

Holding the door open with my shoulder and checking around carefully, I detached the tiny camera from my bracelet. The sticky part was covered by a paper tab. I peeled it off and slid my hand down the outside of the doorframe, gluing it in place so it faced the safe.

One second. I heard the clatter of typing in the background of Ace's transmission. *Perfect.*

I started at the sound of the door behind me opening. Julian Roberts stumbled into the corridor.

"Ah, there you are." He squinted and blinked. "I wondered if you would like to dishcuh the shupiffics of your last contract. I might be able to convince you to submit your next book to my company."

"You wouldn't like to talk to me," I said. "I've got amnesia and I'm not very interesting. If you'll excuse me, I'm going to talk to my imaginary friend." I stepped away from him and into the ladies' loos.

"Annoying man," I said, pulling the camera out of my hair as I went into a cubicle. I shoved it into my handbag.

Nice view.

"Well, I'm not having you watch me go to the toilet." I sighed. "I don't know if he really does believe that author crap, or if he just wants to get his leg over."

Ace laughed.

I washed my hands in the expensive soap and carefully put the camera back in position using the mirror. "I mean, you'd think he could take a hint."

I jumped when a cubicle door behind me, and out came a stout lady looking angry. "You may think it's all right to carry on with your mindless phone call in here, but for some of us it's very offputting!" she berated me. She turned and left without washing her hands, and the door slammed shut behind her.

Miserable old trout, said Ace.

"Stunk the fucking bog out as well. Good job they've not invented a microphone that can transmit that yet," I said quietly, and both of us laughed.

I found Cam by the roulette wheel.

"Pick a number for me," he said.

I picked red nine. Cam put all the chips he had left on it, and it lost.

"Ah well." He slapped his palms on his hairy knees. "No money left. Looks like time to get moving, if that's okay with you."

"Yes," I said. "I think we've got everything we need."

*

Outside, there was no sign of Genghis.

"Where is he?" I said.

"Probably had to take his limo back." Cam shrugged. "We'll hang around a bit, and if he doesn't turn up soon we'll just go back in Zordrak with Ace."

We wandered out of the casino car park and onto a pavement. I shivered in the cold and he put his arm around my shoulders.

"So how much money did you waste on gambling in the end?" I asked.

"About fifty quid."

"Expensive business then."

Cam rolled his eyes. "Well, one has to speculate to accumulate. Let's see if we can make some of it back." He turned to me and opened his sporran, angling his loins towards me in a suggestive way. One of the butter knives from the table lay in there, amidst a pile of yellow and red casino chips.

"How did they end up in there?" I asked.

"How do you think?" Cam glanced away from me, back to the path ahead. Two young men were coming towards us, probably headed for the casino. They had the fresh-faced look of recently graduated professionals, and the conversation the still, cold night air carried to our ears was filled with pompous buzz words and corporate jargon.

"Hey there," Cam hailed them.

Their conversation tailed off.

"Look, I can't talk to you for long, because we need to catch a train back to Edinburgh. We just came out of the casino back there." He indicated over his shoulder with his thumb. "Because my wife here kept nagging me, I forgot to cash some of my chips. They're worth five hundred and you can cash them in or gamble with them and see if you can hit it lucky like I did. It's not very far away."

"What, you giving them to us free?" One man looked incredulous. The other looked sceptical.

"Well, I would rather you gave me something for them. Just whatever you can afford. They are worth five hundred pounds after all."

The incredulous man began to dig through his wallet. "What do you want?"

"Have you got two hundred?"

"Hang on a minute." The man turned to his companion. "Have you got some I can borrow?"

They managed to scrape £150 together, which Cam accepted with profuse thanks. They took their chips and set off towards the casino, talking to each other animatedly. Wherever they'd originally been going had been forgotten, and now they were going to the casino.

"Cheers mate!" Cam called after them.

I frowned. "But you just sold them for half what they're worth. And I thought you lost all your chips anyway?"

"I did lose all my chips." He raised his eyebrows fancifully.

"Then what were those you just gave to them?"

Cam shrugged. "Some tiddlywink things I found in the pound shop this morning."

I stared at him. "How come they didn't find them when they searched us on the way in?"

Cam grinned at me. "Because I put them in one of those plant pots when we were standing in the queue, and I picked them back up on the way out."

I rolled my eyes and I laughed and shook my head.

"Come on." He threw a swift glance over his shoulder. "Let's get the hell out of here before they find out and come back."

7

WHITE LIES

Cam's house was dark and cold, and it seemed the bulb in the hallway had failed some time ago, for he made no attempt to switch it on. He heaved his shoulders and rubbed his hands together as he went to the sitting room and switched on the floor lamp. "You for a drink? Keep us warm, at least."

I followed him into the kitchen. The naked sixty-Watt bulb threw a stark reflection back at me from the uncurtained window that looked out into the blackness of the surrounding Leylandii. He set down two glasses on the shabby countertop and poured something amber and alcoholic into them.

The glass was not quite transparent from hundreds of tiny abrasions on its surfaces, and whichever way I turned it I could feel chips on the rim where it contacted my lips. We stood here in our fine clothes, incongruous in this squalid setting, and I thought of the crystal champagne flutes and the soft lighting and opulent furnishings in the Blue Moon Casino. Why was it right that some people should have these things, should have so much money that they can afford to waste it playing games, when others didn't, just because they'd flipped the same coin and got tails instead of heads? Just because the people in the casino were winning at the gambling game that was life?

"Something for you in the living room," Cam suggested.

I recognised the gold-on-burgundy heraldry of a

passport inside a plastic wallet on the coffee table as I took my seat on the sofa. There were two passports and a sheaf of other documents inside when I opened it. On the inside page of the first passport, I recognised the photograph of myself I'd given to Cam the previous week. I frowned as I read the details under it. "Rowena Griffin?"

Cam returned, glass in one hand and half a packet of digestive biscuits in the other. They looked like they'd be stale, like they were opened months ago.

"Did you invent that? It sounds like a character out of one of those kids' books about magical boarding schools."

Cam sat down next to me. "No, Rowena Griffin is a real person, or rather was. She was born Rowena Blackett on the 5th of October in 1979 and tragically died shortly after, and was then buried in a graveyard in Worcestershire." He lowered his glass and raised his eyes briefly to me over its rim. "Which is where I found her details."

I looked back down at the passport. Rowena Griffin's name wasn't funny any more. "That's awful." I closed the passport and examined the other one beneath it. "Dorian Griffin?"

"Dorian Griffin, born 30th January 1977, died aged three of meningitis. Buried in Stoke-on-Trent. This chap didn't let something as trivial as being dead stand in his way, since he got married last month."

I closed the passports and shuffled them behind the other documents, which turned out to be a marriage certificate and two birth certificates, amongst other things. "I never thought about it that way." I made a mental note to be more respectful of my fake IDs in future.

"If you just want to set up a bank account or forge some identification, I can do it with a stolen ID through a mail redirection scam, or even with an entirely fictional identity if I have enough time to sort it out. But to get a fake passport that's of a high enough standard to get through a British airport, well, that requires more serious measures. These are our good IDs, the ones I suggest we use if this all goes to plan. These are the names we'll escape the country with our share of the money under."

"So you're saying you think I should pretend to be your wife and we should elope together?"

"We just need to make up a story and stick with it. We could say we're on honeymoon. I suggest we go to Norway because it's not a member of the European Union and that gives it some protection should the British government try to exert the long arm of the law through it. We can watch the *Aurora borealis* and lay low for a month or so before we move on somewhere else."

Norway. I'd never been there. An image of a phosphorescent sky over a frigid wilderness full of man-eating polar bears came to mind. I'd been imagining going to New Zealand, to see my aunt and uncle. Perhaps that wasn't realistic. "You've been thinking about this."

"What do you think of it?"

I tried to keep a straight face. "I'm wondering if that's a coward's evasive way of asking someone out."

His expression changed. "And what do you think of that?"

The more I thought about it, the more I liked the idea of pretending to be married and on a honeymoon. Although I've never really seen the point in marriage, it was flattering, and it had the bonus of not including any of the commitment and responsibility involved in a real marriage. It felt like we were talking about a holiday, not a robbery, a holiday where we could go and feel like new people together, and leave the reality of our lives behind and, better still, never come back to it.

I hadn't spoken for a minute, and it seemed to be making him uneasy. "We can always split the cash and go our separate ways once we've got out the country. I just thought it might be less likely to raise suspicion if we went as a couple."

I laughed. "Sorry, I'm just trying to come up with a way a coward might evasively say yes."

I watched him for a reaction, but he put his drink to his lips and masked it. Perhaps he was relieved, perhaps it was wishful thinking. I felt wobbly on the inside. He hadn't dropped his Scottish accent the entire evening. I never knew if his words were at all representative of what he felt, or if they were all just part of the act. Perhaps he didn't really have any feelings under all the façade, and just played people to get what he wanted, like he played with the country's birth records and the tax system, like he played with his magic tricks. If it were so, perhaps I shouldn't mind, and perhaps I should just try to learn something from him and enjoy it for what it was. I wish I could be that way: immovable. Unhurtable. Observing the rest of the world through a logical lens and as stoic as a rock. Yet I wasn't and it bothered me to think that there might be nothing beneath the mask.

I picked up my glass from the coffee table. "To Rowena and Dorian Griffin."

The guilt I felt about using Rowena's identity didn't taste quite as bitter as the cheap spirits. Rowena wouldn't care; she wouldn't even have understood the concept of a legal identity when she'd been alive. But she might have brothers and sisters, parents who'd long ago dulled that sharp edge of grief and buried it deep inside themselves, who would care and would not want it exhumed.

Cam drained his glass and set it down on the table. He leaned back beside me on the sofa. I put my hand on his thick, slightly hairy knee, and slid it up his broad thigh under the hem of his kilt.

"Dammit, you are wearing pants!"

He roared with laughter. "Can you blame me? It's bloody freezing!" He put his arm around me rather awkwardly, and I pushed in close to his body, warm despite the cold of the room. He leaned in closer and kissed me, and I reached up and slid my chilled fingers through his hair and down the side of his warm neck. I put my arms around him, trying to bury myself in his solidity of his flesh, away from the cold room and the nothingness of the world. I sensed him relax, and he slid his hand over the back of my dress and onto my bare shoulder. I could feel that the back of his shirt had come loose from the waistband of his kilt. As my fingers moved up, they touched upon a sudden strange change of texture, as though I'd come across the edge of something stuck to his back, and then beyond that a weirdly rough sensation, as though the grain of his skin had changed direction. Without even thinking, I started and pulled my hand away, and Cam jumped back at the same moment. The sudden expression of horror in his face sent a chill feeling crawling from the backs of my thighs up the length of my spine. His hand sprang upon mine, fingers closing around my wrist.

My guts knotted up. "Cam, what's the matter?"

He regained composure, some of the fear easing out of his face. "It's... it's not anything. I just don't want to take my shirt off 'cause I'm fat."

"You've done something to your back, haven't you?" I remembered it now, when he'd suddenly lost his temper before. It had been triggered when his shirt had come loose at the back.

Cam didn't say anything. He just sat there, like a deer paralysed with fear in the headlamps of a car.

"Please can I look," I at last managed to say, and I gently put my hand on his shoulder, and he did turn so I could see.

The lamp in the room was on the other side of him, and it was not that easy to see with his back cast in shadow when I pulled the back of his shirt up. I could discern a broad, elongated rhombus slightly offcentred to the left of his spine. The skin had a mottled, grainy look to it, and the shape was indented slightly where the flesh beneath had been damaged. Around the surrounding area I could just make out a few dints and small patches of paler skin: scars from something. My breathing slowed as I felt the panic die down. This was nothing. It was just a scar. I'd reacted to his reaction. Why had he done that?

"What happened?"

As I looked away from his back, Cam pulled his shirt down and settled back in his seat. Sweat gleamed on his forehead and around his neck. "Boiling oil."

"What?"

Cam glanced away from me and moistened his lips with a slight movement of his tongue. "I spilt boiling oil. Out of a chip pan."

I stared at him. "How can you spill a chip pan on your own back?"

His eyes closed momentarily, and I feared for an instant he was about to lose his temper. "I dropped the chips. On the floor. I bent down to pick them up and I knocked the handle of the pan, and it spilt over my back."

I glanced from his face to where my hand rested on his bicep. Something here was not right. There was something more to this. I could sense it. "Well, what does it even matter how it happened? Why didn't you just tell me? It's only a scar on your back! Is that what you were worried about?"

He leaned forward and looked at his feet. "Yes." A shudder passed over him. "It hurt... the stuff in the hospital afterwards. I don't like to think about it."

"Why did you think I would find that so shocking?"

"I don't know... I..." As he spoke, I noticed that his eyes had become moist and slightly red. I leaned into him and put my head against his chest to save him the embarrassment of me seeing him like that. His breath shuddered in and out for a moment before calming.

"It's okay," I said, "it doesn't matter."

"I'm sorry." Irony and a slight tremor were apparent in his voice. "I do want to; it's just I... it's not straightforward." He put his arm around my shoulders and gave me a rough squeeze. "I don't know. We're planning to elope together, and then I bollocks it up like this?"

I laughed. A huge relief welled up inside me, that it wasn't because he didn't like me or he was playing games. If he was being frank about things now, perhaps this would be the end of the awkwardness. Perhaps he'd feel safe revealing more things to me now, and letting me get to know him as he really was.

"I thought you would want to go to bed, and I just..."

I looked at him until he faced me and made eye contact. "We don't have to, not if you don't feel ready. Let's just sleep. No obligations."

He moved his face closer, and I kissed him on the mouth. I didn't think about anything, concentrating instead on the feel of his lips and his scent.

Surely he could not be much younger than I was, and yet he seemed so inexperienced. It could be that the scars on his back had made him self-conscious. But then, why always until now? I was too jaded to believe that there had never been anyone before me he'd felt the need to try and get over it for. Maybe everyone else had given up where I was now.

In a way, it came as relief that his behaviour today and before when he'd become inexplicably angry could be explained and it was just because there were scars on his back. That was something I knew about him when before there had been nothing, a piece of the puzzle. At the moment I'd touched his back, in this instant of weakness, had he been truly naked, without his disguises?

*

The elderly hot-hatch lurched over a speed hump on its soggy suspension as I turned in to the one-way system. Pedestrians wandered along the pavements on both sides and spilled onto the zebra crossing ahead. A large man in sports clothes jogged on the outside of the pavement, against the flow of the crowd.

On the seat behind me, Ace pushed his computer off his lap. He wound down the window and leaned out. Cold autumn air penetrated the car's already chill interior.

"Fat bastard!"

Cam glanced over his shoulder at the car and rolled his eyes. I indicated left and pulled the car in to the kerb, slowing so as to coordinate its reaching a halt with his pace. He pulled open the door and threw himself down into the passenger seat. Male sweat mingled with the car's miasma of aging upholstery and old take-away food.

A quavering squeal broke from under the car's bonnet as I eased off the worn clutch and pulled away. I sighed.

"Who did you nick this off, a driving instructor?"

Cam didn't look up from the stopwatch clutched in his hand. "Dick Dastardly? What's wrong with it?"

"What's right with it? The clutch is going, the suspension's gone, the fan belt's slipping. I've been driving it for more than half an hour, and the heating is yet to put in an appearance." I jabbed the button for the heating elements embedded in the rear windscreen. The light was on, but the back of the car remained obscured with condensation.

Cam turned the heating dials this way and that, as though trying to guess the combination on a safe. I tried to imagine driving this car down this street with a fleet of police vehicles following it, and couldn't do it. Did Genghis really expect us to use this car?

"I make that six minutes twenty-five seconds." Cam switched off the stopwatch. "Ace, what you got?"

"Four minutes fifty," replied Ace from the back seat.

Cam scribbled the numbers on the notepad, besides the other four we'd obtained from the earlier two runs. He sighed through his mouth, breath misting the air. "You check out the tower?"

"Yes," I said. "I tried the lift down three times. Averaged a minute and three seconds."

Keys clicked under Ace's fingers. "Is that the mean, the median, or the mode?"

"The mean." I switched off the SatNav.

"What is that?"

"I'm the getaway driver. This is the getaway navigator."

"Mint. Can I have a look?"

"Sure. Cam, can you pass it back to him?"

Cam disconnected the SatNav from its cradle and made as if to throw it at Ace before handing it over the back of his chair.

"It has celebrities' voices on it," I explained. "It calculates a route based on various parameters associated with the voice you select."

Ace thumbed the screen. "What does Jeremy Clarkson do?"

"He calculates a route with no speed cameras on it."

"Mint."

Cam rolled his eyes. "Ace, is there any possibility of you expanding your vocabulary so you don't say 'mint' every second sentence?"

"Shurrup, lard-arse." Ace kneed the back of Cam's chair.

I drove on in silence for a short time, and then Cam said, "You still having your flying lessons, Doc?"

"Yes." I'd told Armitage I wanted to train for my Private Pilot's licence, but now it occurred to me that if things went to plan I wouldn't be here long enough to complete it.

A little kid ran across the road some distance ahead.

"Run her over!" Ace blurted out. He slapped his hand over his mouth. "Fuck."

"It doesn't matter," said Cam.

"No, that was fucking horrible. It just came into my head."

"Ace, it's all right. I know you didn't mean it," I said. In the rear view mirror, I saw him slump back against the headrest, closing his eyes in exasperation with himself. A gust of sympathy for the boy hit me. He hadn't messed up his career like I had. There had been no bridges for him to burn. Presumably he'd always had this impediment. I thought back to what Cam had said, about everyone having nothing to lose, and I wondered if Ace had ever belonged anywhere. He'd mentioned about the teachers in his school, and I couldn't imagine the other students had been any more accommodating. I could see someone like Ace in school, being goaded, being baited; the boy who couldn't modulate what came out of his mouth. I wondered if he ever would fit in anywhere. Then again, if we pulled this off right, he'd have money, and the rich can afford all manner of eccentricities it seems.

"When are we meeting up with Genghis to discuss this?" I asked Cam.

"Tomorrow night, seven thirty. I'll pick you up."

"Everyone's coming?"

"Yes, everyone's coming. We should have the big plan worked out after then."

The big plan. My intestines tensed into an uncomfortable knot of anxiety. That had to be the point of no return, the instant in time when the option of walking away from this was lost. Now was the time to decide where my loyalty lay: did I commit myself to these people and become one of them, or did I go back to being a law-abiding citizen? I thought this over. "The Tweedles as well?" I'd become familiar with the others, but these two were still a mystery to me. I tried to recall if I'd spoken to either of them at the bridge club. Their memory came with a sense of unease, which I tried to reason myself out of. Physical attributes and first impressions counted for nothing in this club — my experiences of Cam and Ace told me that. "Which one is which? I forget."

"They're half brothers by different fathers. Dee is the taller one, with darker skin. Dum's the—" Cam cleared his throat. "He's not the sharpest knife in the drawer."

"Thick as pigshit," Ace added.

"We need them for the heavy stuff."

I recalled what Sage had said in the garden. Working with the Tweedles didn't seem like a good idea, after what I'd heard and the impression I had. Then again, I was breaking the law as much as they were, so who was I to judge? And if this worked, it would be a way out of the futureless rut I'd been stuck in since I'd lost my job, and there would be no more worrying about bills and mortgages, and I could travel with Cam and see my aunt and uncle again. I wouldn't have to be who I'd become any more; I could make a fresh start as someone else.

If I'd heard of this on the news a little over a year ago, when I'd still had my job, I wouldn't have had any sympathy for the people who'd done it. We forget when we see crime in the news, and when *Crimewatch* tells the victims' stories, that the other side have their own stories and their reasons for doing the things they do.

*

Darkness had fallen, and our breath steamed the air in the sodium light of a streetlamp. Condensation filmed the surface of Cam's Rover.

He'd parked near the city, in an old urban area full of scruffy Victorian terraces. What Sage had said about the fragmented gangs of Birmingham returned to my thoughts. This sort of territory was exactly the sort of place gangs operated, where youths were shot and murdered for getting in with the wrong crowd. Was that who I'd become, now? I studied Cam's face as he walked beside me. Was that who he was, the wrong crowd?

Cam stopped where overgrown bushes spilled out of an unkempt garden. A tall gate was buried under the overgrowth. I stared up at the black branches of yew trees against the murky night sky, the moon obscured by cloud. There were no streetlamps. "Is this a graveyard or something?"

"There's one over there." Cam indicated. "That's not where we're having the meeting."

I hunched my shoulders and curled my fists under my arms against the cold. Cam took a step closer to me. His jacket was undone and his presence radiated warmth. I huddled against him and he put an arm around my shoulder in the privacy of the night.

An ellipse of light bobbed jerkily ahead along a path perpendicular to the direction we walked. I could just make out two figures behind it, one tall and upright, the other crooked and shrunken.

"Evening all," came Sage's quivery whisper of a voice.

"Fuck all," said Ace.

The gate grated against the bushes as Cam pushed through. A door with flaking paint led to a ground floor flat. Black mould grew up the walls from the skirting board, and cobwebs tangled around the bare bulb suspended from the ceiling. Men's voices were audible from inside. One door led off to a dilapidated bathroom with a suite in an ugly avocado colour and walled with chipped tiles; another led into an unfurnished room with a frayed carpet covered in dirt and burn marks.

Genghis was in there, with Tweedledum and Tweedledee and some other bloke. Upon catching sight of Cam, Genghis cut short his sentence and gestured for the man to leave. As the stranger pushed past me and Cam, a smell of stale sweat and fags hit me. Genghis's eyes passed from Cam to me, and then back. His irises were nearly black.

Ace kicked some of the disintegrating chairs out of

the way and hauled an electric heater over to the nearest socket. An old gas fire had been pulled out of the wall and broken apart on the floor. It was full of little ceramic tiles.

Cam pinned a street map of Birmingham to the wall. Tweedledum and Tweedledee did not sit down, lurking instead at the back of the room.

This pair still made me uneasy, and there was something about Genghis too. It wasn't an overt sense of danger, as with the Tweedles, but more a mercenary distrust I couldn't pin down. Like many of my old colleagues at work, he gave the impression of only being in this so long as it suited him, with no loyalty for anyone should a better opportunity present itself.

What happened here might decide if I'd end up in jail, or dead. Was jail worse than unemployment? Was jail worse than *employment*? Living in an unheated house in solitude, with not enough to eat? Prisoners have televisions and computers in their cells these days. They don't even have to leave their cells to socialise with whatever unsavoury characters co-habit the prison with them, and even if they did, I doubted such people could be much worse than my old boss.

As for dying, I'd stared that in the face as well. I could have taken my own life. I'd thought about it enough. My dad had done it. Afterwards I'd been consumed by rage at him, rage that he had spurned my love of him by destroying himself. Now, perhaps I understood better. If I died robbing a casino, there would be no-one left behind to suffer for my not being there: my father was dead, my mother also, though her corpse still breathed in a nursing home in Solihull. My aunt and uncle had emigrated.

Often when I used to think about suicide, I had thought of it as a final indignant cry of revenge. In some impotent way at least, I could inflict guilt on my old boss who had initiated the chain of events that had robbed me of my life, of who I was. I couldn't take from him what he had taken from me, but I did have the power to cast that shadow over the rest of his life.

Depression is losing your emotions, one after the other. At the very nadir, you can't even feel despair, just a numb emptiness and a hatred for yourself. I never managed to lose that. Maybe depression can go yet deeper than it did with me. Maybe other people's experiences of it are all different. It's impossible to tell.

I'd already walked through the valley of death. I knew what rock bottom meant. It had made me fearless.

Genghis came to the front and cleared his throat. He indicated the map, on which three routes had been marked in yellow, green, and pink fluorescent markers.

"Right, so here's the plan so far. The security company that collects the cash and takes it to the bank every morning has to pass along this road, regardless of the route they take. Two o'clock or thereabouts on the morning of the twenty-first, Tweedledum and Tweedledee go together on the bikes and set up a road block at this point on the vans' route, making it look like there are roadworks going on. They leave the bikes behind and Sage drops off Baron Greenback, done up to look like a police car." Genghis paused to insert a red tack into the map at the point. "When they reach the diversion at approximately 06:45, they use this." Genghis gestured to a heavy-looking steel concertina thing with vicious prongs sticking up that lay on the floor. "A police stinger, donated courtesy of Sage."

"Just don't ask how I got it," Sage added.

"They impersonate the cops and they arrest the security guards and leave them handcuffed in the back of

Baron Greenback, and continue by bike. Ace is coordinating the operation. He stays in the back of Dick Dastardly with his computer and keeps in touch with everyone. He can triangulate everyone's position using the GPS on their mobile phones. Doc, you're in the tower until you need to drive. Now, in the meantime, Cam and me are in Zordrak, which will be outfitted in the exact same livery as the security fleet. Cam, are the uniforms sorted out?"

"In the boot of my car outside," Cam replied.

"Good. We drive to the casino impersonating the real van and we pick up the money. Doc and Cam's investigation showed us all the security systems we'll be dealing with, so we know not to set them off. Ace's camera plant gave us the time the safe opens and the procedure the staff use to get the money and transfer it to the couriers, so we'll know how to do it without alerting any suspicion. We drive Zordrak to rendezvous point A, the layby on the dual carriageway."

Genghis pushed a yellow tack into the thick green line delineating the road. "Where Sage is waiting with Mumm-Ra disguised as a burger van. We deposit the money with him and he drives to this point here," another pin, this time green, "and ditch Zordrak. Tweedledum and Tweedledee then go via motorbike to rendezvous A and collect the cash boxes. Any suspicion the police are following, dump the bikes and hide the money in Wyre Forest, otherwise head for rendezvous C. Meanwhile, Cam and me run this gauntlet here, where we meet Doc and Ace in Dick Dastardly at rendezvous point B. We drive back to rendezvous A on a different route and pick up Sage. If all goes well, we make the final rendezvous at point C here, off the dual carriageway. There we split up the cash, all seven, all equal, and proceed as planned.

Right. It all seemed enormously complicated when it was put together in its entirety like that, but all I needed to remember was my portion of responsibility: from the tower to rendezvous B, and from there to rendezvous A, then on to C. So long as everyone else remembered theirs, it should all pull together. Cam and Ace and I had made had our own plans to dump Dick Dastardly in Birmingham and leave in our own cars, and about how to launder our money and leave the country after, but what the other members did after was up to them, and we intended no further contact.

"You've been doing trial runs?" Genghis asked.

I consulted the notepad. "Cam averages about five minutes from point A to point B. I average around four from the tower to point B, and it takes about a minute for me to get the lift down from the tower. The moment I see you and Cam leaving Zordrak is my cue to leave. Unless the road is blocked I should be able to synchronise my arrival at the pickup point with you."

"Right." Genghis snapped his fingers. "Forensics, before I forget."

I scanned the brief list on the notepad on my lap. "If we're burning the vehicles, that should get rid of most of the evidence. Wear gloves. Not that it's hard to in the sort of weather we're likely to have. Anything you do touch, rub it with a scarf or something to remove the prints. If we wear hats as well, there's less chance of hair getting anywhere it could be found."

Cam interrupted. "I would like to bring up that Doc and myself do have a few concerns about the roadworthiness of Dick Dastardly."

"What? What's wrong with it?"

I was relieved Cam had broached this topic rather than leaving me to do it, and I felt I should show some solidarity and back him up. "If I have to drive fast, it puts every part of the car under high stress. The fan belt's slipping. If it's not working properly, the battery's going to end up draining and we could lose the engine."

Genghis appeared to consider this.

"It smells like someone ralphed in it an' all," Ace added. His arm abruptly straightened, punching a hole in the plasterboard beside his seat with a bang that made me jump. He winced and rubbed his knuckles. "Sorry."

"Well, Sage, you know some mechanics who can be trusted to keep their gobs shut and not ask questions, don't you? Get one of them to service it. Ace, you'll just have to put up with the smell. It'll remind you to cover your face like you're meant to." He paused, staring into space, apparently collecting his thoughts. "I think that's everything. If all of this goes to plan, I'll see you all tomorrow. If not, I'll see you all in jail." Genghis bared discoloured teeth in a humourless smile and strode past us to the door.

8

BLUE MOON

It was approaching eight o'clock and the sun had not quite cleared the horizon. The air was very clear and still, although the weather forecast had said there was snow on the way. Frosty concrete surfaces coruscated in the morning sun and rivers of traffic glimmered as they flowed through the streets below. If I stood right up close to the window, with my forehead against the glass, I could just about see the roof of Dick Dastardly, parked at the kerb outside nearly thirty floors below.

Some distance to the east, the Blue Moon Casino's car park was nearly empty. It looked different in the daylight, from this elevated perspective.

At an angle of roughly 120 degrees from the casino, I had made a mental note of the location of Rendezvous Point A, a layby on the dual carriageway heading towards the M6. It was difficult to see it clearly without using the telescope I'd brought.

A vehicle had driven into the casino car park. I turned the telescope on it: a white van, with the security company's logo on the side. Cam and Genghis would be in it, although the telescope's magnification wasn't strong enough for me to be able to confirm it definitely was them through the van's windows.

The van stopped very close to the casino's rear entrance. Of the two Kevlar-suited, helmeted men who got out, I could tell one was Cam from his size, although even fundamental traits like his gait and stance he seemed able to change at will. He walked now with a heavy stride that made him appear bigger than he was, rolling his shoulders as the two of them approached the entrance. The door closed behind them. Now all I could do was watch and wait, and hope they had enough from Cam's experience and the information I'd collected in the casino for them to be able to pull it off without rousing any suspicion from the staff.

I found myself staring down at the pattern of the empty parking spaces on the concrete surrounding the casino. Someone in this very location might have looked down on the car park that night and seen the car in which Cam and I were scheming. Such a person could have written down the car's number plate and traced it back to Cam's identity. The police might already know of the plan; it might be doomed before it had even been put into action. They might just be waiting, so they could catch us red handed and have surety of success in the prosecution. If they did know of it, they might even know more about my collaborators than I did. They might know Cam's name and history, the very things he'd refused to tell me.

A sickly tension had begun to cramp up inside of me. I had committed to doing this. There was no turning back, not now. If parallel universes were the result of different outcomes of the same situation, this point in time must be a junction in the insignificant existence of the lump of atoms that was me. In some of those futures I got to go free, and I took back what society had robbed me of. In others, I ended up in jail. What was to happen now would decide which of them came true for the version of me I was about to become.

The door was opening again. I forced myself to focus. I didn't feel like driving. I felt light-headed and wobbly, like I couldn't fit enough breath inside my chest, and it was nothing to do with being at 28th-floor altitude. Cam and Genghis were carrying sturdy metal boxes, two each. They loaded them into the back of the van. Now they were getting in the front. They were driving away, and nothing was happening, and there were no repercussions, at least not yet.

I lost track of the van soon after it turned onto the main road where buildings blocked the traffic from my view. I lowered the telescope, forcing saliva into my mouth and swallowing. I probably wouldn't find it again. I'd just have to watch the layby and wait. I raised the telescope to my eye again and adjusted the focus wheel until the shabby burger van became discernible. That was where Sage hid, awaiting the changeover.

A white form slowed amongst the rush of traffic. Zordrak was pulling off the dual carriageway and onto the hard shoulder. Cam and Genghis had made it to the rendezvous point. Zordrak came to a halt behind the burger van. Both the doors were thrown open, and the men leapt out and ran to the back.

With a feeling of at least momentary relief, I took a step back and pushed the lift call plate, before turning the telescope back on the layby while I waited for the lift to arrive.

But now something else was separating from the flow, another van, smaller, with yellow-and-blue chequered livery covering its flanks.

The sick sensation I'd been feeling ever since yesterday evening began to curdle in my guts. I reached for my Bluetooth earpiece with my free hand. "Ace, we've got problems! Police car at Rendezvous A."

"Fuck!" came back Ace's voice. The connection cut off abruptly.

Cam and Genghis had the van's back doors open, but they'd stopped, noticing the arrival of the police van. I threw a glance around the corridor. *Run*, I willed them. Even if they dumped the money, perhaps there was still a chance to get away. If they tried to fight the police, things would only get worse.

The gadget in my ear clicked, and Ace's voice came back into hearing. "Tweedledum and Tweedledee say they're going to attempt a diversion. We're just gunna have to sit tight and wait."

I raised the telescope to my eye once more. A policeman and a dog had disembarked from the vehicle. The animal strained on its leash as the two of them approached Cam and Genghis. Cam had a box in either hand. Genghis put out his hand, signalling him to stay back. It looked as though he was trying to reason with the dog handler.

Now two motorcycles had joined the three vans, and the layby was beginning to look crowded. Tweedledum and Tweedledee, indistinguishable from each other in their biker leathers, approached the policeman from behind.

The cop turned. He reached with one hand to the truncheon at his waist, with the other towards the dog's collar. One of the two leather-clad figures uncoiled his arm from his jacket suddenly. Something flashed once in his hand, and the policeman took a staggering step backwards and crumpled to the ground. The dog lunged madly against the leash still attached to the man's arm, its jaws working.

Oh, shit...

My hand hovered over the lift call plate. The numbers in orange segments above the lift door slowly scrolled up. This was in too deep. If that man was dead, whichever of the Tweedles had fired the gun was now a murderer, and I and Cam, and Ace and Sage and Genghis were all accomplices to a murder. What did I do now? Did I abandon the whole mission and run for my own freedom? Cam was still out there, and the plan was falling further and further apart by the second. *Damn it*. We'd arranged to go together.

I trained the telescope back on the scene below. Sage had appeared from the burger van. An altercation seemed to have started out between all five of them. The copper lay motionless on the ground, the dog still pulling and barking and trying to get at those who had killed its master.

It looked like they'd come to some sort of agreement. Cam put his hand on Genghis's chest and shoved him back. Then he turned and ran, hurdling the barrier at the edge of the layby and making off into the street. He was going to Rendezvous B. The others were sorting out the boxes amongst themselves. It looked like Genghis was going with Sage.

A sterile, robotic voice behind me announced the opening of the lift doors.

I reached a hand back and leaned against the metal frame. They were continuing with the plan. That meant they expected me to continue with it too. They were relying on me. I couldn't abandon Cam.

I stepped back. I took my hand away. I let the doors close in front of my face. I put my finger to the ground floor panel and the lift began to move. I had to stop panic from overwhelming me. I must take this one step at a time. Once I got to the car, I'd be okay, I told myself. I watched the segmented numbers scrolling down, down, and I concentrated on this one thing to stop my mind from completing the circle it inevitably must.

It seemed an eternity before the counter changed to G and the doors slid back. One step at a time. The foyer, the door to the car park. There was Dick Dastardly. Once

I got into the car I would be okay. My legs felt like lead as I stepped around it to the driver's door, and my fingers seemed unwieldy, as in a dream, when I took the handle. Ace pushed the computer off his lap and shuffled to the other side of the rear seat.

"Doc! What's happened? I've heard nothing since I last spoke to you."

I started the engine and pulled away. I checked left and right before turning on to the main road. I'd practiced this; it was routine; I knew it by now.

"Doc!"

I didn't know what to tell him. If we did get caught, it might be better for him that he truly knew nothing about the Tweedles having shot the policeman. "Something's gone wrong. We're proceeding with the plan to Rendezvous B. That's all I can tell you at this moment. I need to concentrate now."

So long as I didn't think about it too much and I got on with it, I could keep this up. If I could wake up every day to no future and still make myself get out of bed, then I could do this. It was either do the latter now or do the former for the rest of my life. I tried to picture myself, away from here, with Cam, on some tropical beach somewhere, with all of this done and finished and out of the way. I willed myself to believe that a string of reality stretched from here to that outcome.

Here was the street. A heavyset guy stood out on the pavement, in smart trousers and shoes, his dishevelled white shirt conspicuous in the cold weather. Cam made for the passenger door and lurched inside, making the car jolt on its sloppy suspension. His rapid breathing, his sweat-laced scent, and the physical closeness of him served to ease a large proportion of the tension gripping me. Cam was here, with me. We would be all right, for now, at least for long enough for me to hold myself together against the onslaught of things happening for that bit longer until stuff worked out.

"Where's Genghis?" Ace demanded.

"Change of plan. He's going with Sage to get rid of Mumm-Ra," Cam gasped, his head flung back against the headrest as I pulled away. "We're meeting them both at Rendezvous C."

I wondered if they could see the effect this stress was having on me. Perhaps they both felt the same inside. At least Cam was out of breath to hide it.

Still panting, Cam struggled into his jersey and his coat as I drove. He put on a rolled-up balaclava over the crown of his head, without pulling it down. Wavy tufts of hair poked out from under its edge. "You know the way?"

Without answering, I tapped the SatNav screen. "Rendezvous C, Jeremy Clarkson mode."

The map image spun as the computer plotted a route. It didn't take long to get there. Genghis and Sage stood beside the shabby burger van, Sage leaning on his walking stick. Zordrak was nowhere to be seen.

"Where are Tweedledum and Tweedledee?" Cam asked as they opened one of the rear doors.

"On the run from the pigs," Genghis said. "We have to take the loot. Ace, get in the middle."

He and Sage unloaded the cash boxes from the burger van and loaded them into the car, shoving them into the passenger foot spaces. Sage got in one side while Genghis went back to the van.

"Do we leave him?" I said. The rear passenger door was still open.

"He's setting fire to it," Cam explained.

A moment later, Genghis ran out and jumped into the car, slamming the door behind him. "Good old chip fire should give the fire brigade a bit of training practice."

I indicated and pulled out. "Where to?"

"Wyre forest," said Genghis.

The contingency plan, the location of the bend in the road that I had located with Cam.

"Wyre Forest was planned for the Tweedles, with the idea they could hide their bikes down the side of the bank without being noticed," Cam objected. "We can't take Dick Dastardly there. It's too conspicuous."

"What do you suggest?"

Cam turned in his seat to face Genghis in the back of the car. "We go to the big retail park up the motorway and split the money and call it quits. You can get rid of the car."

"The Tweedles need their share."

"Fine, you take their shares and settle up with them in your own time."

"These boxes are locked. We'll need time to open them."

"Fuck you, Genghis!" Cam shouted. "I thought you said you had Tweedledee under control!"

"Please stop arguing," said Sage.

"Fine," said Cam forcefully. "There are four boxes. Does anyone else here object if Genghis takes two, to split with his three, and us four have the other two?"

Nobody spoke. After a moment, Cam said, "Right, let's do that, then. Much as I'm loath for any of us to take a lower cut, I think it's worth it to be rid of you and those two psychos!"

I pulled onto the motorway and into almost immediate congestion. "Go to David Attenborough mode."

Take the next exit off the motorway, said David Attenborough's voice.

The traffic ground to a halt, the car becoming trapped in the middle lane between two articulated lorries. Over the noise of the traffic, I could make out the distant throb of some other sort of engine, maybe a helicopter. Was it looking for us, or just the Tweedles?

"Shit." Cam leaned his head back and squeezed his eyes shut.

"Where are they?" I said.

Ace studied his computer. "They're behind us somewhere."

I indicated left and made for the next exit off the motorway.

"Sage, are you all right?"

It was Ace's voice. I looked into the rear-view mirror to see Sage's face paper-white, contorted and drained of blood. "Sage?"

"I'm all right," Sage wheezed, right hand pressed against his left shoulder.

I slowed to glance back and look directly at him.

"What's wrong with him?" said Cam.

I looked back at the road. "I think he's having a heart attack."

"What do we do?"

"Genghis, I don't know! I've told you before I'm not a medical doctor! He needs medical attention!"

"There's no time."

I reached to the SatNav screen. "Hospital!"

In the rear-view mirror, Genghis rolled his eyes skywards, but said nothing. The route recalculated, directing me to turn off at the next road. The car lurched into the corner and went over a speed hump with a whack that jarred my head on my neck and elicited a sharp groan of pain from Sage in the back. David Attenborough's voice directed me up this road and down through a side-street onto another main road. I could see the hospital up ahead now, a sprawling concrete castle lit up starkly in the weak daylight of an overcast winter's day. I turned into the main entrance and clanked over a line of one-way road prongs. The lane led up a winding route bordered with low concrete walls, to a drop-off point. Two ambulances with their back doors open blocked the exit at the top.

I threw open my door. "Come on, help me get him out."

"We're stuck here!" Genghis pointed at the ambulances. "We can't get out!"

Cam and I took hold of Sage's arms and hoisted him out of the car. "C'mon, Sage," said Cam. Sage's face was tensed up in pain. We moved slowly away from the car, supporting him.

A wail of sirens came into hearing, and blue light flickered upon the concrete surfaces.

"Fuck this!" Genghis shouted. He lunged into the back of the car and grabbed two of the boxes. As the police car hove into view, he sprang away and hurdled the car park wall. The doors on the police car flew open and two cops leapt out and immediately took off after Genghis.

I stared at the empty police car, at Cam and Sage, and at Ace, who crouched on the back seat of Dick Dastardly away from the policemen's view. "Ace, get out! We can't stay here!" I let go of Sage's arm to get back to the car and pull the SatNav off its mount. There wasn't time to remove fingerprints from the inside of the car. We'd been wearing gloves, so we'd just have to hope they didn't find anything. I pulled one of the cases out of the back, the weight of the thing surprising me. Ace took the other one.

As we irrupted into the hospital foyer, I shouted, "Help, I think this man is having a cardiac arrest!"

Immediately two women rushed into a corridor and came back with a bed on wheels. As they lifted Sage onto it, we shoved the cases onto the shelf beneath the mattress.

"You're in hospital," one of the women said to Sage. "We're going to transfer you to the ward as soon as possible." She got behind the bed and ran it forward, like a battering ram, into a pair of doors that flew open on impact. She stopped the bed in the corridor behind. "Wait here." The woman ran through, past the doors at the far end, presumably where they operated on the patients.

I looked at where she had gone, and down at Sage on the bed. His fingers caught mine. His gnarled fist squeezed my hand tight. Through his clenched jaw he choked out, "Thanks for giving an old man the chance to spend his last days doing something worthwhile."

I leant over him, putting my mouth close to his ear so none of the people around would hear me. "Sage, just hold on. The doctors are going to help you. You're going to get better and you're getting out of here, and you're going to the Azores, just like you wanted, and you're going to have many, many more days to do worthwhile things in."

"You can't help me any more. You need to get out of here and save yourselves." Sage managed to force a smile against the tension in his face, the lines on his skin deeper and more numerous than I ever remembered them. He reached his other arm across his chest and clasped my hand in both of his. "This is the end for me, and I'm ready for it. You and Cam have my share. Spend it on dinner services and furniture. That's what my wife and I needed when we moved in. And buy Ace something useful, because he'd only waste it on gadgets if I gave it to him."

I tried to laugh, but it caught in my throat and escaped as more of a sob. A blurry texture had begun to muddy my vision.

I turned away from the trolley, dragging my coat sleeve across my face. There wasn't time to mourn now. I had to hold together for that bit longer. There would be time later to fall apart. Already I was walking down the corridor, and Ace and Cam were following me with the boxes of cash.

I came to a door marked Staff Only and pushed up against the window, shielding my eyes from the lights with my hands.

"Here," I said, when I was sure there was no-one inside. Fortunately, the door wasn't locked. Inside, two walls were lined with vented metal lockers at one end, a few shower cubicles and private changing rooms at the other.

Cam immediately noticed the plastic laundry basket opposite the door. "There might be something in here we can use for a disguise." He pulled up the lid. The box was half-full of medical apparel soiled with vomit and blood and other unidentifiable bodily fluids.

Ace made a noise of disgust. "I'm not wearing those!"

"What about the lockers?" I suggested.

Ace took hold of one of the handles and gave it a tug. "Locked."

Cam pulled a small screwdriver out of the inside pocket of his jacket. He stabbed the point into the nearest locker door and levered the handle down with the heel of his hand.

The door buckled and banged open. Inside, some turquoise garments lay folded neatly at the bottom. Cam took out a shirt and held it up against himself; it was much too small. "That'll have to do for one of you two, in that case." He threw the shirt to Ace and jammed the screwdriver into the next locker.

I made sure I took my keys and the SatNav out of my pockets before I took anything off. I'd not brought my wallet, or anything else of that sort, as I'd thought that would only be an added risk if I lost it and someone found it and traced me through it.

"Hah!" Ace blurted out. "Cam's got moobs!"

Cam scowled and rolled his eyes. "I know. You don't need to announce it like you're a commentator in a game show." I noticed that he kept his back towards me, away from Ace. The skin grafts on his back made irregular patterns of the unsightly sort that nature never does. He rolled up the largest shirt he'd been able to find and pulled it on over his head, tugging self-consciously at the hem of it.

"Doc, what are we meant to be?" Ace glanced up and down at his turquoise garb and his NHS issue trainers. "I mean, are we like surgeons, or nurses?"

"We might be porters," Cam suggested.

"I don't know what we are," I said.

"What we going to do with these boxes?" said Cam.

Ace glanced at the two boxes on the floor. "Can we break them open and stuff the money inside a bed or summing?"

"No, they've got anti-tamper locks." Cam tapped the keyhole under the thick metal handle, where a red glass tube crossed over where the case opened. "We force that, we're going to get sprayed with Smart Water."

I looked again at the laundry bin, its lid ajar from where we had shoved our clothes in it. "Could we make a dummy patient out of our clothes and hide them inside it?"

Cam rubbed his chin. "Good point. Ace, go and get a bed. I think there are some empty ones farther down the corridor outside."

While Ace was away, Cam and I sorted through the clothes. Cam had been wearing a voluminous padded coat with a hood, so we could use that to model the body. We would have to stuff it and build the shape of the legs with other clothes.

Ace arrived outside the door with a bed. He held it still in the corridor and I put the coat on its side on the mattress. Cam put the two cases inside it. I packed my coat around it in what I hope would resemble a lifelike shape and did up the zip. We used Ace's hoodie and my jersey wadded up to make a leg shape with a pair of shoes at the bottom, and I stuffed Cam's shirt inside the hood. When we folded the sheet and the blanket over it, I hoped it would look like an obese patient in a big coat.

"Where are we going?" said Ace.

"I don't know," said Cam. "Let's just see if we can keep out the way and avoid detection until the panic dies down.

We began to wheel the bed down the corridor. We reached a corner and turned. Down at the far end, a number of people clustered, black and white police stab vests conspicuous amongst them. They seemed to be interrogating the hospital staff.

Cam stepped up so his face was close to my ear. "Looks like there's a lift just ahead. Let's use that. I don't want to risk passing them."

We continued down the corridor until we reached the

lift doors. Cam pressed the call plate.

Ace began to twitch and fidget as we stood there. His shoulders jerked, his neck made convulsive movements, and his face twisted into strange expressions. An odd, stifled cough erupted from his mouth. "*Cunts.*"

Cam bared his teeth and glared fiercely at the lad as he mouthed, "Ace!"

"Ace," I said, "put your hands over your mouth!"

Ace began to raise his arms, but his right hand suddenly spasmed and straightened before his face, into a v-sign aimed at the police.

Ace snapped his arm down, but they'd already seen. One of them started towards him. "Don't move!"

Ace turned and shoved past me into the corridor behind us, back the way we'd come. I froze as three policemen came thundering towards us. They barged past the trolley in pursuit of Ace. One of them even barked a hurried "sorry" at us when he jarred the metal guard on the edge of the frame with his hip. Ace and his three pursuers disappeared around the corner of the corridor, and the sudden silence that followed their departure was bewildering. I stared at Cam, and he stared back at me. Then the lift behind us chimed, and I put my hand on the bar on the side of the trolley and forced myself back into focus.

We wheeled the bed into the lift and stood watching the numbers climb.

"What do we do now?" I asked Cam.

He shrugged. Sweat sheened his forehead. "So fucking stupid of him."

"I don't think he does it on purpose."

The lift had stopped now, on the second floor. The

doors slid back and I chanced a look outside. The corridor was empty both ways. "Let's keep moving."

We pushed the trolley out and walked with it about sixty yards down a corridor that, as it turned out, led to a dead end, with just a window in the wall that looked down upon a landscaped garden. A thin, turquoise-clad figure sprinted across a lawn, jumped a bed of roses, and trampled what looked like they might eventually become flowers when the weather grew warmer. Two policemen raced after him.

"Shit," said Cam. "Help me get this window open while he's doing his diversion thing."

I didn't know what he intended to do as we were too high up to climb down, but I helped him force the safety catch on the window so it opened fully. Cam whipped the bedcover off the dummy. He hefted up one of the cases into the window's aperture and shoved it out. It landed in a thicket of rhododendron bushes below.

"What'd you do that for?"

"They're looking for people carrying these. It'll be easier for us to get out without them." Cam quickly pushed the other case out. In the distance, one of the policemen rugby-tackled Ace. The lad landed face-down in the dirt. The other policeman landed on top of him and wrested his arms behind his back.

Cam shook his head. "We can't help him now. Let's go."

We went down two flights of stairs and found our way back to the main foyer. There were four more policemen there, and as I followed Cam to the doors, one of them turned to face us.

"Excuse me," called the policeman. "Have either of you seen anyone acting suspicious? Anyone at all?"

"We saw a lad being chased by coppers out the back,"

Cam offered, making a gesture over his shoulder with his thumb. He glanced at his watch. "We're going out for a fag now. We'll let you know when we come back if we see anything else."

The foyer entrance led to the car park. From here, we skirted around the building, keeping to the lowered path where a wall concealed us from the cars there. We reached a place were ambulance-like vans were parked, bearing the NHS logo and red and white livery that read *Please give Blood*.

Cam looked left and right before stepping up into the car park where the vans were. He opened the back door to one, to reveal a little room with a reclining chair and racks for hanging bags of blood on. A paramedic's fluorescent jacket hung from the back of one of the doors, so I took it and put it on over my medical scrubs.

"Here," he said, pulling a large case with the same decoration as the outside of the vans out from under the bed. "You think one of the boxes will fit in here?"

"I don't know." I couldn't visualise how big the boxes were from memory.

"Those cases are heavy," I said. "I'm not sure I could carry that with one inside."

Cam paused to look around the room. "Perhaps this then?" He pulled a metal trolley bearing bags and needles away from the wall.

"Okay, let's take these."

I helped Cam lift the trolley down off the back of the van. We loaded the case onto the bottom of it and continued around the building perimeter, until we came to the gardens.

I sat on a bench and kept watch while Cam retrieved

the boxes from the bush. He put them on the lower level of the trolley with a sheet covering them and the medical box on top.

He pushed the trolley in front of me. "You can get to your car from here?"

I nodded. We'd parked both mine and Cam's cars in car parks in the city, and planned to leave separately had things gone to plan.

"Okay. We split up and get to our cars. Meet me back at my house."

I turned without speaking, and began to walk, the trolley rattling ahead of me. The disabled ramp led up out of the car park, back to the road. I took my SatNav out of my pocket and checked the distance. It was going to take more than half an hour to walk there. This didn't daunt me as the earlier difficulties we'd come up against had, but by now I was mentally and emotionally exhausted. After what had gone wrong and what had happened to Ace and Sage, all I wanted was to sit down somewhere and close my eyes and have some respite from the world, but I had to keep going. My earlier fears had been replaced by more basal necessities. I was weak with hunger. My knee had stiffened and jolts of pain shot up my leg with every step. The cold winter wind went straight through the thin fabric of my medical trousers. First my fingers, and then my whole hands, began to hurt from the cold. I tried to curl my fists around the handle of the trolley to press my fingers into my palms, but all I felt was the burning cold of the metal bar. I needed to get back to the car and get to Cam's house, and for this to be over.

I tried to focus on one stride at a time, looking for landmarks on the route and concentrating on reaching them: a pedestrian crossing, a tall building, a bridge.

At last I arrived at the car park. I dragged the cases off the trolley and dumped them on the back seat. Then I wiped where my hands had been with the hem of my hospital shirt as best as I could with my cold-deadened grip, and pushed the trolley up the kerb and tipped it over into a bush, the jarring of its wheels on the rough surface numbed through my frozen hands. It took all my effort to concentrate on the road over the pain in my hands and feet and the hunger and exhaustion consuming me.

Finally I reached the street. There was Cam's car, and I pulled in behind it. Up in his house I could see a light in the living room window. I heaved the cases off the back seat.

I crept up to the front door, keeping close to the laurel bush and hoping nobody was watching. The door was on the latch. I stepped inside quickly and immediately pushed it shut behind me.

A sound from the living room, and Cam's head appeared at the door. The tightness in his face immediately slackened upon sighting me. "Thank goodness you're back safe."

9

RED HANDED

I threw the cash boxes down on the floor and flung my arms around his neck. A great swell of relief overcame me, and I found myself laughing as we stood there together in the dim hallway.

"Bloody hell, your hands are freezing!" Cam pulled his head back from me and frowned. "What's funny?"

"It was just how you said 'thank goodness'. It sounds a bit quaint, like something a primary teacher might say."

"Well, okay, then. Thank fuck you're all right."

I laughed again.

"It's because you've been immunised against harsh language by spending too much time around Ace."

This would have been funny had he said it any day before today, but now it wasn't, because Ace was no longer Ace. He was just another statistic, a lad in a cell at the police station, and sooner or later the police were going to find out what his name was, and he would have to face up to whatever had driven him from his identity and become that person again instead of Ace.

"You'd better get changed quickly, and then we'll need to get on with things."

I got changed in Cam's bedroom, where I had a holdall of spare clothes and overnight things: jeans and a jersey over a long-sleeved t-shirt. I opened the door to see Cam coming upstairs, one of the cash boxes in one hand and a steaming mug in the other. He proffered the mug to me: hot chocolate.

I took the mug, making a mitt out of my sleeve and wrapping my fingers around the hot ceramic. "Thanks."

Cam put the cases down on the bed, near a bag of crisps and a packet of oat bars. He propped up one case, balancing it between his legs as he knelt on the bed, and picked up a weird-looking bunch of keys, all long narrow lengths with similar prongs on the tip, from the bedside table. Carefully, he began to insert the keys into the lock one at a time, wiggling them gently.

I stared at the red glass tube that connected the two halves of the case. "What exactly is that stuff in there?"

Cam frowned as he fumbled with the keys. "Most likely Smart Water and a dye. If it gets forced open, something explodes and breaks it, and the dye will go all over anyone standing nearby and the money, making it unusable and marking the person."

I thought I remembered reading something about that sort of thing years ago in a scientific journal — a forensic solution with a DNA-like signature dissolved in it that could be detected and traced back to the person that chemical signature was registered to. It felt like it had been a long time ago.

Cam had one key wedged in the base of the keyhole. He slid a narrower one into the top of the slot and gave the two of them a concerted wiggle. The slot rotated anticlockwise with a click.

"Jackpot." Cam held the keys still with one hand while he pulled the red glass handle gingerly and eased it out of position. The two halves of the case parted to reveal bank notes in red sleeves neatly tessellated inside.

He slid off the bed to land on his knees beside it, and reached underneath to pull out a canvas holdall filled with the paying-in envelopes from the bank and a few more folded-up holdalls. "We need to fill these," he told me. "You need to read the numbers on the slips. They average a thousand pounds, but there's a bit of variation either way. There's a pen over there if you need one."

I took one of the pens from the bedside table and gathered a handful of envelopes. The bundles of cash were each a thousand pounds. The envelopes each contained a paying-in slip that had already been filled in with account details and an amount, and today's date. The first one I read was for a thousand pounds, so I simply slipped one of the wads out of the paper sleeve and stuffed it into the envelope with the slip. Cam climbed back onto the bed and set to work opening the other case.

An hour later, and we had filled two holdalls and finished the crisps and the oat bars. A loose heap of leftover notes from our counting lay in the middle of the bed, like autumn leaves raked into a pile.

Cam dropped an envelope with an infuriated noise and put his finger in his mouth. When he withdrew it, a streak of blood mingled with the saliva. Both our hands were by now covered with papercuts. Mine were mostly on the backs of my fingers and hands where I'd pushed money in and the edge on the envelope flaps had caught me.

"You're getting DNA all over it," I said. "We should have worn gloves."

Cam shook his head. "It won't matter. By the time they work it out, all of the money and the paperwork will be mixed up with the rest of the money and the rubbish."

"Cam, I'm so tired." I leaned my head against his shoulder and closed my eyes for a few seconds. It felt like a month had passed since this morning. If only I could sleep for a while, and in the morning everything that had happened would be easier to come to terms with.

Cam sighed. "We have to finish this today. The sooner we get this part finished and the evidence out the way, the better. Let's have a break for a few minutes and I'll make us both a really strong coffee."

Another hour and four cups of coffee later, we had filled two more bags. Red sleeves littered the carpet. All that otherwise remained was a few grand heaped in the middle of the bed, and a few leftover envelopes in the first holdall. Altogether, there was over two million. I wasn't sure exactly how much over, as Cam and I had both been handling the money and we hadn't really kept track. The dim winter daylight from the window had dwindled away to nothing.

"We'll need some cash, so it's probably best to keep what's left out." Cam wiped his face on his sleeve. The sallow electric lighting revealed redness underlining his eyes. He stiffly rose to one knee and gathered the red sleeves into the empty cash boxes, which he closed and stowed under the bed. Cam shook his head and got to his feet, wincing as he did so. "It's not over yet."

Against the exhaustion gripping my whole body and the ache in my legs and shoulders from sitting on the floor, I forced myself to think. "We should take anything we need, and anything incriminating that'll identify us, with us in the car."

"You're right," Cam agreed after a pause. "We could come back here and find the pigs have got here and staked out the place to ambush us."

While Cam gathered up the computers and all the IDs, I fetched my bag of overnight stuff and the spare clothes I'd been keeping at his house. We put the remaining cash into our coat pockets and inside my bag. I did at least feel a little reassured by the cover of darkness as we loaded our gear and the holdalls into Cam's Rover on the street.

In the car, Cam uncrumpled a piece of paper and handed it to me. On one side was printed a map of Birmingham with a route drawn on it that wandered through each area in a loose circuit. "This is our dropoff route," he explained. "On the back there's a list of what banks are at which point. Every time we stop, we need to take several envelopes to each bank."

"I left the SatNav in my car," I said. "Wait a minute while I go back for it."

When I went back for it, the medical case from the blood bank van was still lying on my back seat. I must have thrown it in there when I'd lifted it off the trolley to move the cash boxes. I thought it was best not to leave it there where it was visible, considering it had been stolen from the hospital where we'd been sighted, so I took that to Cam's car as well.

"Do we need to wear disguises?"

"There's not time for that if we want it done today. We'll just have to risk it. It should be easy to keep your face away from the cameras."

I glanced down at what I was wearing. I'd left my proper coat on a trolley in a hospital pretending to be a patient's legs, and all the disguises were packed away in bags, so I'd had to make do with a spare coat of Cam's, a heavy, baggy thing that came down to my thighs. With a hat on and a scarf pulled up, it would be difficult for a camera to get a good view of my face in the darkness that had already fallen. I could throw away the coat afterwards.

Cam slotted the key in under the steering wheel

and started the engine. "Let's see if we can get as far as Edgbaston, then we'll stop for a break and get something to eat."

I tried to navigate for him as he drove, but my eyes wouldn't stay open or keep focus and my head kept falling back against the seat. An aching hunger burned in my stomach. Cam hunched over the steering wheel, his eyes bloodshot and his face grey, his hair and collar sticking up. I forced myself to look at the map, and at the blurry road ahead.

Cam found a parking space close to the first dropoff. "All we have to do is walk past the banks and post the envelopes through the slot. The idea is we start laundering the money as soon as it's been processed, moving into different accounts, different banks, accounts in foreign countries, shares, other investments. Some of them we draw out physically and pay in elsewhere, that sort of thing. If they do manage to identify any of the accounts we've used, the trail of the money moving around should have gone cold by then."

The cold air and the act of walking served to revive me to a degree. I took Barclays and Lloyds, up the hill, and Cam took HSBC and NatWest, across the road and down another street. With both banks, all the security cameras outside looked to be trained on the ATMs, leaving the dropoff points for deposits — steel vaults built into the walls with a slot above for inserting envelopes — uncovered. I supposed no-one expected someone to commit a crime using a deposit envelope. They were too busy checking for people using stolen cards at the ATMs.

Giving the area where people queued a wide berth, I approached the slots and slid the envelopes through.

Cam and I didn't speak when we arrived back at the

car. I simply opened the door when he unlocked it, and we got back in and continued on the route. It felt like this was going to drag on forever. The end looked unattainable from here, and although my legs felt like they were going to collapse under me and my eyes wouldn't stay open, I had to keep getting up and carrying on until I'd seen it through. It's no good wanting out now, I told myself. You opened this can of worms.

I remember that night as being hazy and numb, as though I was sleepwalking through it. The weak, dizzy pain of hunger. The ceasing of the engine's vibration as the car stopped, the getting out into the cold air, the walking with the envelopes in my pocket, the lighting behind the banks' signs standing out like beacons above the street, looking at the envelopes under a streetlamp to check the symbol on them matched the one above the bank, the sliding of yet another handful of envelopes into a slot, then returning the same way, one foot before the other on legs that didn't feel like they were mine any more, Cam's figure indistinct, the feel of the car door handle, the brief respite of the seat and the hot air blasting out of the grilles by our feet and hands.

At Edgbaston, Cam told me to wait in the car. I must have fallen asleep immediately, because the next thing I knew he was back and pushing at my shoulder, and he had kebabs. By now it was 11 pm. I couldn't feel the hot and slimy morsels of gristly meat with fingers burned by cold and mangled with papercuts. The food cured the sickly faintness of starvation and returned some of my strength to me, but it made the drowsiness worse. Every time I got back into the car I would fall asleep, an unsatisfying sleep that hovered on the edge of consciousness and was filled with the noise and motion of the car. Every time I had to get out, my bad knee seized up and I had to hobble in agony for a few steps before it would start to work again.

Finally we took the last envelopes out of the last bag. I never want to see another DepositPoint envelope for as long as I live.

Back at the car, Cam said, "Just one thing left to do."

We bundled together the holdalls with our coats and the empty envelopes we hadn't filled. Cam led the way down an unlit sidestreet until we reached a canal. The water was frozen, and a thicket of lank bushes grew on the other side. Down here in the shadow, no-one would see us.

Outside a boarded-up factory we broke apart a box of paraffin firelighters and lit a bonfire made of the coats and bags.

I watched the growing flames eat the polyester fabric of the coats, the nylon fibres of the holdalls wilting and shrinking away from the heat.

"That's all we can do, now," said Cam. "Let's go home."

It was almost three in the morning when we got back. We sat on the sofa in the dark and I lay against Cam's chest. I supposed we should have gone to bed, but my exhaustion was so great that even the thought of the stairs daunted me.

"Tweedledum or Tweedledee shot the cop," I said.

Cam twitched beneath me. "You saw?"

I nodded.

"If we get caught, you didn't see. The court might see it as mitigation."

After a moment, he added, "It was Tweedledee."

I must have fallen asleep after that.

10

RED MIST

Although I was utterly exhausted, noises from outside interrupted my sleep several times that night. Drunken youths swore and bellowed outside the window. Shattering glass rang upon the pavement. Once I came awake at the scream of a siren, and Cam too started, his arms tensing around me as pulsing blue light flooded into the room around the edges of the curtains, but the light faded out and the siren Dopplered and died away.

I opened my eyes, still lying on Cam's chest against the sofa's back. The cold, hard light of morning had just begun to show in the narrow wedge between the drooping curtains and the spaces where they hung from the rail. I raised the back of my wrist to my eyes and tilted the face of my watch towards the light. It was a little after eight thirty.

Cam slept with his head lolling back on the arm of the sofa nearest the window. The dawn light that penetrated the room illuminated faint lines on his forehead and under his eyes, and though his hair was dyed black, the roots showed brown salted with silver at the base of his forelock. Oblivious to the world and breathing slowly, he'd unintentionally revealed something of the man he was underneath the disguises, the one I didn't know.

A thunderous hammering broke out in the hallway. I started and Cam's eyes flew open.

"We know you're in there Cam!"

I threw aside the blanket we'd been sleeping under. His hands closed on my wrists as we both got to our feet. "Hide!"

"Where?"

He pushed open the door to the hallway. It only had a small window, high up in the wall above the door. They wouldn't be able to see inside. Without speaking, Cam pointed to the cupboard under the stairs. I ducked through the entrance and sat down, my back pressed against the coats hanging from pegs on the back wall. Cam pushed the door shut as he passed.

I heard the muffled scrape of the front door opening.

"Where's Doc?" someone asked. Tweedledee, I think it was.

"At home, I expect," Cam answered.

"Where's the money?" Tweedledum, probably. The voice sounded different from the first.

"Genghis took two of the boxes."

"We saw that on the news." Tweedledum sounded as though he was starting to lose his temper. "Where's the rest of it?"

"Where's Doc?"

If Cam was feeling threatened, his voice didn't show it. "Doc didn't see anything."

A pause.

"How do you know?"

"She'd have said something about it. I expect she just watched the layby and left for Rendezvous B, like she was supposed to."

Tweedledum's petulant voice interrupted them. "Cam,

where's the *fucking* money?"

"It's upstairs," said Cam. "We were both really tired. The police got Ace, and I think they got Genghis too."

"So we saw on the news."

"It really shook Doc up."

Thanks Cam, I thought. *Make out I'm a wimp.* And yet he was trying to protect me, or at least he thought he was. What did it matter if Tweedledum and Tweedledee knew I saw them shoot the cop? It wasn't like I could go to the police station and incriminate them. We were all in this together.

"I thought it would be better in all circumstances if we lay low for a bit. I couldn't get the safeboxes open anyway."

One of them men made a disparaging noise, and then I sensed feet on the stairs above my head. It sounded like all three of them were going up.

I fumbled around the wall close to the door and found a light switch. The cupboard was full of pirate DVDs and bits of Cam's many disguises. It reminded me of when I was a kid and I used to spend hours playing under the stairs with my cousin, and we pretended it was a spaceship or a dungeon, or a portal to another dimension. There was also there the cardboard box with the leftover chemicals I'd ordered when we'd got the rotavap and the reagents we needed to make the modified Ecstasy. There must be something here I could use for improvised protection if they happened to come back down and find me here. Very carefully, so as not to clink the glass bottles against one another, I rotated each of them in turn, so the labels faced towards me.

Thiophosgene.

Horrid, poisonous stuff, chemically similar to the less smelly and slightly less lethal phosgene gas used in World

War One. If you inhale too much of it, it cross-links the proteins lining your lungs so they don't work, and you suffocate.

An angry, raised voice came from upstairs, and then I recognised Cam's voice in answer. Then an ear-rending bang sent a tremor through the house and made me start so sharply I banged the back of my head on the wall with the coats hanging on it— a gunshot? There came a splintering noise, and something heavy crashed down on the stairs over my head. I seized the thiophosgene bottle and threw open the cupboard door. Cam was lying on his back halfway down the stairs, his feet pointing up and one arm held up defensively over his face. He stared at me, his mouth open. Shattered pieces of wood lay all over the stairs around him, and I realised he must have fallen against the banisters dividing the stairwell from the landing and broken them.

An anguished cry came from above. A man stood at the top of the stairs, his teeth bared, his face an orange rictus. His hands and forearms and all down the front of his shirt and trousers were stained orange, too. They must have forced one of the boxes open. It had sprayed Smart Water and dye all over them.

Cam slithered to the bottom of the stairs and rolled out of the way. I hurled the bottle in my hand at the stairs. Red liquid sprayed into the air as the glass shattered, and reeking rust-coloured smoke began to fog the hallway.

I grabbed Cam's hand and flung open the front door. Bits of broken banister dropped off his clothes as we stumbled out onto the drive. The cold air cut into my lungs. I lost my grip on his hand when he skidded on a patch of ice and fell against the laurel bush, almost disappearing inside it.

I stood on the gravelled area between the paving slabs

to get a better grip. Cam thrust his hand into his jeans pocket as he stood up. "Here, you drive. Get to the car."

"Then let's take my car instead," I protested.

"There's not time. All our shit's in mine."

I got to the Rover and fumbled the central locking fob to open the doors. All the windows were rimed with frost. When I got into the driver's seat, the whole interior was filled with a dingy, pallid light, like the inside of an igloo.

Cam yanked open the passenger door. "Start the engine!" He grabbed a red plastic scraper from the pocket on the inside of the door.

I trod down the clutch and turned the key until the engine started. The heating was already turned up as high as it would go, so I changed the vent dial to direct it onto the windscreen and turned on the rear window heater. I pumped the stalk for the windscreen washers, but the washers didn't work and the wipers were stuck to the surface of the glass.

Cam began to scrape at the windscreen. A small square of daylight became visible. I pulled the stalk again, and the wipers gave with a loud crack, grating unsteadily across the icy surface. Cam swiped with the scraper in between the rhythm of the wiper blades. Gradually, a ragged gap appeared.

He flung himself into the seat beside me. "Just go. There's not time." The door slammed. I opened the window to check it was clear to the rear, and pulled away. The wipers still swatted ineffectually at pieces of ice that clung to the glass and obscured the view, bumping and reverberating when they came into contact. I kept pumping the stalk every few minutes, but the water wasn't coming out. The steering wheel was icy under my hands.

"Where are we going?" I demanded. "We need the SatNav and I think it's in my bag in the boot."

Cam shook his head. He breathed rapidly, and there was a crazy look of fear in his eyes. "Go to the M6. Our best bet's to try to make it to the M1 and see if we can lose them."

"I can lose them much easier if we take the side-roads—"

"No!" he interrupted. "We're safer if we stay in high-density traffic."

"But I can out-drive them!"

"They've got guns. If we go off the beaten track and lead them into desolate places where there are no witnesses, we just give them more incentive to use them!"

I kept my eyes on the road and tried to restrain the panic in my voice. "Yesterday they murdered someone! I don't think it matters to them how many more they murder. Why didn't you just give them their share of the money?"

"Because they wouldn't settle for just their share! They would want all of it! And then they would want us disposed of, because we're witnesses! Genghis could keep them in check. Now he's out of the picture, no-one can. And now they've shot a copper and they're desperate and normal laws don't matter. Tweedledee's a fucking psycho. Tweedledum's thick as pigshit and just does what Tweedledee tells him."

"Why the hell were they in on this? What was Genghis thinking?"

"I dunno." Cam wiped his mouth on the back of his wrist. "Genghis has known Tweedledee a while. He did listen to Genghis. I suppose he never expected it to end up this way."

I was coming up to the slip-road off the dual carriageway,

which led to the main interchange.

"Their car's a dark red Honda," Cam added.

I got in lane for the M6.

The rush hour was more or less over. The traffic on the motorway was heavy, but it kept moving. There are always roadworks of some description, and the M6 is notorious for grinding to a halt. It at least looked as though we were safe from that, for now. Birmingham looked grey and grim in the sunless morning. We passed Spaghetti Junction, cars tearing round its concrete coils like passengers on a helter-skelter fairground ride. Beyond it lay a fenced-in forest of electrical pylons, ceramic discs and steel girders and cables all begrimed from the dirt the passing traffic generated. Clusters of high-rise flats rose from the clutter on both sides, the blank surfaces of their naked concrete forbidding, fortress-like. I don't think there's anyone alive who would honestly be able to say it was beautiful, but it is *something*. It has a character all of its own. And it says something true about the society it's a part of. Unemployed people with no hope and no future live in these places. Often prestigious snobs visit the Midlands and start ranting about how hideous it is and how it should all be torn down and rebuilt, as though they think they can contain the crime and the failure and all the hopelessness by hiding it under some twee, picturesque façade. At least this architecture doesn't pretend to be something it isn't.

We were soon heading out of Birmingham and into the greener areas that divided it from Coventry.

"Cam," I said, noticing something in the mirror. "A dark red Honda."

Cam twisted in his seat. Ahead of us was another car, and ahead of that a Royal Mail van was trying to overtake another Royal Mail van that was trying to overtake a bin lorry. Between the three of them, they had blocked the entire side of the carriageway. When I looked again, the red car behind us was much closer.

"Cam, what do I do?"

Cam wiped his face on the palm of his hand, glancing over his shoulder through the back window. "I don't know."

"Do I go faster? Should I drive on the hard shoulder to try to get around this traffic?"

"Oh shit."

I looked into the rear-view mirror. The following car loomed large, close behind us, and I could make out the shapes of the men inside. It looked like one of them might be pointing at us.

Unexpectedly Cam reached across and took hold of my hand. He put his other hand over his forehead, squeezing shut his eyes and baring his teeth. My free hand tensed on the wheel. What could I do? Should I try to speed and weave in and out of the traffic? Would it be possible even to lose them in this?

I caught sight of a blue flicker in the mirror, and then the wail of a siren started up over the noise of the road.

Cam opened his eyes.

"I'm pulling over," I said. "I don't know if that's for us or the Tweedles, but we can't win this race."

I indicated left and, spotting a gap between two lorries in the middle lane, began to move over. The red Honda tore past as soon as there was room, charging up to the car in front and sounding its horn. The police car swept by in a blur of white-and-fluorescent paint and flashing lights.

Cam exhaled. We breathed for several surreal seconds.

"Let's get off at the next exit," he said.

As the car eased into the inside lane, the wind caught the back corner of the lorry in front, whipping a dirty spray into its slipstream. A slurry of salty meltwater and motorway filth misted the windscreen. Grimacing and squinting to see the traffic in front, I pumped the washer stalk hard. A weak fountain of water burst from the jet on my side. It hit the window and froze into a prickly opaque shape right in my line of sight.

"Shit!"

"Put the wipers on fast! M69!" Cam shouted. "Off here, on the sliproad!"

I pushed the indicator stalk down and crouched in my seat to attempt to see around the mess on the glass. In this way I made it a mile up the sliproad before I pulled the car over onto the hard shoulder. Cam threw open the door and dug through a bag on the back seat. He found a bottle of vodka, which he emptied over the windscreen where it thankfully dissolved the ice. He wiped it off with a pair of his boxers.

"Drive," he said breathlessly as he got back in.

I pulled off the hard shoulder and onto the M69 motorway. Frosted fields drifted by under a gunmetal sky.

"I think we've lost them," Cam said at last.

"I hope the pigs got them," I said vehemently.

For a while, we just breathed in relief, and I drove with my eyes fixed on the road. Then he switched the radio on.

Police have arrested a fifty-six-year-old man and a seventeen-year-old boy in relation to the robbery of the Blue Moon Casino in Birmingham yesterday morning by a criminal gang widely popularised as a modern-day Band of Merry Men. It's been confirmed that a male police officer was shot dead. A seventy-nine-year-old man thought to be connected with the crime was also pronounced dead yesterday in the University Hospital of Birmingham. Neither this person's identity nor that of the police officer shot have been confirmed at this time.

"Shit," said Cam.

"Sage died," I said, and a painful tension came into my throat at the memory of what he'd said to me before we'd left him. I blinked furiously to overcome the blurring of my sight. This wasn't the time for it, and it seemed to me now that there'd never be a time to stop and think and mourn, and try to come to terms with what we'd done.

Just over four million pounds was stolen in the robbery, although it's thought police were able to recover some of the money on the arrest of one of the suspects. At least four of the perpetrators of the crime are thought to be at large.

After a long pause I said, "Cam, what the hell are we going to do?"

Cam shook his head. "We're not going to get out of here for a while. Not with the best fake passports I can make. The police will be watching the airports, and I wouldn't be surprised if the Tweedles were hanging around too. We're going to have to lie low for a few weeks while this blows over."

"Where can we go?"

Cam leaned back into his seat and sighed. "Let's go north. Scotland. If we can get to the Hebrides I think we could hide out there this time of year."

I tried to steady my breathing. "I've never been to the Hebrides. Where are they? Are they the ones to the north, or the ones off the west coast?"

"They're the western ones — Lewis and Harris and Skye."

For a moment, neither of us said anything. Cam seemed

to sense my concerns, and he put his hand out and laid it on my forearm. "Don't worry. We're rich. Just don't think too much about it, and pretend we're going on a holiday. That's all it is, really."

"Cam, our friends are dead or in jail. An innocent man has been murdered for trying to do his job." I thought of the policeman's family, probably a wife and some kids. Policemen who die on the job nearly always have families like that. You have to come from a certain photogenic sort of setting to be a hero. That's why people like me don't become heroes.

I glanced away from the road for an instant and caught his eye. *We can't turn back*, I realised. We had driven this to the point where there was no turning around and walking away from our mistakes. We had thrown the dice, and whatever would come after this would be out of our control to a greater degree than not.

"Let's not talk about it. Just concentrate on driving."

As we drove north it began to snow heavily. The sky became hazy and the fields turned white. The road ahead was obscured by constantly falling flakes that melted as soon as they touched the road surface. I found myself blinking repeatedly. "We're going to have to stop somewhere," I said.

"We can't. Tweedledum and Tweedledee might find us."

"Cam, we're going to have to stop eventually, and they might find us regardless of whether we're here or a hundred miles away!"

"All right. We'll find somewhere."

11

WHITE WEDDING

Cam reached into the back of the car and fished out a road map.

"The SatNav's in my bag if you want to use that," I said.

"Thanks for the offer, but I'm with the old school." Cam tapped his forehead and flipped through pages. After a moment's study, he said, "If you take the next exit there's an hotel nearby."

I indicated and moved into the inside lane. We continued for another few miles in silence before the car came to the sliproad and we turned off.

"Okay," said Cam as we reached the roundabout. "In the left lane here. Now off here, this exit."

I smiled. "Pity my SatNav doesn't have you on it."

"If I was on your SatNav, I'd only lead you astray."

"You do that anyway."

"So if Jeremy Clarkson is the speed-camera free route, and David Attenborough is the scenic route, what niche would I fill?"

"I don't know. Probably the route onto private land and roads where cars aren't allowed."

"Or up dead end streets?"

"No, never up those."

"Ah, here we are. Next right."

I looked across to the other side of the road. A sign protruded from the top of the snow-capped hedge, but below the hotel name a printed strip had been attached:

CLOSED FOR PRIVATE FUNCTION

"This one's no good," I said. "We'll have to look for a different one."

"There're no other ones nearby I can see." Cam shuffled the map. "Turn in. If they won't let us have a room, we can ask them if there's a B&B round here."

I pushed up the indicator and turned across the road. The tyres slithered on snow as I dropped to second gear and continued slowly up the drive. The hotel, a grand Victorian building, came into view. A crowd of people stood about the steps to the front entrance, the men with snow on the shoulders of their suits like bad dandruff and the women with an extra white layer to their hats and dead-bird hair accoutrements. Balloons and decorations fluttered from stone heraldic beasts on the garden wall.

Congratulations Lucy and Adrian.

As I drove in towards where a sign marked *parking* directed us, the people stared at the car.

"There's a space." Cam pointed.

I turned the car about, the steering feeling wobbly and insubstantial against the snow on the tarmac, and reversed into the space. I looked back at the party. "We can't go in there."

"Sure we can. Think of a name."

I hesitated. "What for?"

A scheming leer spread across Cam's face. "Just think of one."

"Yates," I said.

"Yates what?"

"I don't know. Mrs Yates."

"All right, I'll think of the rest myself. Don't say you weren't warned." Cam had opened the door while he was speaking, and he got out. I joined him behind the car, where he pulled up the boot door.

"We ought to get rid of that hospital case," I reminded him, noticing the box we'd taken from the blood transfusion van with its medical stickers and 'Give Blood' exhortations covering the surface.

"That's a nice, strong suitcase," he argued. He unzipped a holdall and began to rummage through what was inside it, until he found a pair of ugly glasses with a tortoiseshell frame and a tuft of hair with a clip in it.

He put on the glasses and raked his fingers through his hair, flattening it with his palms and gathering as much of it as was long enough to permit at his nape. "Untie your hair," he told me, as he fastened the hairpiece to the clump at the back of his neck.

"But I always have my hair like this." I found my holdall in the back of the car and took it out.

He raised his eyebrows behind his unattractive spectacles. "Exactly."

I sighed, untwisted the band from my pony-tail, and put it in my pocket. "You can still tell it's been tied back. And I look like an old hag."

"No, you don't," he said, without even looking. He slammed the boot. "Car locked?"

"Cam, what are you doing? *Cam*?" I lowered my voice to an urgent snarl as he pulled me towards the foyer by the hand. "You can't gatecrash a wedding reception!"

"'Course we can! They'll just think we're two of their own."

"No, they won't!" I had to stop talking, because we had reached the throng at the entrance. The snow on the path mingled with sodden confetti as we pressed through and up the steps.

The hotel reception was overwhelmingly dark after the bright daylight reflecting on the snow outside. As my eyes adjusted, I noticed a glass bowl of punch with floating fruit pieces and a ladle, stood amongst a forest of glasses upon a table with a gold-and-burgundy runner. Behind a large vase supporting a spray of roses and gold twiddly things stood a smiling lady in an elaborate burgundy-and-gold dress, clustered about by a garrulous mass of people.

"Lucy!" Cam shouted, his voice boisterous and Welsh-accented. "You look amazing!" He gave the woman a vigorous wave. She smiled slightly awkwardly, and waved back at him. She must have thought him a friend of her husband.

Cam led me past more people to the desk. He banged his hand down on the little brass bell standing before a rack of pens on chains, even though the receptionist sat there bent over some paperwork on the other side.

"Yes, hello!" Cam bellowed when the man looked up. "Alastair and Merlyn Yates-Middleton. I believe we have a reservation."

"Just a minute, Sir." The man opened a leatherbound book ruled with columns like a teacher's register. After several moments of scanning the columns and sliding his finger up and down the margins, he turned over a page, glanced at it, and looked up at Cam. "I'm sorry, Sir, you don't seem to be on the list. I can't see any reservations under either Yates or Middleton."

"No, it's Yates-Middleton with a hyphen, Y-A-T-E-S."

"I'm sorry Sir, but that's not there either. You say you made a reservation?"

"Yesterday, online with my credit card. It said it had gone through."

The man curled his fingers under his hands where they rested on his book. He looked embarrassed and intimidated. "I'm very sorry, Sir, but it appears it hasn't."

"Well, what are we supposed to do about it?" Cam put his palms down on the reception desk, not hard enough for it to be construed as an aggressive gesture, but just hard enough that it made a noise and commanded the attention of everyone in the room. "We've travelled back here from Ohio to see Lucy and Adrian. We spent good money getting here, and we've little enough time as it is without having to find somewhere else to stay."

The focus of the crowd in the room shifted away from Cam as a man with a burgundy-and-gold cravat and a rose in his lapel entered the foyer.

"Adrian, it's a right mess," the bride declared. "The hotel's mucked up Alastair and Merlyn's reservation."

Adrian glanced at me and Cam. I could see he didn't recognise us, *but he thought Lucy did*. His forehead glistened with sweat in the light from the chandelier. He was under stress, I realised. He wanted his wedding to go without a hitch, he wanted Lucy to remember it as the best day of her life, and he didn't want to upset her guests. He looked back to the receptionist.

"See here," he said, "if Alastair said he made the booking, I believe him. You've got rooms left still, haven't you? When we booked the hotel, there were a few spare?"

The man nodded. He looked confused.

"Well, allocate them one!"

The man fumbled for a pen and began to write on the blank line at the bottom of the list of guests. "Mr and Mrs Yates-Middleton," he said. "You'll be wanting a double room?"

"En suite," I added.

"That's a hundred and twenty pounds fifty."

"Wait a minute," said Cam. "I hope you're not going to be charging us for this, twice. I already paid for it, and I'm not paying for it again."

"With all due respect, Sir, the transaction didn't go through, otherwise it would show up on the system. You mustn't have completed the process."

"But I did! I've got an email with a confirmation number! I'll get it for you once I get my laptop sorted out, if you'll gimme the code for your network!"

I noticed Adrian, who was standing beside Lucy near the entrance, had fixed the receptionist with an angry stare.

"Look," said Cam, "I'll write my address down for you. If there's any problem with the payment, you can write to me and I'll sort it out for you with my credit card company." He picked up one of the pens on chains and began to write on the back of an hotel card. "I'll put my work address on here, too. See?"

The man nodded furiously, his pen strokes gouging the surface of the paper. "Right, you're in the old stable block, room S6." He snagged a key on a wooden fob off a rack behind the desk and dumped it on the table in front of Cam. "Enjoy your stay. Mike, please show Mr and Mrs Yates-Middleton to S6."

The smartly attired man waiting beside the desk gestured to take our bags. Cam and I followed him through a corridor with windows looking out into a snow-filled courtyard and lined with tables on either side loaded with glasses, punch bowls, and wine bottles. Cam snatched up two glasses as we passed through. The man led us out through a propped-open door. Patio heaters were already belching heat into the open air, melting the snow.

"Watch your step here, Sir, Madam." We followed the man down a few steps and between some dead flowerbeds, to an entrance into an old building with a horseshoe nailed above the door. Up a staircase and down a corridor we went, to a door marked S6.

In the gloom of the unlit hallway, I chanced a glance at Cam. He raised his eyebrows and flashed a smile at me.

The man turned the key and pushed open the door. "I hope everything's to your satisfaction," he said. "If you'd like anything, please use the phone." He dumped the bags in the entrance to the room and departed.

I pushed the door shut behind us. "Cam, what are we going to do if they talk to each other and it occurs to them that they don't actually know us?"

Cam began to explore the room, testing his weight with his fist against the mattress and opening the wardrobe door. "They've just got married. They won't get a moment to talk to each other until they're in a cab on the way to their honeymoon."

I laughed. "You're mad. But in a good way."

He turned to face me. "It's a nice room, isn't it?"

I paused to take in the mahogany furniture and the wood panelled door leading to the bathroom and the plush, dark carpet underfoot. Three stairs led down to a seating area by the window with two armchairs, a large LCD television, and a coffee table. The bed, dressing table, and wardrobe were divided into the corner behind the door with a painted Japanese screen, leaving the rest of the room open plan. "And so it should be, for £120 a night!"

Cam set down the punch glasses on a side-table and hefted one of his bags up onto the bed. He dug out his laptop, his face taking on a more serious countenance. "That cash we paid in should all have cleared by now. I need to get started on the accounts."

"The accounts?"

"Ace wrote a program to handle it. It logs on to the online banking services for all the accounts and makes it easy for me to shunt the money around."

"I'd like to have a look at it sometime," I said, "but I think a shower is more important to me at the moment."

He tucked his computer under his arm and stood smartly with a glass of punch in his other hand as I walked past to the bathroom.

I cleaned my teeth first, glad to get rid of the dirty taste that had stayed in my mouth since I'd woken that morning. It was only when I'd got into the shower, with the door shut and the curtain drawn across and the noise and steam of the hot water secluding me that I felt I could finally think and reflect on what had happened.

The force of the hot water massaged some of the ache from the muscles of my back and shoulders. I inhaled the refreshing steam and looked about for a flannel, to find there weren't any. I recalled from my employment days, from the hotels I'd stayed in when I'd been at conferences, there were never any flannels. Perhaps normal people don't use flannels, and I was just brought up weird that way. I can't think what they must wash their faces on instead.

I wet one of the small hand towels under the shower

and blotted my face with the hot, damp cloth. I thought of my house, how it now stood empty and how I wouldn't be going back to it. My car was stranded outside Cam's house. I'd probably never see it again. Those had been the two most important things in my life, the possessions I'd striven to protect above all else. They had been the only real reminders of the life I'd had before it had all gone wrong, and I'd just walked away from them, and it didn't feel anywhere near as significant as my conscience told me it ought to.

Or perhaps things had changed, and I hadn't noticed.

Over the past year, the house had become more like a prison; the mortgage payments had become a burden I couldn't carry. It was just a place where I lived because I couldn't live anywhere else. It had ceased to be what it had once represented. The car used fuel I couldn't afford — but I'd loved that car. I'd managed during my PhD with a disintegrating old Volkswagen while I saved up the money for it. It had been the first thing I had bought by myself that felt as though it was really worth something, an achievement.

But now all that had gone sour. My job, the same thing that had given me the means to buy the house had, in the end, broken me. When I thought of my work, it didn't conjure the same memories it once had. All I could visualise now was my old boss's sneering face. The car was nearly eight years old. It was starting to wear out. I'd only get a few thousand if I sold it. The house was still mostly owned by the mortgage company. I had not really lost that much. They belonged to an era that was finished now. It only felt natural to move away from them.

I wondered how long it would take for my absence to be noted. When I didn't turn up at the dole office, my benefits would be stopped. They wouldn't bother to write a letter or try to contact me, because they did it once before when

I was ill, even though I telephoned them and explained the situation, and I lost a month's worth of benefits and never got it back. The mortgage had a direct debit set up to pay it, so I supposed my current account would go overdrawn first, and it would eat into the overdraft for a few more months before the bank would put a stop on it, and then the mortgage would go into arrears. It might take the mortgage company another few months to notice that. Then it would be letters, and threats, and final warnings. I had no idea how long it took from a mortgage going into arrears to bailiffs being sent over. Probably it would be more months. Conceivably it might be over a year since I had actually left until any of the authorities realised I wasn't there any more. As for friends and relatives, I had none left, and the neighbours tended to keep to themselves. It might be different if I'd died in there and there came a nasty smell and a fly infestation once the summer months came round again, but if I simply wasn't there, I didn't expect people would think it was any of their business.

I forced my thoughts back to the immediate situation. There was no point dwelling on Sage's death. He'd been ready for it and it was inevitable. Ace and Genghis were in jail. They were limited in what they could reveal of us, simply because they didn't know anything much, the same as we didn't know much about them. It had been a wise move on Genghis's part to ensure no-one knew anyone else's name.

Tweedledum and Tweedledee had for some reason decided they were on one side and we were on the other. I found a sick feeling surfacing within me at this thought. Would they still pursue us if we did manage to flee the country? Did they have any idea about where we might be going? I hadn't told them. Had Cam?

I also had to be rational to myself about my standing

with Cam. There was a risk that he too might betray me, and at the moment I didn't have any real stakes in this and I would come away with nothing if he decided he didn't want me with him any more. I'd need to confront him on that, and I'd need to think of a tactful way to do it, to make sure he didn't get the impression I didn't trust him, or that I intended to betray him.

I finished my shower, wrapped the largest towel there around myself, and went back into the other room.

It appeared Cam had finished doing the accounts. He lounged on the bed, propped up on one elbow and eating the chocolate chip biscuits that had come with the hotel drinks tray. His chin was dark with stubble and his hair was untidy.

I sat on the bed next to him. He put his hand on my leg and slid it up, under the hem of the towel.

The sudden intrusion of his touch made me jump. "Cam! At least have a shower first. Besides, we're supposed to be pretending to be guests at Lucy and Adrian's wedding."

Cam arched his eyebrows fancifully. "And I suppose Lucy and Adrian's genuine guests never get up to things in the privacy of their hotel rooms?"

"There are more important things now. What you said about the computer. I think I ought to be more familiar with this." I took a deep breath. "What I mean is, if we get split up, you know where the money is and I don't."

Cam considered this. "You're quite right," he said. "You ought to have half of the debit cards for safekeeping."

"I don't mean to—" I began.

"No, it's a valid point. It's no good if one of us gets captured and we lose the whole lot. All of the accounts we set up have debit cards. The PINs are all 9999, so just remember that." He found a carrier bag inside his holdall and put it on the bed. It was filled with plastic bank cards. "Take half of those for yourself. They average out at about the same per account anyway, so you should get roughly half the money however you choose." He rose from the bed and stretched.

"What are you going to do, then?"

"I'm going to have a bath and make myself presentable for you."

While he clattered about in the *en suite*, shaving and running a bath, I gathered roughly half of the cards, as he'd suggested, and secreted them inside a zipped pocket on my holdall.

"You think it's all right if I wear the same clothes I wore at the casino?" I rummaged through my bag. We had brought along various clothes acquired from charity shops to make up disguises, but none of them were sort of things suitable for a party. "I've not got anything else that's decent."

"I suppose it'll have to be," Cam called back. "Unless you want to be *indecent*." He'd turned off the taps and I heard the splash of him putting his feet in, followed by the sloshing of the water and the squeak of flesh on the enamelled sides of the bath. An urge came upon me to go in there and look at him and touch him, to lose my concerns beneath indulgence. But we still had an appearance to maintain, and I had to keep up my guard. I found myself wondering if I'd ever be able to indulge in anything without constantly looking over my shoulder. Things had become so different overnight. Perhaps it would come naturally in the end, and I'd adapt to it, like I had done when I'd started my old job. I recalled how bewildered I'd felt when I'd started working in that lab with four other people already established there, like I'd lost my identity amongst all the banter and persiflage that went on among them.

And the backstabbing and arselicking, although that hadn't been apparent to me at that early point. Some bosses have the confidence to step back and let their research groups find their own feet, and somehow people take pride in their work and responsibility for the equipment, and everyone gels. Other bosses try to micromanage everything and they bring out the worst in everyone, and they end up with a team of petty, bickering people trashing the lab equipment and trying to do each other over.

As I got dressed I spoke to him in a voice I hoped wouldn't be loud enough for anyone who might be in a neighbouring room to hear. "Will the Tweedles be able to track us here?" I thought of the pair of them breaking in through the hotel door in the middle of the night with their guns. What if people at this wedding died because of what we'd done?

"It's unlikely. But we need to move quickly. We'll be having them as well as the police after us."

I found a comb and raked my wet hair out of my face. "If they've lost us and they don't know where we are, they're not going to find us. They don't know where we're going, right?" I moved to stand in the doorway to the bathroom. Cam was sitting in the bath with his elbow resting up on the side, one of the punch glasses in his other hand.

"The police have an organised network, and they have public services like the news and *Crimewatch*. The nation's criminals have equivalents to that."

I stared at him, not quite sure if he was joking. "What, you mean they have pirate radio stations where they report good places to burgle, and helplines they can ring if their houses are under police siege?"

"It's getting that way. There's a network of organised crime across the country, and disorganised crime sort of feeds into it. You remember the London riots and how the criminals organised it on social network sites?" He gave me a moment to consider this. "Tweedledum and Tweedledee have ways of making it known to other criminals that they're looking for two people of our description, and anyone who can find us is going to get a cut of their profits."

A cold feeling was creeping over my chest. There had been no suggestion of this at the start, when I'd been deciding whether or not to get involved with robbing a casino and attempting to flee the country with the proceeds. "So is there an international network as well, like an illegal NATO?"

Cam raised his glass to the bathroom light, studying the pieces of fruit floating in the pink liquid. "Something like that. Only the real heavyweights are involved in that, though, and that the Tweedles aren't, at least. The amount we've got away with is too insignificant for their likes to bother with. We just need to lie low until the hype dies down and the risk gets as low as it can. Those passports I got I can't get more of, not now. We only get one shot at assuming those identities, and that's when we leave the country. We keep them hidden until then, and we make sure we've learnt them by heart and rehearsed how we're going to play them."

An obsessive compulsive urge prompted me to check in my handbag to make sure Rowena Griffin's passport was still there. "Cam, where'd you learn all this stuff?"

Cam's glass faltered on its route to his lips. A trickle of punch spilled over its rim and ran down his wet chest, dispersing in the bathwater. For an instant, I saw fear in his eyes, and then almost as soon as the turn had come upon him, he regained his composure. "A good magician never reveals his secrets."

I realised too late the question had cut too close to the past he considered off limits. So stupid of me. I should have thought before I opened my mouth. I couldn't afford to have a fight with him now, not like how he'd flared up when I'd first tried to probe too deep. He was just stressed out from all that had happened, I told myself, yet I was fighting down unease, trying to hold my mind back from focusing on the question of why he wouldn't tell me. Surely he didn't still think anonymity would keep him safe if the police caught up with us, of all things, after everything we'd been through together?

I finished getting ready, doing my hair while Cam handled his ablutions. I tried to do my hair up like the hairdresser had done it, sort of in a bun with curly ringlet things hanging out. It wouldn't quite go the same, though. The hairdresser had dyed black streaks and glitter in it and used some sort of spray to stop the ringlets from going limp.

Cam emerged while I was doing my make-up. I watched him in the mirror, over my shoulder, as he put on a pink shirt, a garish multicoloured tie, and a sky-blue jacket. He accessorised his outfit with the ugly glasses he'd put on in the car, the clip-on pony-tail, a belt with what looked like a gargoyle face moulded into the buckle, a slosh of cheap cologne, and a pair of patent leather, imitation crocodile-skin loafers.

Turning back to me after neatening his hair in the mirror, he asked, "How do I look?"

I sat on the edge of the bed, a smile forcing itself unbidden onto my face. "Like an arsehole."

"Excellent." He stepped up to where I sat and extended his arm to me. "Now, would you care to accompany your arsehole of a *husband* to our friends' wedding party?"

I put the key into my handbag after we'd locked the door to our room. There were a lot of people down there. I huddled close to Cam, gripping his arm as we descended the staircase. "I know this just seems to come naturally to you, but I don't know how the hell you do it."

"See Auntie over there?" Cam indicated into the main room, over by the bay windows, to a late-middle-aged woman with a greying pompadour and a bluish-buff dress the colour of doves, around whom the rest of the guests appeared to be orbiting. "She's the grand matriarch; the queen bee. The busybody at the helm of all the gossip who knows everyone's name. Make sure she knows who we're meant to be, and that's the hard part over. Other than that, just try to relax and get into character."

Before I had time to compose myself, we were into the crowded room, and Cam was towing me by the arm into the woman's line of sight.

"Ah, Merlyn and Alastair! I trust your room got sorted out in the end?" The woman made a distasteful expression. "Terrible mess they made of it!"

"Yes, they did, thank you Auntie P." Cam took her hand and squeezed it warmly. I hadn't the faintest idea how he'd found out she liked to be called Auntie P.

"So, you're in America are you now, Alastair?"

"Yes, in Ohio."

"What is it you do again dear boy?"

"I'm an accountant. I'm working for Grieves and Gellars there."

Auntie P switched her cutting gaze from Cam's face to mine. "I don't believe I've met you yet," she said, grasping my hand. She had a shrewd face, with a well-defined nose and sculpted eyebrows. In her youth she had probably been exceptionally handsome. I could see calculations and reasoning going on behind the gracious smile she presented: she didn't recognise Cam, but she'd overheard our names in the foyer and was under the impression we were good friends of the married couple. When Cam had addressed her in a familiar way, she had decided she must know him already, and that I had recently married him. Grieves and Gellars she assumed was some sort of prestigious accountancy firm in the USA.

"I neither," I said. "I've heard so much about you, Auntie P, and it's lovely to finally meet you."

Auntie let out a laugh as sharp as a songbird's voice, and laid a white-gloved hand on Cam's shoulder. "You cad, Alastair!" She turned her attention back on me. "What's this rogue been saying about me? What is it you do?"

"I'm a software engineer," I said.

Auntie smiled, compressing her lips and cocking her head to one side. "All Greek to me, my dear, but I shall take your word for it." Lowering her voice and inclining her head to me slightly, she added, "I'm so glad dear Alastair didn't marry one of those brash Americans he keeps company with. He did leave it rather late, and I daresay he's done very well for himself. Where is it you're from?"

"Stow."

Cam put his arm around me and made a whimsical expression. "She's my little Stow-away."

"Oh really? Uncle Fred and I drive home down the Fosse Way and we always go through it."

Fortunately, the buffet opened before she could ask any awkward questions about Stow, and that served as an excuse to withdraw from the attention. We loaded up our paper plates with quiche and cocktail sausages, and Cam found a quiet corner for us to sit in.

A surly girl in a dark blue dress came and sat down near to us. Her sandy hair was clagged up with glitter, and too much kohl had been smudged around her eyes.

"Hi," I said.

The girl glanced at us. "He your boyfriend?"

I put my hand on Cam's arm. "He's my husband."

"You mind your own business," said Cam.

I hadn't expected him to behave so impolitely. Oddly, it didn't seem to fit with his act either, as if he'd dropped out of character. Surely it wouldn't help our deception if he went around being rude to the newlyweds' guests. I looked at him pointedly, trying to prompt an apology from him.

"Do one of your magic tricks," I suggested, when he didn't respond.

The girl scowled at him. She must have been about ten or eleven, an age where children become self conscious, disowning childish things and aspiring to behave like adults and being taken seriously. I could see she was trying hard to suppress her fascination as Cam made a cocktail umbrella vanish and performed a trick with some ice cubes and napkins.

Then Lucy and Adrian cut a huge cake with coloured fondant flowers that Lucy's grandma had made for them, and we all had some of it. Afterwards, they had a disco. I can't dance, but the object of it seemed to face one's spouse and drape one's arms around his neck and shuffle about in this manner, so I managed to fake it adequately for three songs.

Cam told anecdotes to some men and lads, using exaggerated hand gestures and dramatic tones of voice.

Adrian was talking to his parents and they were both congratulating him. I found Auntie's clique in the garden, sitting about the tables by the swimming pool.

One of them spotted me. "Merlyn! Come and join us!" they called.

All the chairs were taken, so I took off my sandals and sat on the top step of the swimming pool with my feet in the water. It obviously made a great impression on a little girl, who came to join me, strewing her shoes and socks behind her on her route to the pool.

"Oh what a good idea!" Auntie chuckled, getting up in a precarious manner with a glass of sherry balanced in one hand. "Who's for a moonlit paddle, ladies?" She hitched up her skirt and began to wade in the water that smelt faintly of chlorine and beer. The others all declared what a wonderful idea it was, and one by one they followed, some sitting on the sides as I was and others wading in up to their knees and thighs, bantering with each other, and I found myself laughing and joining in with them. The girl Cam had been performing his magic tricks to earlier came down and looked longingly at the relatives in the water, until Auntie yelled at her, "Oh, come on Amelia, no-one from school is going to see!" and then with a forcedly solemn expression, she stepped in with them. A few of them shot off the occasional admonishment that the youngest girl ought to be in bed and that her mother, wherever she had got to, might not approve of her going in the pool in her best clothes. Then a rather large and somewhat tipsy grandma slipped in the shallows and got her knickers wet, and great amusement was had from this incident by all. I found myself laughing so hard my throat ached and my eyes started to run.

When I managed to stop laughing long enough to draw breath, a commotion was spreading across from the main building — people were shouting about something. A blade of fear stabbed up into my chest. Might it be the police were here?

Auntie turned and frowned at the noise. "Oh," she said. "Happy New Year indeed!"

And then people were passing around drinks and raising glasses. Of course. It was midnight, 31st December. It had slipped from my mind completely.

I looked about for Cam and found him standing a little apart from a group of men, staring at me.

Auntie, too, had noticed him. "Alastair!" she called in her sharp, high voice. "Come and get your feet wet!" The request broke off into a raucous cackle.

Cam was striding over now, looking amused. He held out his hand to help me up.

"You're taking Merlyn away from us so soon?" Auntie berated him.

"He's dragging her off to his chamber so he can have his evil way with her," someone else offered, and another swell of inebriated laughter broke out.

"We have to leave early tomorrow, I'm afraid," I said. "It has been lovely to see you all."

Auntie narrowed her eyes. "Susan is up next." She glanced at a young woman floundering about in a skirt with a wet hem, who went red in the face and protested. "Tell Eric to get a move on with his proposal! We'll all meet again very soon!"

For a moment there I wished I was Merlyn Yates-Middleton, and that these were our friends, and that we'd be returning tomorrow to America and the made-up lives we pretended to have. The stupid mess that was my past might almost have been funny had it had happened to someone else instead of me.

We found Adrian and Lucy and said goodnight to them, as was polite.

"What?" I said, as we walked together back into the hotel. "What were you looking at?"

Cam shrugged. His hand brushed against my arm. "You."

"Was I doing it wrong?"

"No."

My hands became clumsy when I fumbled in my handbag for the key to our room. I wanted to get back to privacy, to finally let down my guard and confront the way he was making me feel.

When the door was shut behind us, I yanked his tie off. I don't know if it was because Auntie P. and the crew down at the swimming pool had egged me on, or merely an urge for some sort of release, but this felt right.

"I know you said you thought I looked like an arsehole," he laughed, "but I didn't think you hated this disguise that much!"

I pulled down his jacket so his arms were trapped inside it and pushed him down onto the bed. He took off his belt and shoes in a very straightforward, unpretentious way. We were not kids any more. Last time I'd done this, when I'd been with Richard, I'd still felt young. So much had changed since then.

Being with him was like sinking into a warm tropical sea. He used slow, deep thrusts with all his weight behind him, the softness of his stomach and groin rolling against my skin like the swaying of waves. With each wave that broke I sank deeper into sensation, my sight and hearing becoming surreal and dreamlike as touch eclipsed all else.

He slumped onto his side, dragged the back of his arm

across his brow and laughed. I stroked sweat-dampened hair away from his forehead and kissed him, closing my eyes and stroking my hand down his sticky neck.

He glanced down at himself apologetically. When he rolled over and got up, the mattress lurched back into shape where his mass had been pinning it down, and it suddenly felt very flat and unyielding with just my meagre weight on it.

Perhaps he wasn't as inexperienced as I'd thought. I put my pyjamas on while he cleaned up in the bathroom.

"Do you think it's a bad idea to put this condom in the bin? In case the cops come here and forensics find it?"

"I'm not taking a semen sample all the way to Scotland with us," I said. "Flush it down the loo if you're that bothered about it. Don't expect they'll find out we've been here before the bin gets emptied for the next guest at any rate."

"We'll need a temporary address that's clean to get our new bank accounts set up, so we can put the money in once we've finished moving it around. I have a friend in Scotland. Completely trustworthy. We can use him."

"A friend?" I asked. Cam had never mentioned friends before, outside the seven.

"I'll tell you more later."

After a moment the toilet flushed, and then the bathroom light went off and Cam padded back into the room.

"Why do you think people get married?"

I twitched my shoulders. "I don't know."

"All that money, just for a piece of paper and a few photographs."

"I suppose they do it to make a memory." I rolled slightly onto my back and turned my head to him. "Why did Dorian Griffin marry Rowena?" When he didn't answer immediately, I chided, "You should know! He's your character!"

He got into bed, lying close against my back. "Perhaps Dorian has lots of money and a tragic terminal illness, and he doesn't want Rowena to have to pay inheritance tax when he dies."

"I suppose it's financially advantageous in some circumstances. Some people do it because they think it's the proper thing to do." I thought of my cousin and her partner. "It makes the legal framework easy if you want to have children."

"You think you'd want to have children? Or that Rowena would?"

I tensed. This was how I had lost Richard. "No and no."

"Why not?"

"I don't like them. I mean, not babies and really little kids, not kids like that girl back there. There's no instinct."

I sensed his chest heave expansively as he inhaled. "Instinct?"

This made me feel uneasy. Did Cam like children? "Like when women see babies and they're supposed to fawn over them. I don't get that. My mother always used to say that the instinct would come to me naturally, if it was my own."

Cam yawned. "I suppose it might."

"But it might not. What if I created another life on that assumption, and it didn't happen? That would be selfish, and stupid. There are enough people in the world."

"You're right. There are enough people in the world."

He pressed me closer to him.

"Cam?" I said, after a minute or so.

"What?"

"Do you want kids?"

He let of a short, self-deprecating laugh. "No. Can't stand the things. Besides, a life of crime is no life for a kid."

He said nothing more, but a huge pressure had been released. Whatever reason he had for liking me, it was for *me*, and not because of breeding potential. When Richard had started mentioning it, it had been like finding a bad clause buried in the smallprint of a contract. I drew Cam's hand up to my throat and nestled my chin against it, squeezing with my fingers. He put his face close to the back of my head and sighed, his breath gusting over my shoulder.

I closed my eyes in the darkness. I didn't know what tomorrow might bring, but I didn't fear it, and I didn't feel it would be out of my control.

12

RED TAPE

We left the hotel early the next morning, leaving the key on the dressing table and pulling the door shut behind us. We crept down silent stairs and across the empty foyer to the doors.

Outside, the white-clad grounds and the icicles hanging from the eaves sparkled in the dawn light. Snow crunched underfoot as we hauled our luggage back to the car.

As I started the engine and pulled out of the parking space I couldn't keep my eyes off the front of the house, half expecting to see the hotel staff come running out demanding we pay our bill and reveal who we actually were. As it was, only two people stood in their pyjamas and dressing gowns outside the front entrance.

"There are Lucy and Adrian," said Cam. "Wave!"

Both of us waved as I steered up the curve out of the car park, to the long drive up to the hotel gates. Adrian's arm was draped around Lucy's shoulders as they waved back, smiling in the first rays of the rising sun.

Perhaps it wouldn't be until the honeymoon, or even until they went home and got the photographs back, that they would talk, and they would realise they didn't know anyone called Alastair and Merlyn Yates-Middleton.

"We should be able to make it to Edinburgh if we drive all day," Cam said. I recognised the rugged coastal outline of Scotland sprawling across the centrefold of the map in his lap.

"We're setting up the accounts there?"

"Yes. Tomorrow. We'll find a B&B tonight."

If the Tweedles did come across us at this point, I considered, it would just be extremely bad luck. No; it was the police and the omnipresent Argus of security networks that kept vigil over every corner of the country that would be our main concern for time being.

We pulled off at motorway services around midday, for food and a rest. I went into the shops alone, as we decided that would be less conspicuous. Cam wrote down a list — make-up and hair dye and similar things — that he wanted me to buy from the Boots, presumably to disguise himself with. I loaded them into a basket and paid in cash, trying not to draw attention to myself. Then I bought burgers and chips from the fast food outlet and carried them back to the car.

Cam rummaged through the bag of cosmetics, examining the items with his spare hand while he crunched chips. "So, have you given any more thought to your alter-ego?"

"I need to know who yours is as well. Mine can't exist in a vacuum. She's supposed to be married to you, remember?"

He snorted. "Never proved much of an incentive to my parents."

I stared at him. He'd never mentioned any relatives before. I wondered about them: were they still alive, together, and did he still have contact with them? Did he have siblings?

"Dorian Griffin is the editor of a scientific paper. He got his PhD at UCL eight years ago. He got married and he's moving up to Scotland with his new wife. So what does she do?"

"I don't know. I suppose she should be someone professional to match with him."

Cam crumpled up the burger bags and squeezed them into a ball. "You have a think on it."

After that I let him drive.

"How do you do it, Cam?"

He inflated his cheeks as he exhaled, his hands flexing on the wheel. "Improvisation works to an extent. If you wing it too much, though, you can get caught out."

I closed my eyes and recited Rowena Griffin's date of birth in my head. I looked at her driving licence to check I'd got it right. "How do you make sure you don't get caught out?"

"It's part planning, and part judging the situation as it comes. I suppose it's a bit like being a stand-up comedian."

I shook my head. "I'm never going to get the hang of this."

"You were managing okay last night."

"That was…" I struggled to translate how I felt about it into words. "It was like I was living as someone else."

"There you go, then. You need to work out how to get back into that frame of mind."

Soon we reached Newcastle on Tyne. The A1 passed what looked like a rusting WWII bomber crashed on its tail on the side of a hill. Cam informed me it was called The Angel of the North, and that it was what people in these parts considered art.

By three in the afternoon, we had crossed the border and were into Scotland. Exhaustion overcame me, and I struggled to keep my eyes open. My ears felt deadened from the confines of the car. By eight, we reached the Firth of Forth, and Cam parked in a side-street. "Come on," he said. "Let's go and look for somewhere to eat."

I was tired and stiff, and a dull headache had begun to press on my forehead. I wasn't sure if I'd fallen asleep in the passenger seat while he'd been driving. An incessant wind whined around the car, sending tremors through the chassis and shaking it on its suspension. I had a pain right in the pit of my stomach and a paranoia that someone would notice us and it would give us away at a later time.

Cam seemed to sense this. "It's Hogmanay. There are lots of tourists here this time of year. We won't be conspicuous at all."

"I'm tired," I said. "My head hurts and I just want to sleep."

"Then it's even more important you get a proper meal inside you." Cam rummaged through the glove compartment and produced some water inside an old pop bottle and a packet of paracetamol. "Take some of these and have a drink."

I swallowed the pills and took a few swigs of the stale-tasting water. Sitting in the car beside him while he waited patiently with one hand resting on the wheel, I breathed and looked out upon the dull red steel of the Forth Bridge uplit by night-time spotlights, and the lights of the city on the other side, its reflection glimmering in the dynamic surface of the river. Gradually, the grip of exhaustion and discomfort eased, and my fortitude returned.

I pulled my hair loose and put on a red knitted beret and a black woollen jacket from the bag of secondhand clothing in the boot. Cam linked his arm through mine and we walked along the road parallel to the waterfront, looking at the shop fronts and the pubs, pushing through crowds of revellers, and for now I was in control of this. As long as I was walking with him, I was somebody else. I was someone stopping off with my partner *en route* to visiting Scottish relatives for Hogmanay, and I wasn't a thief and an accomplice to a murder, and I could face this without the urge to run and hide.

We ate a generic starter and a main course in one of the quieter, more upmarket pubs. Throughout it, we managed to keep up a fictional conversation about a made-up mother-in-law.

At ten, we found a B&B with vacancies still available. We gave our names as Susie and Kevin Todd, and were shown to a rather awkwardly arranged room with the ensuite down a step and around a corner. The room smelt musty and the furniture was all torn and bashed about.

I got changed in the toilet and washed my face. The towel was covered in long, orange hairs. When I came out, I checked the passport and the documents in my luggage.

Cam lay partially under the duvet, his back to me and his laptop propped up on the bed in front of him. I sat on the bed behind him. He had on a thin T-shirt and a pair of pyjama trousers. I smoothed one hand underneath, up over his chest, and slid the other down under the waistband of his trousers, to rest with my fingertips at the point just below the crease of his buttock slightly inside the back of his thigh where I knew he was ticklish. I felt him tense minutely, an electric charge of arousal passing over him and quickening his heartbeat.

He twisted to look over his shoulder at me. "You wouldn't make much of a pickpocket," he said.

I laughed. "Have you finished all the transactions?"

He clicked with the mouse a few times, not taking his eyes off the screen. "Pretty much all I can do on the computer. We'll need to withdraw physical cash from some of the accounts later to hide the trail."

Rowena Griffin, *née* Blackett, I thought as I rolled onto the bed next to him and pulled the duvet over my knees. That was who I would be tomorrow. And I had better not screw it up, because it was the one good ID I had.

The bed smelt peculiar, so I huddled up against Cam until his familiar scent drowned out the odours of the surroundings.

*

Early next morning, I coloured my hair ginger with one of the temporary dyes Cam had bought, and used a pair of ceramic tongs that supposedly generated ions that make hair look better to style it into poker-straight curtains that parted dead in the middle of my scalp.

Rowena Griffin, I told myself, studying the effect in the mirror. My reflection looked like some sort of slick, snotty stockbroker. Very well, then, that was who Rowena Griffin would be. I finished the effect using mascara and bronze and brown eyeshadow, with a pair of frameless spectacles, and chose smart tailored jeans and a shirt under a tight-fitting jersey.

Cam had been leaving his stubble to grow for the last few days, but this morning he shaved the sides of his face and under his chin to leave only a goatee and moustache. He shifted his parting to the other side of his head and used silver mascara to add grey streaks throughout it. For his attire, he chose a pair of chinos and a smart-casual patterned shirt. He put his documents and cash into the inside pocket of his good coat, while I put mine into a leather Radley handbag. The rest of our gear went back into the holdalls and we carried it out to the car.

We entered the bank walking side by side, me wearing a

smart coat and carrying an umbrella that matched the bag, Cam with his shoulders relaxed and his hands loosely in his coat pockets. I hoped we looked like a couple who had been married within the past few months: content but not too into each other.

A boy in a suit invited us into an office. I felt uneasy the whole time but, as it turned out, they didn't ask many questions, just very basic ones like our dates of birth and to confirm the things we'd put on the online application. We gave them the birth certificates and documentation, and they checked them and gave them back.

We gave the address of Cam's friend who lived in Glenfinnan, along with some falsified utilities bills as evidence. After Cam's friend received the initial letter with the details on and we picked it up, we could set up online banking and change it as necessary. We paid in a combination of cash and cheques from clean accounts with no electronic trail back to the ones we'd used on the night of the robbery.

After this we split up and tramped off through the cobbled streets to different banks in Edinburgh, where we withdrew cash from a number of the other accounts and set up one new current account each in the names of our new identities. I stopped by some iron railings on the estuary, and I stood there in the wind and put my new bank cards into my wallet with my new driving licence and National Insurance number cards. I took out all the other cards and traces to my old identity, because from today, that person was gone.

I switched on the radio as Cam drove out of the town. We listened for half an hour before we heard anything about the robbery, and it was only a short article:

Police are still searching for the whereabouts and identities of the members of a Birmingham gang responsible for the murder of a policeman and the theft of a large amount of money from a casino. Still missing are two men in their early twenties, one white and one of mixed race, both around six foot one in height, known as 'Tweedledum' and 'Tweedledee', a third man in his early thirties, heavily built and around six foot, known as 'Cam' or 'Chameleon', and a woman in her late twenties or early thirties, about five eight with blonde hair. The Seven stole an amount thought to be in excess of four million pounds from a casino in Birmingham and shot and killed a police officer at the scene. All these people should be assumed to be dangerous and members of the public are warned not to approach them. The police urge anyone with information to contact Crimestoppers *anonymously on 0800 555 111.*

Cam had bought a newspaper while he'd been touring the local banks. There was an article in it: *Mystery of the Modern-Day 'Merry Men' Continues.*

While the hunt for the missing four members of the Seven goes on, information on the three who have been accounted for is slowly becoming available. Whereas tonight's Crimewatch *clearly paints the criminals in a felonious light, the reality of the personal situations for each gang member may turn out to be somewhat different.*

The 79-year-old man who died at University Hospital Birmingham on the night of the robbery was known only to his partners in crime as 'Sage'. Neither of the two members in custody were able to identify him, but identifying material was found on his person at the time he was admitted to hospital.

When police entered 'Sage's' house, they found the place in a squalid state. On the mantelpiece they found the ashes of his late wife, her wedding ring still resting on the lid of the urn, and another urn containing the ashes of a dog he used to own, with the dog's collar on the lid. Sandwiched between them were the numerous prescription medicines Sage took to control arthritis and early Parkinson's disease. Also found in the living room were a glass bong and cannabis in a quantity consistent with personal use. Sage had taken to sleeping on a makeshift bed in the dining room and it appeared had not gone upstairs in some years. More than fifty tins of spaghetti in tomato sauce, and around twenty packets of Rich Tea biscuits were found in a kitchen cupboard. All the food in the fridge was expired, and there was little else in the way of food found in the house.

The youth arrested near to the hospital on the night of the robbery was known to his compatriots only as 'Ace'. His real name has not yet been released. He had been expelled from seven schools, and came from a broken home which his mother abandoned when he was a mere five years old. He spent the rest of his childhood oscillating between care homes and a drug-abusing father. In custody, a police psychologist diagnosed Ace as having Tourettes Syndrome. There is no record of this to be found on his school background, so one can only assume that he slipped through the net. Despite having a high IQ and a gift for figures and computers, Ace never acquired any qualifications and was unable to find work when he reached school-leaving age. It is not difficult to see how a young person who must have been so disillusioned with his life might turn to crime to utilise the fine mind he can find no other use for.

A disadvantaged young black man the school system has failed and a lonely pensioner who it seemed had nothing left to live for — the real lives of these people tell a different story to the one the police might like the public to see. One can only wonder at the realities that faced the other members of the gang in the worlds they had come from.

That night, at a B&B in Glasgow, we lay in bed together and watched *Crimewatch*. Our case was one of the main features. The programme aired a re-enactment of the casino robbery. The lad playing Ace's part didn't swear or make v-signs during the film, and the man they had playing Sage looked too young. The Tweedle actors and Genghis looked the part, but the woman playing me was too glamorous, and Cam's doppelganger was too stout and beer-gutty compared to his tall and broad frame.

They showed the events fairly briefly and from the perspective of the people who'd suffered from it. They started with the security van that the Tweedles had intercepted, before switching to an interview with the casino manager. Then there was the scene at the layby, when the policeman got shot, followed by testaments from the policeman's family and a photographs of plastic-wrapped flowers piled in the layby.

I found my face getting hot and my vision blurring when they got to the part at the hospital where Sage died. I wiped my eyes and leaned against Cam's shoulder, noticing his eyes looked redder than usual, but he didn't say anything.

After the reconstruction they showed bits of information about the cars used and e-fits of the Tweedles and Cam and me, and the clothes in the hospital we had used to make a fake patient and left behind. From what they showed, it looked like they hadn't worked out much about what had gone on after we left the hospital and Ace and Genghis had got caught.

I hoped the B&B owners and the bank manager we'd seen that day hadn't seen it. If they had, we'd only find out when the door came crashing open in the early hours of the morning, or when we went to the airport and got arrested in customs with escape just in sight. They might have been watching us all the way. They could be outside this very building now. That night I found myself staring over where Cam slept beside me, to the grey texture of the curtained window and the unknown that lay beyond it.

13

BLACK MARKET

Glasgow looked damp and grey, its buildings aging and shabby. I supposed it was a lot like Birmingham, really, only the people here spoke with a different accent.

"I think it's going to rain."

Cam shrugged. "Buy an umbrella with some of your ill-gotten gains." He sat in the passenger seat with the SatNav and two decks of bank cards held together with rubber bands on his lap.

A moment later, a thin rain began to fleck the window, not enough to switch the wipers on over.

Cam stretched one of the rubber bands out from the cards and twanged it idly. "I think we need to play it safe and break the trail entirely."

"How do you mean?"

"I mean we need to ultimately withdraw in cash everything we've paid in rather than simply transferring it to the accounts we intend to use, so there's no electronic trail and no evidence to link the clean accounts to the ones the cops might manage to root out now or later."

I recalled with a sense of dread posting the hundreds of DepositPoint envelopes on the night we stole the money. "Isn't that rather a lot of work, and rather a lot of time spent in public where there's more risk of someone identifying us?"

"No hurry to do it all at once. And at least we'd only be paying into three accounts once we've drawn it out. Besides, if we split up, we'll be far less conspicuous. The public are on the alert for a modern-day Bonnie and Clyde thanks to the phenomenon that is arsewipe journalism, remember?"

The suggestion made me feel anxious in a way that took me some introspection to pin down. If we split up, and someone identified him and he got arrested, I might never see him again. I could go back to the car and sit there being cold until it got dark and he'd never return. I might not have the courage or the inclination to carry this on without him. I had no idea how I'd decide where to try to flee to and make it to an airport, and the idea of escaping successfully and being in some kind of Mediterranean expatriate haven alone with a load of money didn't hold any joy. I'd come in on this because I needed money to survive in the rut I'd managed to grind myself into, to pay the bills and the mortgage and to buy food to live off. That was how it had started, at least. Then the goal had moved. My intentions had changed from preserving the status quo to moving on to something better, and now it seemed I'd written Cam in as an integral part of it, and it wouldn't make sense without him.

It had been over ten years since I'd depended on anybody, and it struck me that it was childish and silly to feel this way when I thought of myself as an independent person, when I used to have a career and a lifestyle I'd been brought up to aspire to and respect. There had been Richard, of course, but I'd never felt any sort of dependence on him. I cared about him; or at least I did until that went wrong. We used to live together, in a rented flat, before he started going on that he wanted to have children, and the flat became oppressive to live in with him in it, and we broke up. After that I moved out and bought the house. At the time, the house meant freedom and sanctuary. When I lost my job, the meaning changed.

On the other hand, I'd never plotted a robbery and gone on the run with Richard. Perhaps he had felt dependent on me, and perhaps that was why he had become so clingy and demanding. It could be that what I was feeling now about Cam was what Richard had felt for me, and Cam might well feel the same way as I had in that situation. I could still recall the annoyance and disgust, the suffocating pressure, when I would be watching television and Richard would out of the blue bring up comments about *fertility* and *a baby*, like he'd not heard or completely disregarded everything I had explained to him so clearly a few days before. I didn't want Cam to feel that way about me. I didn't want him to see me as a dependent, demanding person with no regard for his feelings and desires. I made a note to think before I spoke.

I needed to have contingency plans in case this didn't work, for whatever reason.

The rain had become heavier. I switched on the wipers and glanced at the rear-view mirror. I was sure that exact same burgundy Astra had been behind us several junctions ago, and it was tailgating so close I couldn't see the numberplate.

Cam was engrossed in the SatNav. "If I take the north half and you take the south, we can clear out a few of the bank accounts and pay most of the cash into our clean personal accounts at the end. Make sure you leave some shrapnel in some of them, though, to make it less suspicious."

"That car behind. I think it's following us."

I sensed the shift in his focus as he concentrated on the wing mirror. I waited, but he didn't speak.

"D'you think they're plain clothes coppers?"

203

"Impossible to tell."

A rush of guilt assailed me: the image of the police dog handler falling before the leather-clad gunman; Ace sprinting through the bleak winter garden outside the hospital. "What do we do if they are?"

"There's no point trying to run or using dodgy IDs. We'll just have to risk using the good IDs we've got and hope it convinces them."

I looked back to the road with a nauseous, dizzy feeling, my chest tightening. I needed to come down from this and be Rowena Griffin, going about her usual lawful business with her husband, and not someone who had robbed a casino and had come out today to launder money, but my heart was pounding so violently the blood thudded in my ears and made my field of vision quake. I thought back to the composure I'd managed to dredge up at the wedding reception, and tried to make myself return to that frame of mind. I tried breathing steadily and focusing on a point deep in my chest, but nothing was working.

I checked the mirror again after making another turn, and the car was still following. I could make out the shapes of men inside, but the car had tinted windows and their faces were indistinct.

"Cam, I think we should get the fuck out of here instead!"

"We just need to act normal. If we act panicked they'll only find it more suspicious. Turn in here. There's a car park for the shop round the back."

I pushed the indicator up to turn right. The car behind was so close I couldn't see its indicators. "They're going to follow us in."

I heaved the car into the first parking space I saw. The

car behind swept past with a roar of engines and charged around the parked cars, straight back out to the junction, and left.

I looked about the quiet car park. "They went?"

"Looks like it. We didn't give them any excuse to hang around." He shifted in his seat and became pensive for a moment. "It could be something to do with the Tweedles. We need to stay in populated areas and get rid of this car as soon as we're able."

I shut my eyes and leaned back against the headrest. The drumming of the steadily falling rain on the roof and the rhythmic beat of the windscreen wipers surrounded me.

"We'd best get moving," said Cam. "There'll be time to rest later."

Glasgow was cold and wet. The streets and banks were full of miserable, angry people struggling to keep their balances out of the red in the aftermath of the Yuletide frivolities. I was glad of the rain, as an umbrella gave me another layer of impenetrability against the security cameras.

I worked through the cards, withdrawing all or most of the money from each account. At the end, I split the proceeds between the joint account and my Rowena Griffin one.

I got back to the car before Cam did. I sat in the driver's seat and waited, fearing he might not come back. It was with great relief that I recognised his jacket and the hair he'd dyed brown that morning as he walked back towards the car. All I wanted was to get out of here and hide somewhere less public.

"Have you thought about getting a caravan?" I

suggested as I started the engine.

"Caravan?"

"It'd save us keep risking ourselves going into B&Bs. And I suppose it would be less conspicuous. If anyone's looking for this car, they wouldn't be able to recognise it from behind."

He frowned while he considered this. He edged his sleeve up to look at his watch. "The sooner we get rid of this car, the better, and replacing it with one that can tow is a good option. There should be some secondhand dealers other side of the city."

It continued to rain, the sky sinking into a premature twilight. We reached a road along the outskirts of a run-down estate, tower blocks standing on one side like pillars holding up the turgid sky, lights in the windows shining through the murk, the other side a strip of litter-strewn and bedraggled trees. The road had been deliberately narrowed to a single-track width at intervals along its length in order to inconvenience drivers and discourage traffic from using the road.

The Rover's headlamps illuminated a small, slight person in a voluminous kagool walking along the side of the road, but apart from that, the street was deserted.

The pedestrian stumbled and fell off the kerb, into the road in front of the car. I stamped on the brake and clutch, and the car lurched and halted. The person lay on the asphalt, back to the car, shaking violently in the wet road.

"It's epilepsy or some other medical problem," I said. "We have to call an ambulance."

Cam shook his head. He looked on edge. "We can't risk making calls that can be traced and getting involved with the emergency services. Drive on."

When I looked back out the window, I noticed the pedestrian had fallen over just in front of one of the jutting kerb islands. There wasn't room to pass. "You're going to have to get out and help."

"I don't like it! There's something not right!"

"I can't just drive over someone!"

Cam glanced from the person convulsing in the road to me. His hand hovered over the door handle. "Right. You stay here. I'll look."

He was out of the car quickly, leaving the door open behind him. As Cam advanced into the road ahead in the rain and crouched over the body on the ground, I sensed a shadow pass over the passenger side of the car. As I turned to it, a tremor ran through the chassis and a man threw himself into the seat. He was holding his arm up pointing at my face, and protruding from the elasticated opening of his sleeve was not a hand, but what appeared to be a block of cheap black plastic with a hole in it. He didn't speak, but his face was full of threats. Amidst the surge of insensible terror that overtook me, I managed to comprehend that we were being hijacked, that though this was not the police, that it must be connected with the car that had been following us earlier.

Cam help...

When I looked back to the road, the person on the ground had stopped shaking and was pointing a sleeve at Cam, and he was getting to his feet and backing away, hands held up. The other person said something I couldn't make out through the windscreen and over the wind, and Cam moved around the side of the car and in through the back door.

"*Cam!*"

The person who'd been lying in the road got in and slammed the door. The face in the hood was female, emaciated and mottled with sores. "Shut up and drive, bitch!"

If these weren't the police, and they clearly weren't, they could only have come from the Tweedles. A stifling horror gripped my lungs and my legs felt like snapped twigs as I eased off the clutch and pushed the accelerator pedal down. In the rear-view mirror, Cam looked pale and fearful. "Just do what they tell you!"

As I pulled away, the man in the front seat twisted to look at Cam. He was a bullish, thickset bloke wearing a waterproof sports-brand jacket that rustled with the movement, and underneath that he had on a pale grey T-shirt with a printed design of a yellow smiley face with a hole effect in the middle and bright red running down from it, to look like a gunshot wound. His face twisted into an expression of malevolent amusement.

He pulled a mobile from his pocket and thumbed a few keys before raising it to his ear. "We made the pickup. You'll never guess what."

A pause.

"You'll see." The man grinned to himself as he pocketed the phone.

The woman in the back directed us to a run-down estate and told me to pull over at the kerb outside an unkempt house fronted by a disintegrating low wall.

"Now get out," said the man, "and don't try any shit."

I got out and shut the door. Perhaps we should try shit. They couldn't really shoot us here, in a built-up area in broad daylight, could they? I looked about, but I couldn't come up with any sensible ideas.

The woman grabbed me by the coat and dragged me towards a house. She was a full head shorter than me, and it felt ridiculous.

As soon as we entered through the front door, another door opened and a hard-faced, burly man appeared. He looked at me, and then at Cam, and he pointed and started laughing, humourless aggressive guffaws.

"What's going on?" I asked Cam. For a moment, I entertained the idea they might be friends of his, on our side and playing a practical joke, but the expression on his face told me they weren't.

"Aren't you going to introduce us?" the man shouted.

Cam did not answer, and he and the man faced each other. It became obvious from the stoic stare of both that they didn't merely know each other, they *despised* one another. The man regarded Cam as though he was an anathema, the scum of the earth, and Cam in return looked at him like the man had murdered his family and he was salivating for revenge.

"No matter," the man said at length. He threw open a second door, revealing brick steps leading down to a cellar illuminated by a naked lightbulb. A wave of warm, damp air loaded with a familiar herbal fragrance hit me as we were jostled towards the opening. My memory of Ace's garden surfaced unbidden, Ace on his knees grubbing in the soil and Sage on the bench, smoking his bong.

The unplastered walls had been partly covered with Styrofoam and makeshift insulation. There was no handrail and the bricks gleamed with condensation. At the bottom of the stairs the path turned left and ran alongside a partition wall with two doors. The man opened the far door, and we were forced inside. This room was even warmer, and it was lined with Styrofoam and reflective baking foil. Fierce lights shone from boxes on the ceiling, and serried rows of cannabis plants took up every horizontal surface. These weren't the old school variety that Ace had grown in his cold greenhouse; they must have been skunk or one of the other more potent modern cultivars.

"You, turn your pockets out," said the man. He set his hand against the back of Cam's neck and shoved him against the doorframe. "And you."

A moment later, we had turned over all the bank cards and passports. I couldn't see a future any more. We were fucked if these people decided to kill us, and we were fucked if the police caught them first and us with them.

"Siddown." The woman stared fiercely and aimed her gun at me. She might not even have been old enough to call a woman. It was hard to tell. Her face had probably never been attractive, and drugs had made it emaciated and sallow, her eyes bulging in their sockets and looking too big for her shrunken face. Auburn hair hung in greasy strands over a forehead pocked with sores and acne, like sodden pondweed sticking to a toad's back. Her jaw was overshot, uneven teeth brown-edged with decay jutting over her bottom lip. Her expression reminded me of a gerbil.

I took a seat on a pile of grow-bags near the back of the room. Something caught my attention amidst the plant pots on the foil-covered table. An orange-and-black hazard sign, a chemical warning. It was a tin of plant fungicide with an irritant symbol on it. *Copper sulphate*. Water-soluble and acidic.

The man looked through the passports and shuffled a few of the cards. "So, *Mr Griffin*, you were planning to flee the country with your new passport?"

There was something familiar in how he addressed him. "Cam, do you know these people?" A slight hope kindled inside me. Perhaps there was some other reason for their apparent aggression if that was so.

Cam didn't answer, but his face betrayed both fear and anger.

"Cam, huh? So that's what you call yourself now." The man glanced at me. "Don't expect he told you what they used to call him in jail."

I stared at Cam through the cannabis fronds. The expression on his face now was almost a cringe.

"Now be a good boy and tell me what the PINs are." He glanced from Cam to me and back. "And if you lie, I'll cut your bollocks off and make *her* eat them."

Cam held up both hands. "All the PINs are 9999. Please just calm down."

The man pulled one card at random out of one of the decks. "Metcalfe, take this up the road and check it."

The other man took the card and left. The first man threw the other cards down on a table with our passports and wallets.

"I told Tweedledee I wouldn't kill either of you. I think he wants that privilege for himself." The man leered at me, and then he turned to Cam with a look of disgust. "But scum like you gunna get what you deserve, whether it kills you or not." He grabbed Cam by his jacket, spun him round, and flung him through the door. He charged after like a bull, and I heard a sound of bodies crashing together, and a protesting shout from Cam, and the door slammed shut.

I started to my feet, but Gerbil Girl levelled her gun at me. "You just chill," she said. "You're turn'll come soon enough."

After I'd sat back down, she stuffed the gun back into her kagool and glanced back at the door. I had to *think*;

I had to do something. There must be something in this room I can use as a weapon just for an instant, so I could disarm her. Then I realised what it was.

I reached into the pots and seized the copper sulphate tin. The lid was only balanced on and it fell off as soon as the tin moved. A cloud of blue powder flew into Gerbil Girl's face as I pitched it at her, launching from my seat at the same time. She let off an anguished cry and threw her hands up to her eyes, but before she could raise the alarm I spun her around and drove her headfirst into the breeze-block wall beside the door with all the strength I could muster. I lost my grip and she rolled over on the wall, her arm flailing, and slid down to the floor. Now she was even less pretty. It looked like I'd broken her nose, and her skin was covered in abrasions from the rough concrete. Her neck straightened in a lethargic, unconscious sort of way, the same way a weed slowly recovers after you stand on it.

My hands shook as I reached into her coat pocket for the gun. It was painted black and it looked cheap and plasticky, but the weight of it told me it was mostly metal. On the handle there was a manufacturer's logo, a bird-thing with an R inside it, and it said, *Ruger*.

I thought back to when I'd shot game with Paul years ago. You had to hold the shotgun right when you fired, push the butt up firm against your shoulder, otherwise you'd hurt yourself on the recoil. This gun had no butt to brace it against. I could only assume the recoil would be too weak to need it. I settled the handle into the heel of my right hand and slid my finger into the trigger position. That man was outside and he was going to hurt Cam, and this was a weapon and it was the only one I had.

I opened the door and went out, holding the gun in front of me. Cam and the man were in the next room, and he hadn't bothered to shut the door. I put my other hand to the grip of the gun to stabilise it, but it still wobbled and made circles in the air before me. I could see through the doorway Cam half sitting, half lying on the floor, and the man was standing over him, a crowbar in his hand.

I didn't know how this gun worked. The safety catch might be on, or there might not even be any cartridges in it. There was no time to try to work it out. I'd shot animals before, but never a person. It went against everything I knew and the first things I'd ever been taught. I once read that even soldiers in the army, even when they've been trained, when they go into warfare situations and they see a man and fire a gun at him, they aim the gun over the man's head, and they had to develop special training so they wouldn't do it.

I imagined the man was a rabbit and I was starving. I focused only on the spot on his head I was aiming at, so he ceased to be a person in my understanding, and became instead a few inches of stubbly scalp. I imagined a point deep in my chest and concentrated on pushing inwards against it, making a black hole to sink my emotions into. I used to think the opposite to cowardice was courage; now I wondered if it was insanity.

Then Cam looked and saw me, and the man must have seen his expression change, because he started to turn, and adrenaline kicked in. The ugly black thing made of plastic and metal kicked into the bones of my wrists, the noise of it palpable, hitting me in the face like a brass cymbal. The man reeled back and crashed to the floor, and a slash of mess came into being on the wall behind him.

Cam was still on the ground. He locked eyes with me for a moment, before he rolled over onto his knees and got to his feet. He stumbled against the wall as he made his way to the door. The air suddenly smelt like Bonfire Night and the room had become murky with a red haze. It took me a minute to work out it was an aerosol of tiny droplets of blood, scattering the light cast by the ceiling bulb. The bullet must have penetrated one side of his skull and come out the other. I could see where it had etched a scar into the bloodstained bare plaster on the wall before it had come to a stop embedded in the brickwork.

It wasn't just blood either. Bubbly, rubbery, pale chunks stood out against the spatter, like the white of a fried egg amidst a plate of baked beans and ketchup. It didn't seem real. I couldn't reconcile the mess on the wall as being what rightfully belonged in a person's head. It looked more like someone's fried breakfast had exploded. The normal laws of cause and consequence didn't match up when I tried to connect the act of moving my finger a quarter of an inch to the result of an inert man with two bloody holes in his head and eyes that no longer saw, and bad conceptual art up a wall. Perhaps I was losing my mind. Perhaps this was how psychopaths felt, and how they could live with themselves after they'd done the depraved things they did.

I took a faltering step back through the door and came up against the wall. The rough brick against the palm of my hand felt solid and ordinary, like this didn't belong here.

A dull thud of footfall conducted through the ceiling. I turned to where the corridor bent into the stairwell at the squeak of the handle on the cellar door.

There was Metcalfe, one foot on the third step down, the other hovering mid-way to the one below it. He stared at my face, and then his focus shifted to take in the gun in my hand. In the glare of the hundred-watt uncovered bulb, I noticed his eyes were a stony grey colour. The stark lamp made his face different: craggy and somehow more human.

And as he stood there, the realisation hit me. He was a witness now, and he'd go squealing back to the Tweedles, or maybe the police. He must not leave this building...

I meant to aim for his head as I had before, but some involuntary reflex prevented me from raising my arm enough. The noise of the gun echoed off the bricks of the narrow stairwell, its recoil jarring from wrist to elbow to shoulder.

Metcalfe staggered and fell on his arse. His body tobogganed down the stairs, leaving a dark, wet trail on the lip of every step. I pressed my back to the bare wall as his Caterpillar boots came at me. He came to a stop at the foot of the stairs and let out an unnatural choking noise that segued into a long groan. Blood was spreading from a hole in middle of his T-shirt, the fabric wicking it into an expanding dark circle that oddly didn't match with the fake wound in the garment's design.

A shudder crawled through my flesh. I sensed the low ceilings and narrow walls of the cellar shrinking around me. I blundered into Cam as he emerged from the room.

"What did you do with the other one?" he said.

I didn't understand what he meant. I looked at the gun in my hand. "Other gun?"

"The kid. The one who was supposed to be guarding you."

Of course. I wasn't thinking straight. "We need to get out before the Tweedles get here, and we need to call an ambulance for them."

Cam looked stunned. He kept blinking and his hands shook. His voice was low and not quite even. "No, we can't call an ambulance."

"I mean just do it anonymously from a phone box."

"It's no good. They'll grass."

It was like a fog had descended. I couldn't make sense of anything he was saying. "Why would they grass?"

Cam threw a trembling arm in the direction of Metcalfe's feet. "Because a gunshot wound to the stomach is usually fatal! If he's going to die, he's got nothing to lose. He just took one of our cards to an ATM up the road. If the police link what's just gone on here to the heist and that card, and we used that account anywhere on the way from the night of the robbery to here, they'll have a massive lead on us and on all the other accounts we've been using by association."

I turned away from him and took a few deep breaths. The cellar was silent, apart from the sound of Metcalfe gargling his own blood. I looked down at the thing I was holding, and I tried to clear my head.

"These drugs gangs all have feuds with other gangs, right? If the cops find them and they're all dead, it will probably look more like there was a disagreement of that sort, and someone from a rival gang killed them, won't it?"

Cam wiped his sweaty face with both hands. "We'll have to hope so. I can't see any other option."

"We're going to have to kill the other two," I said.

He didn't reply.

I considered for a moment. "Then we do our best to clean up any forensic evidence we've left, and we get out of here as soon as it's dark. And we get rid of your car to be safe. That must have been how this lot recognised us in the first place."

He still didn't speak, but he lowered his eyes and gave a barely perceptible nod.

I turned to the far door, dread curdling in my guts. Gerbil Girl's number was up.

She was lying awkwardly on the floor when I entered, one arm bent under her body, head slumped back. Her face was badly grazed from when I'd crashed her head against the wall, and her nostrils were clogged with partially clotted blood.

I put the gun to her forehead and tried to squeeze my finger against the trigger, but I couldn't do it. I feared the tension on the underside of my knuckle, feared this dead piece of plastic and steel roaring to life again. The tendons spanning my fingers began to cramp up and the gun shook in my hand. I exhaled and lowered my hand.

When Cam spoke, I could detect a quaver in his voice. "Do you want me to do it?"

"No, I'm all right." The idea of handing the gun over to him seemed preposterous, although I couldn't fathom why. It was as though the act of forcefully taking it and using it to kill had made it rightfully mine, and now only my own death would release it from my ownership.

The back of Gerbil Girl's head was against the floor. I told myself at least it wouldn't shoot up the wall again. I'd killed animals before. I'd killed the man in the room with Cam only a few minutes earlier, so why was this so difficult? Perhaps I'd already killed her with the blow to the head, and she'd never regain consciousness at any rate. Then it would make no difference whether I shot her or not.

I imagined the person lying on the floor was not a person, but a rat. I concentrated on breathing and on a point deep in my chest, and I shut my eyes and I turned the real situation of flesh and blood and emotion into one of chemicals and mechanics and mathematics in my head.

$$4 \; KNO_3 + C_7H_4O + 2 \; S \longrightarrow 2 \; K_2S + 4 \; CO_2 + 3 \; CO + 2 \; H_2O + 2 \; N_2$$

$$f = ma$$

I closed my eyes and inhaled, and my finger squeezed the trigger until the tension went over that invisible ratchet-point, and the gunpowder deflagrated inside the gun's aperture, and the bullet of mass m exited the barrel with acceleration a, and burst its way through Gerbil Girl's skull with force f.

Now Gerbil Girl was just some dead criminal with a hole in her face. There was no time to think about it any further than that. I couldn't afford to analyse things now, and there was still Metcalfe.

Metcalfe's eyes were shut, but his breath rattled grotesquely and blood bubbled from the corners of his mouth. I imagined he was a pig in an abattoir, waiting to be put out of its misery. When I raised the gun to his forehead, his eyes opened and he moved lips wet with blood and saliva.

"Fucking *no*—"

His heaving chest and noisy breath ceased the instant the blow of the gun pounded the walls of the cramped brick-walled space.

The two of us stood there alone in the cellar, our breathing loud in the close heat of this subterranean atmosphere. When Cam faced me, there was something in the way he looked at me that had not been there before. I felt sweat slide over the side of my forehead and run down my temple. I put the gun in my coat pocket.

"We need to find everything we've touched with our hands and wipe it," I said.

I left him to deal with the corridor and the other room, and went back into the room with the cannabis plants and Gerbil Girl's corpse. I searched her pockets without looking at her face, and found a plain cardboard box of gun cartridges. The tin of fungicide had rolled against the foot of one of the benches. It being the only thing I could recall touching in the room, I picked it up and wiped it before putting it back in the same position.

The only other place I'd put my hand was the wall, when I'd backed out of the other room. The surface was probably too rough to leave a reliable print, but I rubbed it with my sleeve as best as I could.

I met Cam in the room with the weed. We put all our bank cards and IDs back into our pockets, and I wiped down the table where they'd been. "Done?"

Back in the corridor, he searched Metcalfe's pockets and recovered the bank card he'd taken from us. He bent it in half, back and forth, ruining it, before putting it away with the others. "We can't use that account again." He looked at his watch. "It'll be dark out by now."

I clambered over Metcalfe's corpse, stepping gingerly on the edges of the steps and trying not to look at him. I opened the front door with my hand inside my sleeve. Cam was right: it was already dark, and still raining.

The freezing air outside met the sweat on my forehead and sent a clammy shudder crawling through my scalp as I hurried down to the car.

14

BLUEPRINTS

Cam pulled off the road a few miles later, into an area crudely surfaced with rough hardcore. Rocks crackled and twanged under the tyres. Rubbish overflowed from a skip to one side, a heap of rubble in the ditch beyond it. At the other side stood a prefab building with a luminous sign announcing it was a café. He parked the car next to the skip.

"What if there's CCTV?"

Cam regarded the car park and the shabby prefab, the foundations of which looked to be propped up on breeze blocks. "There won't be CCTV here. Let's get something hot inside us. It'll help us get our heads together."

I got out the car. He shut his door and came around to my side, and put his arm around me. My coat felt out of balance from the weight in my pocket. I imagined I could feel the gun, a lump of hard, cold metal lying against my thigh.

"Okay?"

I didn't know if he was doing it in case anyone saw, or because it would help me 'get my head together'. I nodded.

The prefab's flimsy door opened to a narrow corridor, toilets on one side and café on the other. Inside, fridges hummed and a noisy electric fan heater blew warmth into the room. Cam went to order while I took a table that put the heater between us and the till. Hopefully it would prevent anyone from eavesdropping on our conversation.

As I waited for him to return, I studied the myriad stains and scratches on the table surface, the pattern of holes in the cheap paper napkins, the congealed sauce on the condiments basket, and the way the glass bevels of the salt cellar scattered the colours of the electric light. Someone could shoot me in the head and all these things would be over, at least in my interpretation of the universe. I imagined how it felt, a sudden cold, hard pressure on the skull, an instant before release and then nothing, not even any noise, because bullets travel faster than sound. I wondered if other people saw and reasoned exactly the same as I did, if we were all no more individual or indispensable in the grand scheme of things than are microbes multiplying on an agar plate.

Cam brought two mugs of coffee. "There'll be fish and chips along in a moment." He cleared his throat as he seated himself opposite me.

I took my mug, feeling the heat through the ceramic and breathing the coffee aroma, somehow more lucid than I had noticed it before. I couldn't think of anything to say. Cam sniffed. My nose was running from the change from the cold air outside into warm. I wiped it on my sleeve.

A waiter came with our fish and chips. "Foul weather for driving tonight," he commented as he set down the plates. We made grunts of assent, but refrained from starting a conversation. I hoped he'd assume we were simply exhausted instead of murderers on the run.

I picked up a packet of tartar sauce without opening it and squeezed it between my thumbs and index fingers, as I once remembered doing a very long time ago as a young child. Cam watched, expressionless. The mushy peas steamed, unappetising in their creased paper cup.

"You were in jail?"

Cam lowered his eyes to the food, saying nothing.

I suppose it didn't surprise me. Sage and Ace had intimated something had happened to him in the past, and considering the situation he'd been in I hadn't expected him to come up smelling of roses. I'd heard of what men do to other men in jail, but it would embarrass both of us if I asked directly or laboured the point trying to get him to divulge more.

I pushed food about my plate with my fork. It was stupid, sexist, really. If a woman was a rape victim, people felt sorry for her, sympathised with her wrecked confidence and the ruin it made of her life. Raped women get counselling and support. If a man gets raped, it's somehow seen as an embarrassment and reflects something on him rather than his attackers. Men don't get kindness and sympathy. They just get left to deal with their shame alone. I wished I could give him that, but in the end he wouldn't allow himself to be vulnerable enough to ask me and I probably didn't have the strength to take that role. I feared that he would always wear a mask in that respect, that there would always be these aspects of him that must stay hidden from me. It must be hard to trust anyone to be intimate once other people had violated that and polluted one's whole perception of it. Perhaps that was why it was so often awkward with him, and he'd been so volatile about the skin grafts on his back.

I thought of Richard again, and how irritating the suffocating pressure he'd put on me had been. I didn't want to be that person to anybody else, but there was yet one fact I had to know.

"Please would you answer me one thing?"

He looked back, eyes fixing upon me, mouth stiff.

"Did you kill someone?"

In the slight pause that followed, I thought I saw tension in his forehead, an urge in his expression as though he was wrestling with something in the privacy of his thoughts, and then he shook his head ever so slightly. "No."

So whatever he had done, it was not as bad as what I had just done. Was it murder? Manslaughter? I wasn't sure on the specifics of the law. Perhaps the first time could be excused as manslaughter. But the second and third, when I'd shot to kill those who were already wounded and lying on the ground? I tried to recall my old life, going to work every morning, my boss demeaning me. It felt distant, unreal, like I was recalling a dream or a documentary I'd watched about someone else.

"It doesn't matter," said Cam. "Mallory should have the bank stuff tomorrow. After we've been to Glenfinnan we can get to the ferry. It'll be easier once we get to Lewis."

I managed to force down the fish and most of the chips, against the nauseous meniscus in my oesophagus.

"Let's at least make some of the journey to Glenfinnan tonight," Cam said.

Back outside in the car, I asked him, "Can you see any other way I could have acted?"

He ran his thumb and forefinger down over the sides of his mouth and exhaled. "No. I can't see anything else either of us could have done. Thank you. For doing what you had to. If you hadn't... well. It just doesn't bear thinking about."

I couldn't think of anything to say in response to this, and as Cam pulled away I tried to speculate what would have happened had I not, if they would have sent the police and the Tweedles after us had I not put bullets through their heads. Gerbil Girl might have been dead already, and

Metcalfe's fate might already have been sealed, but now I would never know.

Neither of us felt it would be appropriate to risk a B&B. Cam pulled off the road somewhere near Glenfinnan and we spent the night in the car, sitting under our coats. I leaned back and closed my eyes, but I couldn't find sleep. The noise of the wind never ceased. I don't know if Cam slept. His eyes were closed, but it could be he was feigning it in fear I would talk to him.

Although he sat right next to me, I'd never felt so distant and cut off from humanity.

At last the starless sky began to lighten, lending texture to the dark landscape. I flexed limbs gone cold and stiff under my coat. I sensed the weight of the gun inside my pocket and took it out. In the predawn pallor, I examined it.

Ruger. Prescott AZ, USA.

An American make. They're legal over there. Under the bird with the R symbol — a phoenix, maybe — at the bottom of the hand grip, there was a part that looked like it was designed to pull out. That must be where the rounds went in. There was a sort of button thing behind the trigger. Perhaps that was the safety catch.

I ought to get rid of this thing. If the police caught us, it would link us straight back to the shooting in Glasgow. On the other hand, if the Tweedles caught up with us and we didn't have it, and they did have one...

I put my hand around the body of the gun. It felt solid, real. An alien thing, with a hole in one corner where things came out and killed people. And yet, I felt a strange affinity for it, as though I could rely on it when my faith in the world was failing. Moreover, by killing its owner and taking it, a deep, almost subconscious responsibility had stirred in me. A cycle had been set in motion, and this instrument of death belonged, rightly or wrongly, to me.

I'd made this thing a part of myself.

We moved at dawn. Cam kept watch over the occasional buildings we passed off the side of the road. Shortly after he spotted a suitable used car sales venue, I pulled over into a layby. Cam threw his jacket into the back of the Rover. He pulled on another as we walked, and he took off his glasses and put them in his pocket, and out of the same pocket came a cheap plastic comb, with which he combed his hair a little differently from before. By the time we reached the main gate to the garage his stride had already changed, and he was flexing his facial muscles and shrugging his shoulders, settling himself into yet another identity.

A thin drizzle fell on the road and its cold verges, and on the menagerie of old cars parked on the broad polygon of tarmac within its aluminium palisade fence. A blocky prefab building at the centre seemed to be the only housing for whatever persons staffed the sales court. I couldn't see anyone else. I was wearing a pale grey hoodie I'd picked up at the motorway service station and a pair of Cam's plain-glass spectacles. The plastic of the glasses was sticky and heavy on the bridge of my nose, and fine raindrops flecked the lenses, adding a smeary, surreal dimension to the drear scene. I pulled the hood up, glad of anything more I could use to obscure my identity.

"Let's try to make it look as though we're not in a hurry," Cam said. "You take that side, I'll take the other. See if you can find anything suitable."

When he walked away I stayed for a moment, and I watched his back and the way he walked as he went along glancing at each car. If we got caught and went to jail, then I wouldn't be able to look at him any more.

As I wandered between the lanes of parked cars, a rear-mounted tyre with a cover sporting a name in cursive font caught my attention. Dulled dark blue-green where metallic lustre had once been, speckles of rust sullying the tailgate edges... it had been a special edition, for when I wandered around the side, a name, like that of a boat, was inscribed on the side.

Nautilus

When I looked at it, I found a strange nostalgia creeping up on me. Sensory memories hit me with the shock of a vodka shot: music by *The Lightning Seeds*, the scent of cheap cologne worn by a teenage object of unrequited lust, the odour of chemicals and paint flaking under the hot sun in the deteriorating science block of the school I used to go to, where I decided I wanted to do Chemistry for a career, because I thought it would mean inventing wonderful drugs that would save people's lives.

I remembered one of these cars had pulled in at the school, its rich green paint glowing, some yuppie parent picking up her kid in her Chelsea Tractor, and back then it had been the newest, flashest thing I'd ever seen. When I grow up, I had thought, I want to have a car like that. And now here it was, or one very much like it, worn out and discarded, bereft of its former splendour. And that resonated with me. This car and I had both seen more hopeful days, and both of us stood here in the rain now after our fair share of abuse. I felt a pang of aching regret for all those unfulfilled ambitions and naïve expectations I'd had proved wrong.

I took a step back and glanced around to locate Cam. He was examining a Volvo estate. Sensing my attention, he turned his head to look at me.

"I want to buy this car."

He stepped over to stand beside me and looked the Vauxhall Frontera up and down, his eyes lingering on the price posted in the window. "It's a diesel, so it should be up for towing. And the price is certainly within reason. Wouldn't you prefer something newer?"

"No, I like this one." I cast about at the other cars. For the length of time we would likely be using it, it was probably as reliable a bet as anything else here.

Cam turned and made eye contact with the cheap-suited salesman who had recently emerged to hover like a vulture on the periphery. He hurried over.

"Hi." Cam shook hands. "We're on holiday here, but our car's broken down and we need another at short notice."

"The timing belt went," I elaborated.

The man cringed. "Diesel, was it?"

I nodded. "Write off."

Cam continued. "The insurance company will pay for a new one once we get home, but we're looking for something cheap that we can manage with for the rest of our break and get home on."

The salesman gestured to the car. "The Frontera? Good choice. They built those diesel engines to last." His expression changed to slight disgust. "They certainly didn't build them for refinement."

Cam shrugged nonchalantly. The motion of his shoulders inside his jacket sent an electric charge surging into my chest. I wondered if there was room in the back of a Frontera to do things other than reading maps. Odd that I should think of *this* of all things when I had murdered three people yesterday and not slept last night. "Can we inspect the paperwork for it?"

The man went away to get it. I put my hand on the car's

right wing. So, today I would own a piece of the past. The man returned with an odd haste to his step, as though he feared we would run off and buy a car from somewhere else. An assortment of paperwork flapped in his hand.

Cam flitted through the documents while the salesman stood picking at his hands. "It all looks to be in order."

I leaned over to see. "When was the timing belt last changed?"

The salesman locked eyes with me confidently, and jabbed a page with his index finger. "Last service."

Cam snapped the Frontera's service book shut. "We'll take it."

*

Cam lifted a petrol container from the back seatwell of the Rover. He splashed streaks of the liquid across the seats, and the fierce pungency of the volatile fuel cut through the more muted scents of damp earth and leaves. He emptied what remained over the front seats and dumped the empty container in the passenger seatwell.

It occurred to me that this old car had done nothing to deserve destruction, and a strange sorrow came upon me. This car had no doubt once been someone's pride and joy. Probably it had been built years ago in the Midlands, in one of the factories of the now-extinct British car industry, by people there were no jobs for these days. To immolate it in an act of such wanton destruction was not merely disposing of evidence of crimes, but destroying a little slice of history and disposing of evidence of better times. And here I stood, having just killed three people of flesh and blood in person, feeling sentimental about a car, a pile of steel and plastic and rubber. I couldn't understand it. There must be something wrong with me.

Cam snapped a lighter over the damp stain on the fabric. Flames rippled across the surface of the upholstery.

I stood by him and watched as the fire rose, eating into the seats and sending roaring tongues of flame licking up through the open doors. The paint on the car's roof began to discolour and peel away from the bodywork.

Did my victims have families to miss them, people who'd hate me for what I'd done? I tried to picture who they might have been, before they'd become criminals. Somebody's son; somebody's daughter. Could they once have been something more, having a career, having hope for a better future, as I once had? Could there still have been the potential for them to turn their lives around and become better people once again, like the hope I'd dared to nurture when I'd started working for Genghis... when I'd come to know Cam... when I'd made the choice to cut the losses of my old life and go with them to rob a casino?

I still felt nothing for them. They were criminals, like me, and they had killed, as had I. Despite this, I could not countenance any similarities between me killing in desperation and what they had likely been intending to do to us. I could not imagine myself ever becoming like them.

Had I even believed what I felt, back in the car with Cam outside the Blue Moon Casino? It seemed so distant now. I didn't think I could be that person any more. I was back in the shadows, no idea where I was going or how I was going to get there.

It was only when I thought of it in these terms that I felt something: a small thread tautening inside. Was it guilt? Remorse? Pity? Self-loathing? I couldn't tell any more. Perhaps I was a psychopath, unable to feel any empathy for other people, and perhaps that potential had always been there in the girl I used to be, my father's daughter. Could be he had planted that seed there when he'd torn himself from my life forever.

Oh, Dad... if only.

I glanced at Cam, my eyes burning, seeking any kind of reassurance. His posture was rigid, his expression, illegible. I thought back to the way he'd behaved in front of the car salesman: a character he was acting, not Cam himself. Was everything an act? Was there nothing behind the mask, just another shadow-person, like me, no saviour to pull me out? Was this as deep as I could go?

With a miserable realisation, it occurred to me that he wouldn't stay with me if we ever did manage to flee the country and get to a safe place. And I didn't know what I'd do then, alone with a stash of money and a bigger stash of guilt and regret.

The wind swept a plume of smoke from the fire into my face. I blinked against the acrid sting, my eyes watering more.

The heat from the fire pressed against my face and throat. Cam reached an arm towards me. "Move back a bit, just in case the tank blows."

The sky was growing darker, the air cooler. I folded my arms, pressing my fists into my sides to keep my fingers out of the cold. We watched the car burn a little longer before turning to make our way back to the Frontera. After the dry heat of the bonfire the air felt cold, wet almost, against my face. The burning car cast long, flickering shadows ahead of us as we walked.

By the time we got back to the road, the fire had really caught, and the harsh Scottish wind dragged the flames in long stuttering plumes through the open windows. There wouldn't be any evidence left when the fire had burned out.

Cam checked his phone. An expression of relief came over his face. "Mallory's texted me. He's got the bank stuff."

*

It was already dark by the time we reached Mallory's house, a crumbling council end-terrace that faced directly onto the pavement, with no garden to speak of.

Mallory was a weaselly little man, short and thin with receding curly black hair. He hurried us in as soon as he opened the door, without even greeting us. We weren't there for very long, but for the whole time he sat uneasily on the shabby sofa in his own home, keeping his voice low as though he was listening out for something. There was a hopeless look in his eyes, and as he sat there I noticed a moulded plastic object fitted around his left ankle — a police tag.

Cam and I checked through the documents from the bank. Cam gave Mallory some bank notes, shook hands with him, and wished him well. We left as quickly as we'd come in, and went back to the car.

"Did you notice he had a tracking tag on?" I asked.

"It's a condition of his bail," Cam answered, without looking up from the bank letter he was double checking on the steering wheel.

"It means the police are keeping tabs on him. Are you sure it's safe?"

"He's completely trustworthy."

I sensed he didn't want to be drawn on the matter. Likely it had something to do with his time in jail. I said nothing more.

15

BROWN TROUSERS

We picked up an off-road caravan smelling of damp from a secondhand dealer's forecourt on the way out of Glenfinnan. By 7 PM we had made it over the Skye bridge and into the Hebrides.

"Why is this safe? Is there not organised crime here, like in Glasgow and Birmingham?"

Cam scratched his jaw. He still had the goatee from the banking tour, but the rest of his beard was starting to blend into it. "Crime does happen, and sometimes quite sophisticated crime, but you don't have the gangs like you do in the cities. Probably because there's just not the population density to support it. Criminals on Lewis do still have connections through the Internet and so on, but it's less likely they'll be able to track us here."

We stopped at a supermarket and Cam got out and bought pies from the deli counter. Parked in a layby, we heated up the pies in the caravan's microwave and ate them off plastic picnic plates.

I was tired, and I did manage to go to sleep, despite the musty smell of the caravan's fold-down mattress, finding respite at last in oblivion.

In the morning, Cam wanted us to both dye our hair black. He shaved, and then we used a combination of fake tan and foundation to make ourselves look more like we came from the near East. He claimed it wouldn't matter if we didn't have authentic Indian clothes and that I couldn't do an Indian accent, because we were to pretend to be third or fourth generation British Indians from Leicester, called Rakesh and Rupinder Singh, which were the names on two fake IDs he'd made that he thought would fit the situation best.

It didn't take long to drive to the town of Uig on the far west coast of Skye.

Wind ripped at the sails of boats. The facades of the buildings overlooking Uig harbour made me think of a time several years ago, but recalling it now it felt like another world. I'd been to Swansea with friends, a couple I knew and a man who had seemed very important at the time. I'd been much younger, and whenever I'd looked at him I had felt ill with dread and anticipation and fear and longing about what might be and what might not. I remembered everything about that holiday in lucid detail, the palm trees swaying in the wind before the white stone of the Victorian hotels, the shabby piers and the concrete groynes all along the coast, the blue skies, the haze over the ocean waves. The way I'd felt the whole time made that summer vivid. We had talked and talked while our friends were off together, but it had never clicked into place. It was something with him, or something with me, and it hadn't happened. I wondered where I might have been now, instead of here, if it had. It seemed silly, now, to get worked up into that sort of emotional state about someone who didn't reciprocate my feelings, and who in retrospect was not that special.

I wondered if in a few years' time I might feel the same way about my memories of Cam. Perhaps in retrospect, a less risky solution to being unemployable would become obvious. I would have time aplenty for that kind of regret if we ended up in jail. And yet we had heard of no breakthroughs by the police on the radio as we'd been driving. Perhaps we could still walk away from this. It's easy to think criminals always get caught, because the media gives solved cases the highest profile to make the public feel good. It would have been so much easier if the Tweedles hadn't shot that poor copper. The police might have cut their losses earlier. But they'd turned it into a murder, and whereas a casino's profits might not be worth taxpayers' money, a man's life was.

"There's the ferry," said Cam. A shape had become visible on the grey ocean's horizon.

I watched the ship draw closer, men in fluorescent jackets scurrying around the dock, moving barriers and cones. When the gangway was in place, they began waving the traffic up into the road within the boat. Cam started the engine and joined the queue. I stared at a security camera as the car climbed the ramp, the caravan wobbling behind.

Cam parked the car where he was waved to. "Well," he said, switching off the engine. "I suppose we'd better go and see the ship."

We went up to the top deck, where there was a lounge with windows offering a view out into featureless grey ocean and mist the ship travelled into. There was a restaurant and an outdoor area where masochistic people had gone to look for birds.

Cam sat and read a newspaper he'd brought. To disguise my discomfort I sat beside him with one of the provided paper vomit bags clutched in my hands, pretending my unease was from seasickness.

We talked quietly for a bit about what we were going to do on our holiday. Cam got up and walked up and down the width of the lounge, stretching his legs and looking more relaxed than I thought I'd ever be able to manage, not even if I practiced this for a year.

Finally, a darker grey shape took form against the paler grey sky, and the boat approached a cluster of lights at the base of this dour headland.

Soon, we were off the boat and heading into a wintery, twilight land where ceaseless winds tore across a barren land devoid of trees beneath a sallow sky.

"You know where you're going?"

Cam nodded.

We drove north-east. The night was drawing in by the time we reached the long road that passed between the mountains dividing Lewis from Harris. I could only just discern the derelict whaling stations down against the desolate land where it met the sea.

Cam drove on until darkness fell completely. There were no streetlamps, just catseyes in the road. Several times he had to brake when sheep crossed in front of the car. Once or twice the car trundled over cattle grids with the caravan rattling behind it.

"There should be somewhere along here we can park," Cam said after some time. The headlamps showed level ground on the left of the road. He slowed the car as we passed a sign, and turned the wheel to steer off the road and into what must have served as a caravan park in the summer.

"Well," he said, switching off the engine and pulling on the handbrake. "Let's call here home for the night."

We'd parked on a level grassed area. Although it was too dark to see, I could hear the ocean over the noise of the wind and make out the glisten of wet sand in the opposite direction to the road, from which a damp wind tore. The caravan door felt rickety and insubstantial when I pulled it open.

"You want to use the shower first while I sort out the generator?" Cam offered.

I dug the towels we'd pinched from the hotel out of the bags. In the shower it was impossible not to get water on the toilet seat. I managed to scrub off most of the fake tan, although it clung on in the crevices on the backs of my knuckles. The hair dye didn't quite come out after two washes, remaining as a murky brown colour with a tinge of green.

"It might be an idea to cut your hair," Cam suggested to me as he squeezed past on his way to the bathroom. "It would be less conspicuous shorter."

I went back to the caravan's main room and found a comb and a pair of scissors in a bag. After adjusting the mirror so I could see, I combed my hair from the side where it naturally parted. I didn't really know where to start. I'd never cut my own hair before.

Cam emerged from the shower with a towel around his waist. From the difference in tone on his face and chest, he hadn't quite managed to get the fake tan out either.

"Do you cut your own hair?" I asked him.

"Yes. Have done for a while."

"You'd probably do a better job of it than me, then."

He studied the back of my head. "You want me to try?"

"Go on, then."

"You're not going to moan at me if it looks horrible?"

"I don't know. I might do, I suppose."

He took the scissors off me and gathered my hair behind my shoulders. After examining it for a moment and flattening it with the comb, he slid the lower blade underneath it, against the back of my neck, and snicked slowly across, holding on to the loose end to keep it taut. He put the dismembered length down on the table. It gave me a weird feeling to look at. Cam angled the scissors diagonally and used them to trim it shorter where it fell over my face and ears. He cut layers into it by separating off parts on the sides and back, one at a time.

"How's that?" he said after teasing it out with his hands a few times and snipping off a few bits he'd missed.

I ran my fingers up through my hairline, sweeping damp locks back from my forehead. It looked a bit choppy and scruffy, and it probably wouldn't dry looking naturally tidy because of the wave in it, but that was what seemed to be the fashion these days anyway. What surprised me most was how much more youthful it managed to make me look. The past few years I'd started to look old with it loose, and tired and strained when I tied it back. Like this, it had a similar effect on my face as it had when the hairdresser had styled it up for the casino. I wondered why it had never occurred to me to try this ages ago. We all get stuck in our routines, reassured by what's familiar, to the point where we get daunted by the thought of trying anything new or different.

"Is it all right?" Cam sounded nervous.

"I really like it." I turned my head side to side, marvelling at how much more freedom I had in my neck and how much lighter my head felt. "Thanks." He put his hands on my upper arms and leaned his chin on my shoulder. In the mirror, I watched him kiss me on the neck.

He'd seemed so distant and cold since what I'd done in Glasgow, and his touch came as a relief. Perhaps I'd been reading too much into it, and he'd been that way because we were both tired and under stress, and now the shock had worn off, things between us were getting back to normal.

I'd just have to make sure I didn't mention jail, or Mallory's tag, or the fact that I'd murdered three people.

"Have I got bits of hair stuck down my back?"

Cam brushed my neck, shoulders, and upper back with brief strokes of his palm and blew hard on my skin so it gusted over the edge of the towel I was wearing. "A little bit."

When I turned to face him, I noticed he had offcuts clinging to his front. I tried brushing them off, but they were stuck in his chest hair. So I resorted to trying to comb them off him with a nailbrush, and we both started laughing.

"I've just thought." Cam raised a hand to his forehead. "There's nothing to eat."

I sat up again and sought about for the bag with my clothes in. "I'll take the SatNav and find a supermarket," I suggested.

"Wait a minute. I need to unhitch the caravan before you go."

I found myself laughing. "Well, are we going to put on some clothes first?"

In the Frontera, I suctioned the SatNav to the inside of the windscreen and marked the current location to make it easier to navigate back to. Cam disconnected the coupling and made a thumbs-up sign at me through the rear window in the dark.

It wasn't far to the nearest supermarket, although it felt it with all the sheep in the road and no streetlights most of the way.

Immediately when I entered the shop, some black-and-white e-fits on the front page of a broadsheet arrested my attention. Standing out of the way where I hoped no-one would see me, I grabbed one of the papers.

Four of Seven Still at Large

While Tweedledum and Tweedledee of the Blue Moon Casino robbery in Birmingham have been identified by police and the manhunt continues, the romantic story of this modern-day Band of Merry Men who met in a Jobcentre in Birmingham has been sweeping the country. The identities and whereabouts of the remaining two unknowns, 'Doc' and 'Cam' have become the latest public obsession.

It wasn't good, although at least they still hadn't tracked down our real names. I would have felt better about it if the Tweedles had been captured. At least that way, they'd be one less thing to worry about. I folded the newspaper in the basket so the headline faced down.

I grabbed some microwave meals and basic food that should last us for a few days. Reading the front page had shaken my concentration too much for me to be able to manage any more. I paid for the shopping quickly and left.

On the drive back, I switched on the radio and caught the back end of a report on Cam and me. The reviewer compared us to Bonnie and Clyde and the Scarlet Pimpernel, and claimed the fascination of the public owed a lot to the knowledge that we were supposedly masters of disguise and thus could potentially be anyone.

Back at the caravan, we ate our microwaved Indian food over the article, on the bed.

Cam sighed. "It'll have to blow over eventually. People will get bored of it and they'll run out of stuff to write. I mean, look at this." He pointed to a section on the inside page. *Cam's ability to disguise himself confused even his peers. Genghis and Ace were unable to reliably say what colour eyes or hair he had, and were only able to place his height at around six foot and describe him as being well built. It may indeed be that even this information may be unreliable, which is why the police description released specified Cam only as being a six-foot white male.*

Cam swallowed his rice. "Do they think I've spent all this time faking being fat? Like I wear some sort of silicone prosthetic bodysuit like Hollywood actors wear because it's politically incorrect to be fat these days?"

I chewed for a moment and considered. "Perhaps they think you went on a of diet to help blend in when you're on the run."

"Ha. They think it's that easy?" Cam grimaced.

I reached across and patted his waist. "You're fine just the way you are."

He smiled at me. "Well, if you want me disguised as someone thin, you're going to have to rely on your own imagination."

The caravan wobbled on its suspension, the wind shrilling around its shell, but inside it was warm, and I fell asleep with my head on his shoulder.

*

A grey dawn gave way to a sullen day, in which the sun seemed to struggle even to clear the horizon behind a curtain of rain. The wide, flat expanse of sand that led down to the sea was so wet I couldn't discern where the beach ended and the sea began, the surface stretching endlessly into the mist.

"Where is it we're going?" I asked Cam.

"Crosbost. It's a hamlet over the other side of the isle. I know somewhere we can hide out there. We should be safe if we lie low for a month or so."

"Even so, if there are likely to be people there, we

should wait until dark before we move."

"Yes, let's wait until dark. It's not like the days last long this time of year and with this weather anyway."

At lunch, I made us toast with a tin of sardines on it. Cam looked on his computer, but there weren't any wLANs for him to look at the bank accounts on. By three o'clock it had started to darken. Cam drove. He took the road back to Stornoway and took the south road out once we reached it. He drove through Crosbost and into a side road that didn't lead anywhere — the tarmac just stopped. He turned around at the end and we parked facing back up the road. I couldn't see any lights over the land's incline on either side. To see the caravan, you'd probably have to either come down the road or walk over the heath.

"The house is back there," he explained. "Can't risk parking outside it."

We gathered up all the luggage from the car and caravan. Cam wore the laptop bag across his shoulder and carried the medical case in one hand and a holdall in the other. I had the other holdall and my handbag and a torch. We walked in the dark and the wind, feeling along the road before us more than seeing it. Back on the main road, we passed bare, pebbledashed houses with lights on behind their curtains and cars pulled up on the drives. Others had boarded-up windows and no lights, some very dilapidated and looking more like disused outbuildings. In one place there was a pile of rubbish lying beside the road. We came upon a gap in the houses, and my arm ached and my face itched from having my hair mangled about it by the wind, and I wondered if it was much farther.

At last we came to a high wall with flaking white masonry paint. I could barely make out the house behind it, just the dark polygon of the eaves against the slightly less dark sky, and some trees near to it. Cam opened a metal gate and I followed him through to find myself in a concrete-paved path between two walled-off gardens, tree branches overhanging on the left. I switched on the torch. There was another gate ahead, attached to the side of the house, and beyond that, a solid wooden door into a porch jutting out from the side of the building, with an old swan's neck light full of rain on the wall above it.

"Here." Cam showed me through the gate and into the garden facing the porch. I found a forlorn rockery, covered in moss. Cam crouched down and picked up a concrete fish, pushing aside the gravel beneath it. A dirty key lay there. He dusted it off and used it to open the door.

The porch had an old lino floor and undecorated walls. There was a slight smell of damp and some cheap plastic chairs stacked on top of each other. I went through to the inner front door, the handle squeaking stiffly in my hand. Behind it was a cold hallway with stairs that led up halfway, turning a corner 180 degrees to face back the other way. Underneath the upper flight of stairs an open door led to a bathroom.

As Cam lugged the cases in, I opened the door on the left to a sitting room and found the light switch. Probably it would have really been a lovely house, had it been refitted sympathetically in a style befitting its character, but unfortunately it looked to have been redecorated on the cheap in the seventies and untouched since. The walls were covered with a garish patterned paper that gaped apart and frayed at the joints between sheets. An ugly Modernist mantelpiece had been built around the open fire. The furniture was universally shabby and consisted of a sofa and two chairs, a few standard lamps and tables, and a beaten-up piano in the corner behind the door.

I crossed the hallway again to inspect the room on the

right. The kitchen was similarly badly appointed with ugly green-patterned wallpaper and battered cupboards and ancient plumbing. Behind the door there was a yellowing fridge and an old Rayburn oven, the enamel on it all chipped. A white-painted table and chairs stood before a window with a deep sill into the thick wall.

"What a shame," I said.

"Hm?" Cam entered behind me, raising his eyebrows.

"It could be such a nice house. But the only thing decent is the cooker, and that needs restoring."

"Property's not worth much out here. This used to be one of the original blackhouses. They built it out." He leaned against the horrid wallpaper. "That's why the walls are so thick."

I looked again at the window. He was right; the walls were probably more than three feet thick. I didn't ask him how he knew these things and what connection he had to this house: I knew him too well by now to interfere.

"I'm going out to get some peat," he said. "Why don't you have a look upstairs?"

The two bedrooms had sloping ceilings from the roof angle. They were in better condition than the downstairs rooms, being decorated in old pastel wallpaper and equipped with ancient wooden furniture. They were also freezing cold and I couldn't locate any radiators or other means of heating them.

When I went back downstairs, Cam was busy loading bricks of what looked like dried black mud into the fire and the Rayburn. He'd turned off the main light and put on one of the lamps instead. "Let's try to keep the lights off as much as possible," he said. "I'd rather not risk people noticing there's someone here. Probably not a good idea to have fires going during the day either."

We had sandwiches for dinner. The bedrooms were just too cold to sleep in, and we ended up taking the duvets and pillows downstairs and making a bed in front of the fire in the living room.

I lay with my back against Cam's chest, staring into the glow of the fire and trying to oust cold and hunger that had settled deep within me. The burning peat gave off an oddly sweet fragrance, almost like incense.

"Where do you get peat from?" I said.

"Heap under and old tarp out the back."

"I mean, before that?"

"They cut it every year. It's just rotting plants and stuff. I suppose it's like what oil is before it gets fossilised."

"So I suppose you could solve Britain's renewable energy problems if you could turn the whole country into a barren bog."

He chuckled slightly.

"Do you really think this media crap is going to blow over?"

"I don't know."

*

With the light of the next day, I could look outside and see the place we'd come to. The house was screened from the surroundings by a number of yew trees on both sides, their hairy foliage a handhold of green in contrast to the surrounding winter desolation. The little gardens at the front of the house looked like someone had once cared very much for them but, now abandoned, they'd fallen into decay. Beyond the porch and on the other side of the house to the entrance gate there was a long, low outbuilding where Cam said there was a deep freeze and a load of junk, and beyond that was a swath of empty land, and then the water of a loch.

We waited until dark before starting the walk back to the car so we could go out and buy food. I was looking forward to getting a real, substantial meal inside me.

As we drove along the coastal road back to Stornoway, Cam insisted on stopping and stealing two lobster traps from a pile. After we'd parked, Cam went to the supermarket while I paid for the parking and dealt with the banking.

When I returned to the car, Cam still wasn't back. I took my place in the driver's seat, glad at the respite from the wind despite the dirty, fishy seaside smell the lobster traps were giving the car, and switched the radio on.

The words I heard made me start as violently as though I'd electrocuted myself on it. The police had discovered my identity. As I listened, shock turned to nausea. They'd dug up that I'd been having treatment for depression and that there'd been friction in my old job. They made it sound like I was some sort of unhinged mental case.

Cam was walking back across the car park, a plastic bag in each hand. It seemed as though he was a mirage, a hallucination. Now my identity had come into it, the reality of everything seemed too serious, too ridiculous, to be believed. How did I get from being a girl who liked science and wanted to make drugs that would save people's lives to *this*?

Cam reached the car and the door opened. Wind noise rushed in as he threw down the bags on the back seat.

"Cam, they've identified me!" I said as he sat in the passenger seat, the door slamming behind him and muffling the wind.

Cam took one look at the radio where it was installed in the dashboard, and pushed the button to turn it off. "I don't want to hear it."

16

BLACK AND WHITE

I turned the key in the ignition so we could go home, but my hand was shaking so much I couldn't seem to hold it for long enough for the engine to pick up from the starter motor.

"Let me drive," Cam said.

"I'm all right." I tried again to turn the key. Once again the tremor of the starter motor vibrated against the unsteadiness in my arm, and the car didn't start.

"You're not. You'll feel better after you've sat down for a bit, but we can't stay here." He opened the door and got out.

My legs didn't feel steady enough to carry me. I climbed over the transmission to get into the passenger side.

We drove in silence. I couldn't think of anything to say, and Cam's stare was fixed ahead, his mouth tensed into a line. At last the headlamps illuminated the sign for Crosbost and the cattle grid thundered under the tyres.

Cam pulled up by the wall outside the house. "Here's the key. Take the shopping in. I'll park and walk back."

I lugged the carrier bags through the two gates and fumbled the key into the lock with weak fingers. I dropped most of the shopping on the porch floor. In the kitchen I tried to sort out something to eat for dinner, finding a packet of bacon and some mushrooms, but I couldn't seem to think of what we could have with them or remember what I was supposed to do with them to make them into a meal. I ended up sitting with my elbows on the table and my hands on my forehead, taking deep breaths and concentrating fiercely on the pattern on the plastic surface. All I could think of was how everyone I'd ever known must be talking about me now. My ex-boss was probably on the phone to his horrible girlfriend, laughing and saying I'd had a screw loose the whole time, and being a lackey in a crime gang was all I'd ever been fit for. I couldn't ever have my life back now. Any modicum of public dignity I'd managed to retain through the ignominy of the past few years was lost forever now. It always had been, I supposed, but it was only now that I could grasp the reality of it.

Cam returned after a few moments. "Where's the stuff for the freezer? I ought to take it out now." Either he genuinely didn't notice the state I was in, or he pretended not to out of politeness. It appeared he'd found the bag with the freezer food in the porch, because I heard the front door close and the scrape of his feet retreating on the path outside.

A newspaper lay on the edge of the table; today's, the one Cam had just bought. I grabbed it and opened it on the surface in front of me, concentrating fiercely on the black-and-white of the type and trying to use the meaning the words contained to block out what was running through my head. Yet there was more:

NO SYMPATHY FOR VICTIMS OF GLASGOW GUNMAN

I read on with a sensation of floating dread.

In recent days the public have warmed to a romanticised ideal of crime as portrayed by the modern-day highwaymen of Birmingham. However, a recent triple murder in Glasgow demonstrates an altogether different public perception.

While it seems nobody has much sympathy for the 'Glasgow

Gunman' who was, in all likelihood, simply a member of a rival gang, it's hard to find anyone who has anything nice to say about the victims he or she cold-bloodedly executed.

Forensic evidence suggests the gunman entered the house and descended into the cellar, encountering 47-year-old Luke Garrett in a partitioned-off room. The gunman shot Garrett on sight; the bullet struck him in the head and killed him instantly. The gunman hid in another room and awaited the arrival of the second victim, 19-year-old Alice Feasey. Feasey was beaten, possibly to get her to divulge information, before being executed with a single shot to the head. The gunman encountered Iain Metcalfe, 42, on the stairs, probably en route to the exit, and shot him first in the stomach and then in the head, again possibly to disable and question him before his murder.

Adrian Feasey, a 52-year-old car mechanic, described his daughter's murder as 'an act of senseless violence' but then admitted Feasey had 'messed up her own life'. Metcalfe's sister and only surviving relative declined to comment, but it is understood has had no contact with her brother since 1996 and does not intend to attend his funeral. Garrett has two sons in foster care, whom for legal reasons cannot be named. The eldest described his father as a 'c**t'. The youngest upon being informed of his father's death grunted to confirm he understood and went back to his Playstation.

I shouldn't panic about this, I told myself. It implied in the newspaper that the police thought it was the work of a member of a rival gang. That was good, wasn't it? That meant what we'd done had worked... well, unless it hadn't, and the police were pretending it to the public in order to give us a bogus sense of security in the hope we'd get complacent about things.

Cam came back, but he didn't say anything. He was carrying a metal bucket with peat in, which he used to stoke up the Rayburn. Then he went over to the counter where I'd left the mushrooms and bacon and found a chopping board and knife, and began to slice up the mushrooms. The cold wind from the loch had made his nose run, and occasionally he would sniff, or the steady tapping on the knife on the board would cease for a few seconds as he paused to wipe his nose on the back of his hand. I listened to him clattering about filling pans and standing stuff on the Rayburn, and tried to reason myself out of the fear that had closed upon me.

I turned a page. The name *Glenfinnan* caught my attention with a stab of renewed fear.

PAEDOPHILE EXECUTED IN VIGILANTE ATTACK

Police are appealing for witnesses to come forward in what is believed to be a hate crime. Steven Mallory, 43, was violently assaulted and brutally murdered in his home in Glenfinnan on Wednesday. Mallory was released on bail in 2009 following a ten-year sentence for an assault on an eleven-year-old boy. His name was on the Sex Offenders' Register, and this is believed to be the motive for the attack. A post-mortem is to be carried out early next week, but Mallory is believed to have died from multiple stab wounds and blunt trauma injuries.

Steven Mallory. Paedophile. *Murdered.* A memory of the man, sinister and haunted, returned to me. I felt sick. The tag on his ankle. That was what the tag was there for. I looked at Cam's back. Did he know? I couldn't say anything to him. I didn't want to ruin the tenuous harmony that existed between us when these things were forgotten.

And yet there was more to this. *Violently assaulted and brutally murdered.* Could it be that it wasn't a hate crime as the police thought? If he'd been released from jail in 2009 and had been under police surveillance and not offended again, why would someone want to suddenly brutally murder him? Could it be that the murder was for something else, that someone had given someone else a tip-off, and the someone else had tortured Mallory to get information from him and then killed him?

Cam had finished doing the cooking. He set down a chipped glass plate in front of me: fried mushrooms and bacon on two slices of bread and half a tin of heated-up chick peas. He sat opposite me and ate, and I watched him and the steam that rose from the food. I reached for my knife and fork and I put food in my mouth, and I chewed it and forced myself to swallow. In this way, we pretended to be normal, even though we were anything but.

Cam finished his meal and pushed his plate aside. I had eaten barely half of mine, and yet I already felt the urge to throw up would overcome me if I had one more mouthful.

He rose and went into the living room. I picked up the paper and followed him, switching off the kitchen light behind me. He sat on the sofa.

"You once told me," I said. "About how you live with your mistakes."

He looked down at his hands on his lap and sighed through his nose.

"You build a wall," I said. "In your mind. You keep getting up every morning and putting one foot in front of the other, and you don't look back, and eventually, by the time the wall starts to crumble, whatever happened behind it is too far away to hurt you."

He considered this.

"My bricklaying isn't good enough," I said. "If I try to build a wall, it's full of holes, and the holes are always over the worst parts. My memories fester. Bad things happen to me, and they just grow like weeds in my mind until they get all blown out of proportion."

I wondered if other people lived their lives hating themselves because of the past. Did great men and women lie in bed at night racked with guilt and consumed by embarrassment, or balk halfway through eating their breakfast cereal at a sudden intrusive memories of their past mistakes?

I would have liked to watch television, to fill my thoughts up with banal rubbish, but there wasn't one, and even if there had been, I'd be afraid of seeing the news. My mind wouldn't keep still. Perhaps every criminal felt this way when the police closed in, and that was why some of them were eventually compelled to give themselves up.

I didn't want to bring it up. I didn't want to ruin the illusion of safety. But I couldn't not tell him. "Mallory's dead. I think the Tweedles did it."

He twisted to face me. I handed the paper over.

A horrible tension filled up the room as he sat there reading the article. A tremor passed over him. "Poor Mallory. This is my fault."

"It says in there he was a paedophile."

He didn't look at me, but I could see the tension spreading through his shoulders and down his thighs. He knew. He'd known all along. He'd trusted a convicted sex offender, and he hadn't wanted me to know this.

"I don't think this is going to blow over after all, Cam. They're going to find out we're on Lewis before long. They're not going to forget about us and let us escape, not now. We're going to be running from them until they find us. I don't know if there's any point in going on with this."

"There's always hope."

"But if we did surrender willingly, our sentences would be reduced. Surely it would be better than not knowing?

Surely... if the Tweedles did this... if the Tweedles find us first? The police and the law have got to be better than the Tweedles, right?"

A rigidity had suffused his entire body. "Do you have any idea what it's like in jail?"

"No. But it can't be that bad. I mean, what's a modern jail cell like compared to a house with no heating, or a caravan? There'll be proper food there. And the Tweedles won't be able to kill us!"

"The Tweedles don't know we're here. And we don't know it was them who murdered Mallory."

"No, but the police haven't caught up with them yet either! And what do you think's going to happen when the police work out where we are? The Tweedles are going to use what they hear on the radio to track us down."

"You've never been in jail. There are people there who make Tweedledee seem placid and reasonable!"

I sat down hard in an armchair, fighting the urge to ask him about jail.

"All that matters is that it's full of violent criminals. Oh, you'll get off a bit lighter. Women's jails are more like madhouses, full of suicidal nut-jobs who spend their time smashing toilet bowls and trying to exsanguinate themselves on the shards. Men's jails are in a different league."

"It's still food and a place to live! I mean, you get a cell, don't you? If you don't like the other people, you can just stay in there!"

"It doesn't work like that!"

I gripped the arms of the chair. This was digging too deep. I knew he didn't like it, but silence was worse. "Well, how does it work, then? Cam, what is it you've done?"

"You don't want to know!"

"How do you know I don't? You can't unless you tell me! Look, I know you. Whatever you've done, it can't be that bad. I mean, you can't possibly be a serial killer or anything like that."

"How can you know? You can't unless I tell you."

"Then say it!"

He turned to face me, eyes fierce. "The police can't find out who I am!"

"Why not?"

"Because, if I have to be that person again, I'm as good as dead anyway!"

From the expression he was making, I feared he was going to lose his temper and shout. I dared not speak, willing it not to happen, not wanting him to become the person I couldn't recognise and take from me Cam whom I knew and trusted.

Just as I began to think we were doomed to stay there in silence, he breathed in, and the answer came in a shuddering voice. "My original name is on the sex offenders' register."

I stared at him. Eventually I said, "You're a... a rapist? A *paedophile?*"

"Please don't be disgusted. I can't take it, not from you." Cam's shoulders began to shake, and then the first sobbing spasm of breath broke from him.

Behind the heavy curtain of shock, ugly memories stirred in the back of my mind: children's bodies rotting in woods, a little boy's beaten and broken corpse on a railway line, police photographs in the newspaper: haggard men with pale, sinister faces and soulless dark eyes.

A vision came to my mind, of me running out the door

of that house in Crosbost, running to one of the other houses for help, pleading for the police to be summoned, begging the police to keep me safe, to lock me up, away from the monster the mask had revealed. "Cam, what the *fuck* have you done?"

At last he breathed out. "Doc, I have tried so many times to tell you this, but the words won't come. However I try to say it, it's the same."

It was only now I noticed his voice had changed, to an accent I didn't recall him using before, a Scottish accent, but milder and different to the one he'd used for Hector Macleod in the casino. It occurred to me that my lungs had stopped working. I forced myself to exhale. "What is it? What did you do? What?" *Tell me it's not true!* His face was the face I knew, the face of the man I loved, not the face of a soulless child molester vilified in black and white on *Crimewatch*. How could he be someone else, something else, when I knew him, when I laughed at his jokes, when we kept each other safe, when I slept beside him and shared his warmth, when I cherished the scent of him on me when he went away?

Cam's voice came out as a gulp, almost a whisper. "When I was at school, I was this fat dork who was picked on and ridiculed all the time. There was this group of girls who used to piss about and play pranks on me, standing me up on fake dates, daring each other to grope me or do whatever stupid things they could come up with to embarrass me the most. I got away from them when I went to university. I studied Law. I never had any luck with women. I think I was just too beaten down after what had happened. I was back home after I'd finished my degree. I'd just found out I'd been offered a job in a solicitors' firm. It was the career I'd always wanted.

"I'd had a skinful. So had she. She was... I didn't realise

it then, but she was some kid sister of one of the older ones at a reunion of my old school mates. One of them must have dared her, or she'd listened to their *funny stories* and wanted to join in with their fine old tradition. She decided it would be entertaining to try to lead me on. I decided I was going to teach her a lesson, that what she thought passed for humour wasn't funny when the shoe was on the other foot, to tell everyone that I wasn't going to take shit like that from people any more, that I wasn't going to let them define me as an object of ridicule. She shouldn't have gone outside with me. They saw me as something so beneath a man that I could never be a threat, and I refused to play that role any more. I needed *respect!*" Cam took his hands away from his face and let out a hoarse breath. "She said no, but I did it anyway, in the kids' playground, in the dark outside the pub, to see how she liked being forced to play a role she didn't ask for. The judge threw the book at me. I got three years.

"While I was inside, word got round, like it does. Some of the other inmates heard that I'd sexually assaulted a girl. The screws just acted like they didn't notice. They thought I deserved it. That's how I got those burns. Someone threw boiling chip fat over me in the prison kitchen. I ended up in hospital.

"It was the worst pain I've ever felt."

He looked at me for a moment, and now he was shaking visibly. I thought the word, I knew what they must have done to him there, but I dared not say it.

"In that place, Mallory was the only friend I had. There are people who think child molesters deserve worse than death. There are people who think anyone who is unfortunate enough to have sexual feelings directed at kids — even if they never act on them — is something beneath human, a scourge that must be annihilated from the face of the earth. They're afraid to even ask for help. In jail, no-one cares what happens to them; not the screws; certainly not the other prisoners.

"It didn't matter that in his case his crime was what he desired in the depths of his soul, or that mine came from drunken indignation and the need to be respected as a man. In there, we were just two blokes. He's a human being, not some kind of monstrous demon in a man's body, just a person like you or me, with something inside him that got wired up wrong when his sexuality switch got flipped on at puberty."

How could he defend something like this? "He might have been, but he had a choice not to do it." And I thought it, but I didn't say it, *You had a choice!*

Cam sighed. "He went to his GP years ago. Asked if they would castrate him, like a dog. When they wanted to know why, he lied and told them he was gay and religious, and his sexuality was not appropriate and he wanted those feelings removed. They refused. He managed to repress it for years. Can you imagine what that must be like? The thing you want most being not only legally and practically impossible, but deeply immoral and disgusting? Thing is, he was never particularly academic and he worked a string of low-qualified jobs that occasionally brought him into contact with children. And then it happened, in an instant of weakness, and once he'd found out he could get away with it, he did it again, and again, until he got caught."

As he'd been saying this, it had felt as though his boundaries were expanding, as though the room was shrinking around us and forcing him into my personal space. I was aware of the wall against my back, although I didn't remember getting up from the chair. My heart pounded in my chest and I felt as though I couldn't breathe. A cold, prickling feeling was beginning to spread through my limbs, and a burning ache pressed behind my eyes. I couldn't cope with this. I had to get out, now.

My hand found the doorhandle, its mechanism suddenly heavy and unwieldy. I managed to get it open and stumbled into the hallway. I groped my way to the other side, found the kitchen door, staggered into the sanctuary behind it.

With my back against the closed door, it was utterly dark. Without the light, I couldn't see the ugly wallpaper. The only sounds were the whining wind outside and the occasional sound of hot peat crumbling within the combustion chamber of the Rayburn. I tried to concentrate on the sounds, tried to use my senses to anaesthetise my consciousness. My heart ran into jarring palpitations that made me fear it would stop entirely of its own accord. I bent my knees slowly, reaching out for something solid as the vertigo began. I didn't know where the ground was until my fingers touched the sticky surface of the lino flooring.

All the muscles in my chest and diaphragm had locked, stopping me from inhaling. I was choking to death on my own panic. I was going to die on this floor, crouched in the dark next to the Rayburn. I squeezed my eyes shut, but an hallucination of popping red and blue blobs possessed my vision. The buzzing cold had spread inwards through my fingers and hands and feet, and it was encroaching up my legs and arms.

I dug my knuckles into the lino and managed to force a sharp breath in and swallow the saliva flooding my mouth, forcing down a swell of rising vomit against the pain in my sides. Only nothingness lay before me, only horrors behind. The darkness closed in.

The memory of what had caused me to first start having the attacks was resurfacing. I wanted to build a wall, like Cam had said. I didn't want to think about what had happened, but I found myself unable to look away in disgusted fascination. The first time this had happened to me, I'd been in the lab, at my old job. Everyone around me had been working, and then the boss had come in, and everyone had stopped working because this boss used to criticise people's technique if he saw them working. He used to complain that when he went into the lab, no-one ever seemed to be doing any work, but that was preferable to what he would say if he caught us doing work. This time, however, I was in the middle of something and I couldn't just drop it like that.

I was transferring a solution from one flask to another without letting the solution come into contact with the air. There's a special technique to this: what you do is put the two containers in place with pure nitrogen gas flowing through them and close them off with rubber bungs, and you take a long, dry, flexible stainless steel tube called a cannula and poke each end through the septa on the flasks. Then you increase the nitrogen pressure in the flask you want the solution to come out of, and it makes it flow into the receiving vessel through the tube.

I knew he was watching me, and my hands were shaking so much I slipped, and the tip of the cannula punctured the glove covering the back of my left hand. The steel tip was stained with blood when I pulled it out, and a dark patch began to spread under the blue nitrile. I'd put a spare cannula in the lab's drying oven in case anything went wrong, so I'd had to go and fetch that one. This time I pushed it into the septum correctly. Then I reached for the tap that controlled the nitrogen and turned the wrong one, the one to the vacuum line, and solvent shot up it into the trap, and the boss saw everything. The sneer of contempt on his face and his harsh words came back to me there and then as a twisted flashback. I'd ended up gripped by this same terrible prickling cold, heart pounding and struggling to breathe, and I'd hidden in the staff toilets, afraid of anyone seeing me like this.

I'd often wondered if my boss had somehow known about the way I'd reacted. I was so ashamed of myself. I sometimes thought how he'd behaved more and more unreasonably towards me was to punish me for doing it. People don't lose control of themselves like that at work, not normal people at any rate. It might be understandable if someone behaved that way if they'd been recently bereaved, or diagnosed with cancer, but it's not right or proper for an employee to do it for being told off by her boss for making a stupid mistake.

After that it had only got worse. One of the last incidents before I lost my job had been when someone had left a chemical in a flask — we never found out what or whose it was — and it blew up during the night and took the fume cupboard out. As the lab manager, my boss was responsible for it, but he told the health and safety people it was my fault, and I took the fall for him, partly because I thought it might improve his opinion of me, but also partly because I was too afraid to stand up to him. He'd had a go at me in front of everyone else for the error both of us knew I hadn't made, and it had come over me so bad I'd had to take the rest of the day off work.

By the next morning, I'd still felt shaken, and I couldn't face going to work and having to see my boss again. Instead I'd gone to my GP. I told him I thought I was losing my sanity and asked for drugs to help me. He told me it was a reaction to stress and instead gave me a medical note saying I was unfit to work for the next week. I phoned work and told them, and I spent the next week at home, worrying about what I would do when I did go back. When I did, I was given notice: I was being made redundant, with the excuse being that there was no research funding to continue my employment.

I didn't even manage most of the short time I had left there. I filled it in with more sick notes. After I left for good, I got better for a bit. I was, after all, rid of the boss at least, and I hoped I could find another job where I could start afresh and things might be better. But it wasn't to be. After three months' solid applying, I found that my old boss was writing bad references or not bothering to write them at all. As the situation became more and more hopeless, I found myself going back to the GP and asking for help, but when it was at its worst I couldn't even face going there and having people see what I'd become.

They say losing your job is like bereavement, and that you grieve for it in the same way you'd do for a deceased loved one. There are five stages of grief, or so my therapist used to say: denial, anger, bargaining, depression, and acceptance. I went through them in the wrong order: denial that my boss was victimising me and suspecting that it was all in my imagination, bargaining that it was my fault that I had lost my job and thinking it wouldn't have happened if I'd not been so crap and I had done so-and-so instead of such-and-such, then a long sink into depression, and finally anger. I suppose I'm a passive sort of person. I don't like confrontation. My dad was the same, pretending he still had his job after he'd lost it to avoid a fight with my mother as much as for the shame. Perhaps that's why the anger came later in the sequence than it's meant to.

I was managing to breathe more steadily. The coldness was starting to recede from my arms and legs. Perhaps it was the warmth from the Rayburn, but these memories seemed so much more distant, so much less significant now all this had happened. I didn't cringe inside with guilt and self-loathing like I used to when I recalled them. It was like those events weren't relevant to me any more, as though they happened to someone else I'd known a long time ago.

I stayed there, and I breathed, and ominous fears that had surrounded me slowly drew back, replaced by a lack of any emotion; a lucid dead calm. It didn't matter who I had once been. That didn't define me, not what I was now nor what I might be in any future version of events.

The past is another country, and we need to dissociate from it and live by the choices we make in the present if we're to have any hope for the future.

I got to my feet slowly, feeling for the solid back of one of the chairs. I could barely make out the shape of the uncurtained kitchen window. I didn't know what time it was, but dawn would be a long time coming. Stars showed through a break in the clouds above. It was as though I looked at them through eyes I hadn't used for a very long time, and as I stared out into the sky my old job and my boss and my home in Birmingham seemed very distant, as though time had eroded them away and I would never touch them again.

Cam must still be in the living room. He hadn't come after me, and I hadn't heard anything from him since I'd run out. He must be sitting there, still, a stranger to me. I tried to think what it meant, I tried to feel something about what he had revealed to me, but my emotions had gone dead, like I'd sat on them while I'd been on the floor. I didn't know if it was because I was insane or because I genuinely didn't care about what he had done in his past. I tried to rationalise what I should feel. Relief, perhaps? I'd known there was something since that first night; probably I'd known subconsciously since I'd first met him. It meant I wouldn't have to feel frustrated about it any more, or be afraid of the unknown within him. Perhaps I should have felt disgust about the nature of what it was he'd done; obviously he thought it disgusting and was embarrassed by it, and everyone else who'd known about it had thought him disgusting from his account. Perhaps he was lying to me still, and he really had done something seriously, unforgivably perverted, and his explanation had been highly sanitised to make it sound more acceptable.

But I didn't feel any of these things. Why would he lie now, when the truth could be exposed in a newspaper tomorrow? He'd made a bad decision in his past, and he'd been punished for it, and it was so long ago he wasn't that person any more. I tried to imagine how I'd feel if it transpired he'd murdered a little kid or something horrendous like that, but I couldn't countenance him doing that. I knew him too well. That wasn't what he was. When we'd been together... like that... he had never been in any way aggressive. It had always been me who'd had to initiate it. What he'd said in the living room made sense. It was the truth. A kid, yes, but an older kid on the borderline between a girl and a woman. He might not have realised she was underage at the time, like he claimed, and I supposed I'd never know, and the judge wouldn't have known either. A girl who had goaded and manipulated him by his account, as part of a pattern of long-term abuse...

I'd never even liked kids. I hadn't enjoyed being one, had never had anything to do with them, and I'd never wanted them for myself. That wasn't to say at all that I thought anyone who meant harm to kids was ever justified, but me being with him wasn't putting any kid at risk from him, even if there was the remotest chance he might reoffend. Which I couldn't believe there was.

When I went back, he was still sitting on the sofa, his elbows resting on his thighs and his head bowed. He didn't look up when I entered.

"Cam, I believe you. I don't care what you did. It's done now."

He looked at me, his eyes glistening in the light of the lamp. He exhaled a shaky breath and wiped his face on his sleeve. After several moments, he spoke again. "You don't want to be with me. Everyone I'm with I poison. When I got out, I went back to live with my mother. It wasn't long before it was bricks through the window and... and words on the door in orange paint, and rough elbows and scowls and threats to my mother whenever she went out to buy groceries. I went to the police and they agreed to help me. They gave me a new identity. I was never allowed to see my mother again. I had live in another town. But less than a year later, some insider in the police decided to blow my cover on an anonymous blog, and the whole thing happened again. They stuck a lager bottle full of petrol through my letterbox while I was asleep. I woke up and tried to get out the back, but there were more of them there, and they attacked me. If the police hadn't turned up, I'd probably be dead.

"After that, I'd had enough. I couldn't live this way any more. So I built a wall. I put one foot in front of the other and I didn't look back. I stopped updating the police like I was supposed to. I kept moving and reinventing myself, hoping the trail would go cold, that no-one would ever be able to trace who I was to who I am today."

I sat beside him. I didn't look at his face because I knew he was embarrassed. "I'm a terrible research scientist and a bad person."

"No you're not."

I ignored his reply and continued. "I did something stupid in my past as well. I used to have this job."

"You don't have to tell me," he whispered. "I don't need

to hear it."

I paused to consider. "No. I've to say it and be honest, and you've to hear it and know it. Because if you won't hear it and you won't know me for everything I am and everything I've been, then you'll only have the façade that's the me the rest of the world sees, and I'll be no better than I was when I lived the way I did before I met you, and I won't be able to finish this so I can start again any more."

After a long silence in which he ventured nothing more, I continued. "I had this job, working in a lab. I wasn't much good at it, and one day the boss decided he was going to make things hard for me, and I let him. Don't know why. I thought I deserved it, I guess. And this got out of control, and I ended up taking the fall for something he'd done, and I lost my job and ended up unemployable."

It sounded far more reasonable than I remembered it when I summarised it like this and spoke it to someone else. I wondered why it had seemed such a big deal, such a source of guilt for so long.

"I don't think... I think I'm not right. I never managed to stay long enough for a diagnosis, but I've got panic disorder or something, social anxiety and stuff. I had depression after I lost my job. I think you probably know what I mean. You lose what makes you who you are. You don't want to live, but there's no courage left to kill yourself with."

We sat there in silence a little longer.

Cam said, "It's late. We should try to sleep now."

I agreed.

It was only after we had lain down under the duvet and the lamp had been turned off, leaving the peat in the hearth the only source of light in the room, that his breathing began to shudder and his shoulders started to shake. I lay against his chest and held him to me, and that night we both mourned what had once been, and I think we both finally let go of it for good.

17

SILVER LINING

I remember surfacing into consciousness a few times that night, each time touching him, making sure he was still there. I don't think either of us slept particularly well. We stayed there until dawn came, and grey daylight broke through the gap in the curtains, the same wintry kind of light I remember from the morning after we robbed the casino, cold and brutal in its penetrating candour. It fell upon the squalid, faded room and the worn-out duvet and the torn pillowcases we lay within upon the floor, and on the greying roots of Cam's hair and the lines that had started to form at the corner of his eyes. And nothing had ever seemed so real, so serious, as it did right now in this morning.

I didn't want to part from him, not even for the shortest moment. Every second we had left together was precious. I didn't fear any more, but I felt as though I stood, still and calm, staring into an abyss of chaos and insanity, unable to look away, and with no route out.

Cam opened his eyes. I'd known he'd been awake for a while, but only from the way he breathed and the way he'd reacted to my movements in his arms, but he hadn't looked at me before now. He tilted his head a bit to look at the curtains. "We need to get up?"

I looked back at him, considering. "And do what?"

"Keep walking."

He was right. The situation might be overwhelming and have no clear solution at this moment in time, but there was no point staying here in indecision and waiting for us both to come to terms with it. The overarching concepts of 'getting up' and 'getting ready' seemed too hard from this perspective, so I tried breaking them down into sequences of routines. Usually the first place I went in the morning was the lavatory. Well, I could at least do that.

The fire had burned out during the night and the room had grown cold already. We'd agreed not to use it during the day, not wanting to risk the smoke from the house's chimneys being noticed. I shivered in the bathroom. The only room that had managed to retain any warmth was the kitchen. The fire in the Rayburn had gone out before dawn, but its iron husk still radiated heat. I spooned instant porridge into a bowl of milk and put it in the microwave.

The past few years had been like sleepwalking. I felt as though I'd just woken, as though I saw a refreshed world, different in the morning light. It hit me like an epiphany. I was still alive, and at least that was one thing.

Cam moved an old Roberts radio with a teak case from the bookshelf in the living room onto the kitchen table, and we sat there listening to it.

He sat at the table stirring his porridge, his face intense as he concentrated on Radio 4. I knew he was afraid to hear his identity had been uncovered. After we'd listened for five minutes or so, the topic came up on the news and it was apparent they hadn't yet. There was just a brief mention and speculation about who Cam might be and where we were.

I studied his expression and found myself wondering how he'd coped the first time, maybe the morning after he'd made his drunken mistake. Had he sat in much the same way as now, listening to the radio in dread of what the airwaves might reveal? Perhaps he'd even gone to the police and admitted it, thinking he'd be able to explain, that they'd be reasonable and lenient. Perhaps I'd ask him some day, but not now.

"Why have they said nothing about Tweedledum and Tweedledee?" I said. "I mean, they shot that policeman. Surely they're a bigger priority than we are."

He swept his knuckles across his jaw, unshaven skin rasping. "Quite probably to the police they are. But this is the media, and I suppose we must be the bigger story that's of more interest to Joe Public. And I suppose the police think if the media can create enough hype, someone will recognise us, and that when we get caught, we'll lead them to the others."

"It's hard to tell how much they do know. I mean, if they had any idea whereabouts we were, I don't expect they would say on the radio, would they? They probably wouldn't make it public at all, because if we heard it they'd know we'd start moving again. What information they do release is probably carefully calculated so it won't make us do anything they don't want if we hear it. I mean, they might even be trying to manipulate us through it."

Cam sighed. "It doesn't bear thinking about too much. Perhaps it will die down."

It didn't sound as though it was going to die down.

At length he rose.

"I'm going outside to sort out the lobster traps," he said.

While he was out I switched off the radio and got dressed quickly in the living room. It was too cold to sit in here. I gathered up the duvet from the floor and pulled it onto the sofa, curling up my legs beneath it and crushing the thick wadded fabric around myself.

I heard him come back in; he went into the kitchen. I think he was eating his cold porridge. I sat there clutching the duvet, listening to the slight sounds of him moving pots and cutlery around.

He came into the room, shutting the door behind him, and stood peering out through the gap in the curtains. It had begun to rain again, drops specking the windows and drumming tunelessly on the porch roof. The daylight was so poor, so colourless, I could make out no details of Cam beyond his silhouette. His shoulders were hunched, and the light coming through the window illuminated a vapour blossom around his mouth and nose when he exhaled.

"I wish it would hurry up and get dark, so we can put the fire on."

Not only that, I considered, but it simply felt safer with the dark closed in around the house. Even though this place felt like the edge of the world, there were still people here, and there was still the risk. I thought about the car and the caravan and the dead-end road where we'd hidden them. What sort of people lived here? Did they keep to themselves, or would they talk if they noticed an unfamiliar vehicle? How was it Cam had known to come here?

"How did you know about this house?"

"It was my grandparents'. My grandma died while I was in jail and left it to my sister. She got married and went to live in Fife, but I knew she didn't want to sell it. Last I knew she was using it as a holiday retreat in the summer. I wasn't adamant it was still unoccupied, but I knew there was a strong likelihood."

A sister. Perhaps she had known his victim. I wondered what she was like, if she'd stood by him, like it sounded as though his mother had. I wondered what Cam had been like against the background of the family he'd had, and about them growing up together. What had they thought when he'd been convicted? When the urgency to stay safe from an angry mob changed his identity and took him away from them. "I suppose if they discover your identity, they'll think to look here."

"They might."

He didn't look at me, and neither of us spoke for a while. The dripping of water was prominent in the silence. We would have to deal with that if and when they did uncover his identity.

We'd talked about waiting for it to die down and fleeing the country, with those passports Cam had made. I'd believed it, but I couldn't see it any more. I couldn't see anything beyond us being trapped in this house now, with the media sensationalising it and the police finding us here. We'd run to this place in a bid to hide, but now we were trapped here like some wretched fox gone to earth in a hunt, and there was nowhere else for us to run to when they started closing in.

"Cam, if it goes wrong — if we get caught — I'll wait for you. They can't lock us up forever."

I sensed a shudder pass over him in the dim and musty room. "If we get caught... if I end up in jail again... the only way I'll come out of there is in a black bag. I don't know if it'll be by my hand or by someone else's, but that will be the way of it."

An image came into my mind of Cam stripping off his shirt to make a noose, alone and hemmed in by blank gunmetal walls, away from the eyes of others where pride or modesty might protect him, the scars on his back exposed like a brand to the world. He was quite right. Even if we did both survive that institutional hell, that gauntlet of ignominy, we would not be the same people we were today. Even if we were to meet after all that, we wouldn't know what to say to each other any more. It might even be a condition of our release that we weren't allowed contact with one another. Neither of us would have anything, and we'd both be unemployable. I couldn't see us queuing up for the soup kitchen, or applying together for a place in some mouldy council flat with rats. Not because we burned the bridge this time, but merely because too much water had passed beneath it.

"There's nothing else we can do?"

"I'm all out of ideas." He turned from the window and pulled up the duvet to sit on the sofa beside me. "The only option left to us is to sit and wait, and hope it blows over before the pigs gather enough evidence to find us."

I thought again about the police and the media. Perhaps they were playing mind games with us, and they had teams of psychologists working for them. Perhaps they'd intended me to feel this way. Perhaps we could play mind games with them back. After all, they could only go on the evidence they had.

"Unless we can make it look like we died."

Cam snorted. "What? Like, you mean, write a suicide note and post it to the police? Your media portrayal has made us terribly depressed, and as a result of this we've conveniently killed ourselves, so you can stop trying to hunt us down."

I thumped him gently in the shoulder and pushed out a halfhearted laugh. "You know what I mean! If there was an accident and we planted evidence there that made it look like we were there at the time. Or if we could make it look like there'd been an accident."

"Trouble is, someone isn't usually considered dead

unless there's a body. That one person can die without a trace is unusual, but for two people to die together and leave nothing, unless it's in a bomb blast or an aeroplane explosion, or a shipwreck, or something else catastrophic, that takes plausibility too far."

"I might be able to make a bomb," I said. "I suppose I know all the theory about it."

I leaned my chin on my hand. As I considered the options, I found myself becoming aware of the sharp aroma of the spent peat fire and the smell of damp and old, disused house, and the not exactly pleasant smell of rooms people had slept in. I studied the dust on the faded fabrics and aged wood, the discoloured books decaying slowly inside a glass-fronted cabinet in a corner beside an armchair. Wedged between the side of the chair and the cabinet was that big solid case, the one that we'd inadvertently stolen from the blood transfusion van at the hospital. The one I'd told Cam to get rid of.

"What if we staged an explosion and put our blood in it? They'd find a huge mess and maybe some bloodstained scraps of clothing or something."

Cam shook his head. "I still don't think it would be enough. There'd be pieces of flesh and bone if that happened. And I don't think cutting bits off ourselves is going to help us. That and we'd be risking giving them more information by showing them where we'd been. We'd still be waiting for the media storm to die down. And then there's still the Tweedles."

When he said these words, a dim, barely formed inspiration started to gather into a mass in my head. "We could make it look like the Tweedles caught up with us and killed us."

"They'd only deny it if the police found them. And the

police might not even find them, so they'd still be after us."

Involuntarily, I found my eyes drawn to my coat, draped over the back of an armchair, and the gun I knew resided in its pocket. "Not if we killed them."

Cam didn't reply to this. I didn't look at him, but I could sense him looking at me, and his discomfort from the slight adjustment in his posture.

I found myself staring at the medical case again. "What if it looked as though the Tweedles murdered us somewhere and there was really *loads* of blood at the scene? More blood than anyone could survive losing at once, in fact?"

"Wait a minute, you're not making any sense." He was frowning. "If it's more blood than someone can lose, how are we going to survive losing that much?"

I got to my feet and crossed the room to the case. "You lose about a pint, and then you regenerate it, and you can give blood again in a few weeks." I pulled the case out and set it down on the coffee table. "What happens when you donate blood?"

I opened the case to reveal various tubes, needles, and empty blood bags. *Yes, now perhaps I could just make out a path out of this.*

"We put our blood in these bags and freeze it, then freeze some more in a few weeks' time, and we'll build up a supply of it that will be more than we could lose at a single point in time."

Slowly, hope dawned in Cam's expression. It was rapidly replaced with scepticism. "I thought you said you weren't a medical doctor?"

"I'm not."

"And how exactly are we going to get it to look as though the Tweedles did it, once we've got this blood?"

"I don't know yet. But if we start now, we have it as a contingency. It's better than anything else we've got. Gimme your arm."

Cam laughed abruptly. "What, so you can stick needles in my arteries?"

"It goes in your vein, not your artery." I peeled open one of the needle packets and fixed it on to a tube.

"Why should I trust you to stick needles in me?" He was still laughing, but nervously and without any real hint of humour.

I rummaged in the case. "There aren't any tourniquets."

Cam tut-tutted. "Haven't you ever shot up?"

I frowned. "No. Have you?"

I watched him slide his belt off. He wrapped it around his arm just above the elbow and pulled it tight. "The things I put up with."

His arms were twice as thick as mine. The skin on the inside of his elbow felt very smooth where I traced the bluish form of a swelling vein there. It wasn't difficult. I'd had various medical complaints throughout my life, and I'd never been squeamish. I'd watched and learned every time someone had stuck a needle in me.

Cam looked away and winced as I pushed the point in. A dark meniscus rose into the tube and moved steadily down the length, until it spilled over into the bag, leaving a filmy stain on the inside of the plastic.

"Do I get tea and a biscuit?" he asked.

I shrugged. "Suppose. Depends if you bought any biscuits." I separated a piece off a wad of cotton wool and pushed it around the base of the needle so he didn't have to look at it.

He studied the bag uneasily. "What if too much comes out?"

"It can't, because the bag only holds a pint. A pint's considered safe for an adult to lose. Bigger people have more blood in them."

He laughed. "So you're saying I can probably give three, on account of being a six-foot fat bastard?"

After several minutes the bag was beginning to look full. I pressed the cotton wool down on top of the needle and pulled it out, as I'd observed the nurses do every time I'd had a blood test. "You have to press that down for a minute or so," I said.

Cam sat with his thumb pressed to the inside of his elbow while I held up the tube to allow the remainder of the blood to run into the bag, and sealed it. I spread some tissues on the coffee table to stop blood going on it.

"You needn't think I'm doing yours," he said as I sorted out another bag with a tube and needle.

I scoffed. "I wouldn't trust you to do mine, considering you can't tell the difference between a vein and an artery! Can I borrow your belt?"

He winked at me and handed it over. "Only if you hold the strap in your teeth like a real heroin addict."

I sat with my forearm exposed to the chill air and watched the bag fill. Cam brought me a glass of water as I was pressing down on the pinprick waiting for it to seal.

"Can you get some chips out if you're going to the freezer?" he asked as I gathered up the bags of blood.

I fetched an oven tray from the kitchen and made my way out the front door and along the path beside the house to the outbuilding in the direction of the loch. The light was very poor by now, and to reduce the visibility further, the wind had dropped and a mist had rolled in from the sea. It hung over the loch as a damp veil of murk. My knees wobbled and my head swam a bit. I didn't know if it was from blood loss, or merely from stress and an overactive imagination.

Inside the outbuilding I put the blood bags into one of the freezer's hanging wire racks. Freezing the blood in a domestic freezer would almost certainly disrupt the structure of the cells in it, and if someone studied it closely enough, it would probably be possible to tell. I supposed, at the end of the day, it all depended on how much money they were prepared to invest in forensics, and how easy we could make it for them to come to an obvious conclusion and close the case without digging too deep.

There weren't any scissors, of course, so I had to stab the chip bag with a key to get it open.

I went back with the chips in the tray held out in front of me. It occurred to me with a sense of ironic self-disgust that I'd never thought I'd end up freezing samples of my bodily fluids so I could stage my own death to escape capture for a crime.

Inside, I put the bloodstained tissues and the needles into the peat as kindling. I sat huddled on the hearth trying to light a fire while Cam fetched the lobster traps in and dealt with the Rayburn and the dinner. We had oven chips and lobster with a salad. The taste of the lobster reminded me of expensive meals at scientific conferences. It didn't belong in this shabby old kitchen with its dated, disintegrating décor.

Afterwards I sat in an armchair as close to the fire as was bearable, a pen in my hand and a notebook resting on the arm, and tried to brainstorm. Back in my old job, I had done this often, and it was the same problem-solving technique as working out a synthesis. You've got a molecule to make and you know various reactions to make chemical bonds, so you break the structure down into smaller units and work out how you can assemble them from simpler reagents and in what order it needs to be done. I used to enjoy this, but now I looked back, it seemed I'd spent most of the time impatiently anticipating future events: waiting for exams to be out the way, wishing I could write my thesis faster and for the viva to be over and the corrections done, so I could be a doctor; waiting for a job, waiting for the day I'd have money. That turned out kind of ironic. The only time I'd had money, I'd been too busy and stressed to appreciate it.

Well, now I'd arrived at the future, and I might not have much of it left. I'd thrown away my halcyon days fantasising about what might be yet to come. Youth is wasted on the young.

I ended up with a scribbly diagram. It would need some more local geographical knowledge before I could really solidify it, as we needed to find somewhere to face them and somewhere to dump the bodies. If it went wrong, they would end up killing us, but with no plan that risk would eventually become a certainty, and it might just be worth it to get them off our backs for good.

Could I kill them? I'd killed three times before. I'd got past it by dehumanising them, seeing them as pigs and rats instead of people.

"You come up with anything yet?" Cam asked.

"Not quite yet." I put the book down. "But it'll come to me eventually; it always does. I suppose we ought to put the lights out, in case someone sees it from outside."

"We can't sleep all the time it's dark," he chided.

"Then perhaps we can find some other way to entertain

ourselves and pass the time, as well as keep warm." I reached up and switched off the light I'd been using. Sliding off my seat, I sank to my knees on the floor and crawled over to where he lay, on the floor under the duvet. He put down his book when I nestled alongside him.

"Turn off the light if you prefer it that way."

He reached behind and switched it off, leaving only the light from the fire. I unbuttoned his shirt and trousers, fascinated by the shape of his shoulder and chest in the flickering orange glow.

The world around us melted into insignificance as I touched his body, planing my hands over his flanks and back and the now-familiar rough surface of his scars. He kissed me and put his hands on my waist, catching my shirt and pulling it up. As I submerged in the sensation of his flesh, I knew who he was better than I knew anyone, and I'd revealed to him more than I'd ever revealed before. And I had never felt more alive than I did now.

*

It was still dark when I woke, but when I checked my watch with a torch, it was half seven already.

I lay for a while beside Cam and tried to go back to sleep, but a restless unease had come upon my mind. I'd dreamt about something, but I couldn't recall the specifics of it now, just a sense of a deadline passed and impending doom. I'd shifted into high alert mode and now I couldn't keep my eyes shut, and the bed on the floor had become uncomfortable.

At least the fire hadn't gone out entirely, and with the room still warm-ish, now was a good time to rise. I crawled out from under the duvet and found my clothes in the dark. I'd go into the kitchen, sit there and read or do something to occupy my mind, so as not to disturb him.

The cold in the hall hit me in the face when I opened the door. The kitchen was better, but it still wasn't warm enough for me to want to sit in it. I'd go upstairs and find another duvet, I thought. There was a battered old armchair shoved in the corner behind the fridge, and with a little more insulation I could be comfortable enough there.

I felt my way around in the dark and cold. None of the curtains upstairs had been drawn. Dawn hadn't yet broken, but the horizon was starting to become visible against the overcast sky. Through the window I could see blotchy irregularities and dark patches upon the landscape.

I lifted the catch on the window and leaned out against the hinge, a gale shoving its way into the house. It wasn't much colder out than it was in.

My eyes were fully adjusted to the dark, but I could only just discern the paler shapes of the statues down in the decaying rockery. Water was dripping from something onto the path below, audible over the bluster of the wind. I couldn't make out the surface of the loch on the right, but on the left the stone wall lay as a black shape, and the hedge behind it quivered under the wind's onslaught.

I squinted as I looked at it. A blocky whitish object stood behind the hedge, a black shape pulsing at the top. It was a van, I realised, and the black thing was one of those rotating ventilation things that spin in the wind that some vans have, I think when they use them for transporting dogs. As I leaned a little more, I saw another, almost hidden behind the angle of the house wall, and a queasy, sinking feeling came over my insides as I looked at them. They had to be police vans. There couldn't be any other explanation.

18

WHITE FLAG

Cam was still oblivious to the world when I went back into the living room. I knelt over him and shook him by the shoulder.

"Cam, wake up."

His breathing changed and he stirred under the duvet, raising an arm over his face in protest.

"Cam, get dressed. There's a van outside."

The next instant he was up on his knees, making incoherent noises and groping about the furniture like a zombie. Perhaps if this had happened before today, I would have panicked and stood about uselessly, but now I found myself clear-minded, and I thought quickly about what I could do to speed our escape. I found his rucksack underneath an armchair. "What else do you need? Are your documents in here?"

"We need the computer as well. The evidence is still on it."

I found the laptop in an armchair with a book on top of it, and shoved both of them into the bag. I knew where my documents were. I put on my bag and my coat over it. While Cam put on his coat and sorted out his bag, I went to the back of the living room, to the small window set deep inside the thick wall, that in this light was just a slightly lighter shade of dark. I fumbled for the catch and pushed it open. "Out here."

Cam hesitated. "Well, you'd better go first in case I get stuck."

I put my knee up onto the sill and got my shoulders into the gap, feeling my way over the lip of the casement and reaching out into empty air. I lost my balance as I groped for the floor and fell headfirst with my arms in front of me in a flash of panic before I landed on soft soil strewn with yew needles. I wormed my hindquarters clear of the window and rolled to one side.

Something bulged out of the window next. When it fell to the ground I realised it was the rucksack. I could see only the vaguest motion as my eyes strained to make out the blank face of the wall in the dark. I felt his emergence by clutching at his hands.

"I *am* stuck," he muttered.

"You're not stuck. Hurry up." At the same time, I feared he was stuck. What if he got caught like this, and the police had to call the fire brigade to knock down the wall so they could arrest him? I bent my knees and reached around his chest under his arms, and pulled. I don't think he really was stuck — it was just the angle of his back and the length of his legs that made it difficult for him to get leverage against the sill. Once his waist was over the edge and he got his hands down, it was easier.

Cam got up, picking up the bag, and pushed the window shut. The yew branches stood out inky-black against the dark sky. I felt a strange *déjà vu*, remembering the night at that churchyard when we'd plotted in the scout hut, before Sage died and Ace was arrested, before the plot had all gone wrong and a policeman had died.

"Come on," said Cam. "Let's go."

We pushed through the undergrowth, making our way down past the back of the outbuildings, away from the road. The loch was black, unseeable, but the lap of the water was growing louder over the roar of the wind.

I wasn't sure we'd reached it until my shoe hit wet ground. The water came sloshing up the shore in halfhearted waves. I clutched his hand as we pushed on, the wind tearing at us.

"Shit," I realised.

"Now what?"

"The blood. We left the blood in the freezer in that outbuilding."

He turned back and pressed forward against the wind. "Forget it. Let's go."

"No Cam! If they find that blood and analyse it they'll pick up your DNA. They'll have a record of it from before, from... what you did. They'll identify you."

He faltered mid-stride, but he didn't look back. "They will identify me anyway, in the end. We can't risk it."

I stopped. "Look, I'm going back. I'll meet you at the car." He turned to face me, walking backwards. I saw him only as a shape, his features indiscernible. "If I'm not there in ten minutes, go without me."

"What if the police have found the car and they've laid an ambush?"

"Just be careful. If there's anything not right, stay back and I'll find you when I come back down. Now go."

I turned and walked away, the wind at my back, carrying his voice to me. *Fuck*, he said.

I crouched, keeping my body low as I approached the house and its ramshackle outbuildings. Using the slope of the land to conceal myself from anyone who might be looking out the windows, I made my way up to the stone wall bordering the garden. I crept along to its edge to peer past and get a cautious glimpse of the side of the house. The porch jutted out from the wall, blocking my view of the path down from the front gate. Its door was on the opposite side.

I caught motion around the edge of the porch, black-clad figures moving down the path, swift and controlled. There came a reverberating crash and the sound of wood splintering. Booted feet pounded the porch floor. I heard the clatter of the plastic chairs falling and the bang of the inside door flung open so hard it struck the porch wall. For an instant I couldn't move. My breath lodged in my throat and my limbs wouldn't respond to my intentions.

The raiders were all in the house now. I gathered all my courage and bolted across the path to the outbuilding door. There was no lock, only a latch, but it was unfamiliar and in the dark my fingers couldn't make sense of it. I struggled with it in panic. At last I found the position and felt the mechanism, pulling the door open just wide enough to duck inside. I didn't dare risk the light. Using the hum of its motor and my sense of touch, I felt my way to the freezer and pulled up the lid, fumbling inside for the frozen stones wrapped in plastic. I put them into the inside pocket of my coat, on the opposite side to the gun, and flailed back to the door, pulling it shut behind me. I feared the police had got to the caravan first, and that Cam might have been captured already, that I'd never see him again. I'd lost all composure and didn't even check before I broke cover, diving behind the wall and charging back down the slope to the loch's shore.

They'd see our footprints. They'd know how we escaped. Every second wasted was a second in their favour. But they wouldn't be able to begin until it was light. The night was on our side.

As I came over the rise of the land, I recognised the blocky, pale shape of the caravan against the road, and relief welled up in me. Yet I still had to be careful. There might be an ambush waiting down there.

I crept down to the car. He was sitting inside, in the passenger seat. I could just make out his shape. When I opened the door, the car's damned internal light came on. I slammed it shut behind me as soon as I was in, but the light remained a few seconds longer, revealing and awful, the night without made black and impenetrable by the contrast

"You drive," he said. "Let's get away from here. Quickly."

"The police not here, then?"

"If they are, we'll soon know it."

I trod down the clutch and turned the key in the ignition. The bags of blood weighed against my thigh like icy rocks. I reached them out of my coat pocket and passed them to him, and he stuffed them into his rucksack.

"Where to? The ferry?"

"That's no good. They must know we're here. It's the only way off the islands and they'll be camped out there. No doubt they'll be stationed on the road through the mountains between Lewis and Harris too. Our only chance is to come up with somewhere to hide. We'll have to get rid of the caravan soon, but for now it's all we've got to make do with."

As a colourless morning dawned, we drove a lonely road through an empty moor. Lewis was too small and it would take too long for this to die down once they realised they had us trapped here. It was only a matter of time. I thought again of my father, who'd spent life striving to improve, and in the end had ended it by his own choice, and of my mother, who had wasted her life to stagnation and apathy, allowed it to slip through her fingers unheeded. What did it matter, ultimately, how we hoped and toiled?

Whatever choices we make, the end is always the same.

I supposed we could shoot ourselves. But if Cam wanted me to do him first, I wouldn't be able to.

A car had joined the road some distance behind us. I could only see it in the wing mirrors, as the caravan was in the way.

"You see it?"

Cam sat with an odd stillness about him. "It's the Tweedles."

Dread gripped me, and I stared at the reflection of the blue car in the wing mirror, too distant to make out anything of the people inside it. If it wasn't one thing, it was another. "Are you certain?"

"I'm sure of it." Cam's face was full of tension and his voice came out angry. "The police must have led them right to us!"

I held the car steady on the road, maintaining the needle at fifty. "How can they even know it's us? I mean, they don't know who we're disguised as, or what we're driving."

"They might not." Cam ran his fingers over his stubble. "Turn off when you can. See if we can lose them."

I indicated and turned at the next junction. Cam's oath told me the Tweedles had done the same.

I kept driving. Occasional houses passed on both sides, several in ruins. Then the houses began to grow sparser, petering out. A sheep wandered across the road, and its retinue followed it. I braked and used the horn as the car drew closer, but the sheep didn't respond.

"Stupid buggers! Get out the way!" The car had come to

a stop now, but the sheep were just standing there, and the Tweedles' car was coming up behind. If they wouldn't get out they way, I would have to push them out the way.

The Frontera's roo bar hit the nearest sheep, and even though I was going as slow as I could, the impact still made a noise, and the sheep did a sort of backflip off the edge of the road. The other sheep scattered, bleating in a confused sort of way.

"Shit. Is it all right?"

Cam was looking about, an uncomfortable sort of recognition apparent in him. "Damn it, we shouldn't have gone down here."

"Shit!" I said again.

The road ended ahead. The surface just tailed away into exposed hardcore and then unsurfaced rough ground beyond that. It looked like whoever had been building it ran out of money before it was finished.

I couldn't turn, not with the Tweedles behind us. This was supposedly an off-road vehicle. The Tweedles' wasn't. Perhaps we stood a chance.

Soil slithered under the Frontera's tyres as it left the road, the caravan rattling and bumping behind. "The SatNav." I threw it to Cam. "Here. See if you can use it to find where we can join up with another road."

The car shook and the noise got louder. Behind, I could see the Tweedles' car reaching the end of the road. They were following, although they seemed much slower.

"There's another road I think we can reach," said Cam. "We'll need to cross this dip to get there."

I nodded, gritting my teeth and clenching my fingers around the wheel. As the car descended the slope, the landscape ahead opened up, revealing a shallow valley with a trickle of water running over its rock-strewn bottom.

Cam pondered the ground ahead. "You can do it. Just take your time."

Yes, I thought. I tightened my fingers on the steering wheel. *Frontera, I trust you.* Stupid of me to initiate telepathic communication with a fifteen-year-old Chelsea Tractor. Perhaps I am stupid. Or mad. Once upon a time, I used to be someone who drove to a lab in the rush hour every weekday.

I scanned the debris littering the the base of the valley, looking for a way through that wouldn't involve scraping the bottom of the car or ramming the tyres up against insurmountable boulders. I found one. Steering gradually, I let the car slide onwards. The front tyres hit the water. I hoped it wasn't deeper than it looked. The gradient eased off and the engine began to take over. Then there came a thud from behind and I felt something snag.

Tyres sloshed in the water and the car made a juddering fishtail motion. I pushed the accelerator harder. Pebbles and debris rattled in one of the wheel arches and the fishtailing intensified.

"Cam, it's stuck!"

"Put it in four-wheel-drive!"

"It *is* in four-wheel-drive!"

I breathed and forced myself into focus, putting down the clutch again and shifting to second gear. With only the slightest pressure on the accelerator pedal, I eased the clutch back up. I could hear the engine running and the wheels turning, yet could sense no traction through the car. The view from the wing mirror showed the rear tyres had slurried black mud up the beige chassis of the caravan.

"It's stuck." Cam was reaching down for the red release

button on his seatbelt. "We need to ditch the caravan."

"*Cam!*"

Wind roared through the open door, then it slammed and he was gone, the suspension lurching slightly in the wind and the wake of his sudden departure. Through the windows, I saw him hurry to the rear of the car, and crouch down over the relay that joined the caravan to the Frontera's tow bar, the wind ripping at his coat and hair. His fumbling with the coupling sent a tremor through the car's wheelbase. His hand rose from behind the car, palm pressing against the back windscreen as he pulled himself up. He groped around the corner of the tailgate, and then a loud *crack* pierced the sound of the wind and he dived alongside the left rear tyre, out of sight.

I couldn't breathe. I couldn't look away. All I could do was stare at the rear-view mirror and the caravan with the empty sky around the edges. It had to be a gunshot. They'd shot him, and now they'd be coming for me, and I was paralysed and couldn't act.

The door flew open and Cam flung himself into the seat. "Drive!"

I turned to face him. He was a bit breathless, but unharmed. He looked ridiculously normal. I turned back to the road and stamped down the clutch. My hand found the gear lever. The engine roared as I jerked my foot up through the bite point, but this time the tyres caught and the car lurched forwards, over the boggy ground at the bottom of the shallow ravine and up, back to the road. It was only when it got there that I realised how hard my heart was pounding, each pulse sending tremors into my elbows and knees.

"Where to?"

Cam picked the SatNav up off the floor. "North, to

Stornoway. They won't follow us into a populated area."

"I thought you wanted to stay away from populated areas because of the police!"

He sighed through his nose. "Which is better — no, which is worse — which do you *unprefer*, the police or the Tweedles?"

"I... I don't know. Isn't there a third option?"

An abrupt laugh escaped him, and then he shifted in his seat, his breath coming back with a shiver. Unexpectedly he reached across the car, bridging the gulf between us with his arm. His hand squeezed my knee.

I kept checking the wing mirrors, but I didn't see the Tweedle's car again. Hopefully it was stuck on the moor. And they wouldn't be able to call roadside assistance for fear of being recognised, so they'd have to walk until they found another they could steal.

Police cars were parked up in the ferry port as we passed, white and fluorescent yellow and all no-nonsense letters and official badges. There would be no exit that way.

As we turned the curve in the road, bollards and moored boats overlooking the harbour on one side and shop-fronts swept by wind and rain on the other, the dull roar of a motor blurred into hearing, and a helicopter flew across the sky and whirled out to sea, curving across the waterfront.

I sensed Cam follow it in my peripheral vision. "We can't stop here. Just follow the road around."

The seafront was full of police uniforms. A tense knot formed inside me as the car approached the traffic lights, but they stayed green and the traffic kept moving. After a few minutes, we were back out of Stornoway on another road. There was a clock tower up ahead, a brown stone thing, indistinct in the rain, a concrete building next to it. We passed a park with bare trees in it, and a roundabout. It would probably have been quite pleasant in summer, but now it looked drear and cold, and the empty heath surrounding the town seemed to be threatening to get in.

As we passed the last of the buildings before the road reached out into the undulating moorland, the throb of the helicopter once again rose above the Frontera's engine.

"You've got the SatNav. Think of something."

I glanced sideways to see him leaning back his head, eyes closed in a futile gesture. He was wearing spectacles and had dyed-ginger hair that was showing a darker colour at the roots. It occurred to me how, when I'd first met him, I'd been unable to recognise him in his various disguises; how skilful I'd thought him at maintaining the façade. Yet now, I felt I would know him however hard he tried to look like someone else. Perhaps he'd let down his guard around me, or perhaps I'd simply learnt to see through it.

And now at any moment we might be captured and separated, and I'd never see him again, except perhaps just before the judge passed sentence in the courtroom.

Looking ahead, a smudge on the drab terrain stood out, blocky buildings catching my attention. "What's that?"

Cam conferred with the SatNav for a few moments. "Stornoway Airport."

I gazed upon the approaching buildings. Flying. I used to do that, back in Coventry. I remembered the bright autumn morning I'd first flown. It felt like someone else's memory, from another world, even though it had been only a few months ago.

Something flashed in the rear-view mirror. A siren made me start.

"Game over," said Cam through gritted teeth, his eyes still closed.

The policeman behind me was flashing his headlamps and sounding his horn. I looked again at the airport, getting closer now so I had to look sideways through the passenger window.

"Is your seatbelt on?" I said.

"Yes?"

I took a deep breath.

Then I braked, hard, and swerved off the road onto the embankment. The tall wire fence that separated the airport from the surrounding land loomed, the buildings close behind it. I put the Frontera in four-wheel drive, third gear, and prepared to charge, but the next thing I knew, everything was whirling sideways and the air was full of the crunching of glass and the buckling of metal. Sky and moor turned over.

I opened my eyes. I was upside-down, suspended by the seatbelt, and the engine had stopped. The car's windscreen was full of cracks, like an enormous spider web. The ground ahead was covered in tiny fragments of glass and bits of Frontera.

"Cam!"

I heard broken glass moving on my left. "I think I'm all right," he said.

"Get out the car!"

I unfastened my seatbelt and crawled through the broken window on elbows and knees. Behind the Frontera, the police car lay on its side, sandwiched between the perimeter fence and the embankment, just ahead of where the fence had been torn open by our entry. It must have hit me from behind, either by accident or as a deliberate attempt to immobilise us. The broken wire sagged from its supports, swaying in the wind. Up in the sky, the helicopter still kept vigil.

Cam emerged from the other side of the car, SatNav in one hand and rucksack in the other. I turned back to face the airport. Out on the tarmac a windsock wiggled, and beneath it were parked two familiar aircraft: Piper Cherokees.

I ran to the nearest plane and grabbed the handle on the door. "In, quickly!" I told Cam. "Don't step forward of the line." I looked back to see another police vehicle had arrived. A muddy tan shape moved wolflike down the embankment. *Shit*.

He was in, and I climbed in after him. The key was on the ledge above the instruments, the same place they kept them in Coventry airport. I started the engine and began the preflight checks.

"We need to go now!" Cam had seen the police and dogs running around the outside of the fence. I looked out the window to check the rudder, and a man burst from the doors of a nearby building, waving his arms. He looked *incensed*.

I put the headphones on and pressed the communication button, reading the plane's ID from the label on the controls. "Control, this is Mike November Twelve, requesting taxi, over."

"What the fuck? Just go!" Cam shouted.

I panicked and took the brake off, and the plane began to move forward. The man behind was running after it. I used the rudder to steer around the corner of the building, out towards the main runway.

Mike November Twelve, please hold your position and

await further instruction, replied Control.

"Sorry," I said, and I checked carefully for any planes on the runway before I moved out. As soon as the plane was straight, I pushed the throttle up and the plane began to gather speed. The police and the dogs and the man whose plane it presumably was were all out on the runway behind us, but it didn't matter now, because the plane was going faster and faster, and the runway was rushing underneath and falling away, and the horizon was within reach...

I looked to Cam briefly. His eyes were wide, his head pressed back against the seat. I could see in him the same exhilaration I'd felt when I first flew.

And then the clouds closed over us, hiding us from our pursuers, and I could barely make out the east coast of Lewis below us through the mist. Even the helicopter couldn't match out speed.

"We can escape in this? We can go back to the mainland?"

I studied the instruments. "No. There's not enough fuel."

"What? How much fuel is there? Are you sure?"

"I wouldn't want to find out over the ocean. Look, we probably wouldn't be able to get that far anyway, not before the RAF got to us."

Cam sighed.

"Every minute we stay free is another minute to come up with something better. Starting with a flat place to land."

"Will a beach do?"

"Fine."

He looked at the SatNav. "There's a very flat beach up north, on the west side of the island."

"Tell me where to go."

*

The beach was beautiful, serene. Its position wedged between cliffs and the conditions we chanced upon that day had even conspired to make it sheltered, and the wind was not a bother as it usually was everywhere else on this barren isle.

White sand spread from the distant edges of the land down to the pristine ocean. I walked around the front of the plane to take it all in, and I breathed deep the clean air.

Cam paced around to stand behind me, and he leaned against the plane's fuselage.

I closed my eyes and listened to the sea, and I thought.

Then I studied our location on the SatNav and I took my mobile out of my pocket and switched it on.

"What are you doing?" said Cam.

"I'm calling the Tweedles. This is the one chance we're going to get of getting the police off our backs for long enough for us to flee the country. We have to kill them and make it look as though they killed us. If the police intervene before we've finished, perhaps they'll see them as higher priority than us."

Cam stared at me for what seemed a long time, his breath sounding ragged, but he didn't raise any objection.

Perhaps there's a monster in all of us. I selected Tweedledee's name from the list and pressed the green call button.

"Doc?" came Tweedledee's incredulous voice.

"We're near the Butt of Lewis," I said. "We've had enough of contending with you as well as the police. Meet us at the lighthouse and we'll make a deal."

I hung up.

We climbed up from the beach and hiked over more heath, avoiding the roads. A spire became visible in the distance. Fog had begun to roll in, and I couldn't see it clearly.

"I used to do Duke of Edinburgh on the cliffs round here when I was a lad, and kayaking in the sea." Cam narrowed his eyes as if to peer through the fog. "It's the lighthouse on the Butt of Lewis."

As if to confirm his answer, the tower flashed.

"There aren't lighthouse keepers, are they?"

"No. All the lights were automated years ago."

"Good."

Up close, the lighthouse revealed itself to be a plain tower made from red brick. It looked like a chimney from a furnace built during the Industrial Revolution. There were some white-walled, single-storey buildings within a complex of low walls, and an empty parking area. I gazed up at the slowly rotating machinery of the light behind the glass walls, before movement down on the ground, in the distance, caught my attention.

"There's a car coming." It was a blue car.

Without speaking, we ducked behind a wall. I fumbled for the solid shape of my mobile in my coat pocket, held down the button that powered it on. I waited for the signal to pick up, and I thumbed nine three times, my hand already becoming numb from the windchill.

"Hello? Police!" I shouted into the phone. "My name's... never mind. I'm the one they call Doc." The way it came out felt like a confession, a forbidden truth. "I believe you want to speak to me."

I almost laughed. "We are on the Butt of Lewis, close to the lighthouse. Tweedledum and Tweedledee are here with us, too."

19

TRUE BLUE

An engine came into hearing, drawing closer. It stopped and a handbrake rasped. Doors opened and slammed. I heard voices but couldn't make out the words.

I must take out Tweedledee first. I couldn't afford to falter and miss, like I'd read they trained soldiers in the army to overcome their natural human instincts to do. What animal should I try to visualise him as? A crocodile? A vicious, rabid dog?

A man appeared around the side of the wall. It was Tweedledum. "Bro!" he called, glancing back the way he'd come.

Tweedledee appeared, a gun in one hand, arm slack inside his Adidas jacket. "Get out," he ordered us.

Despite his manner, he looked fidgety and nervous. His attention seemed to be focused on Cam's hands. I suspected why: he thought Cam had shot the Glasgow drugs baron and his gang. He assumed I, a fallen academic, a female science geek who was so far divorced from the world he knew, didn't have it in me to use a gun.

He walked towards us, herding us to the edge of the land, where the grass and mud gave way to bare rock, and bare rock gave way to empty air. Nothing else, only the eroded edge of land jutting out, and below that, the fierce sea, tearing at the rocks it hadn't yet devoured.

"Go and stand over there. Turn around, you sack of shit."

Cam turned around, keeping his hands raised. I set my feet apart to steady my balance against the wind. Tweedledee shifted his weight from foot to foot, gun shaking in his hand.

"So where the fuck's our money, bitch?" I could see the heat rising in Tweedledee's face. If only I could put some pressure on them, it might force them into making the decision to postpone what they were going to do. Everything seemed to be procrastination now; staying ahead of the police that bit longer, stopping the Tweedles from killing us that bit longer, to wait for the chance I needed.

"All the money Genghis didn't take is laundered and in bank accounts."

I took a deep breath. "We called the police."

"*What?*"

To my side, Cam closed his eyes and lowered his face in a grimace. Wrong choice. I'd said it now, and I couldn't unsay it. There's a parallel universe and all that crap...

"They'll be here soon."

Tweedledum and Tweedledee exchanged glances. "Fuck."

Tweedledee refocused his attention on me, raising the gun, still pointed at Cam, and closing both hands on it. "Give me your phone!" His voice shook with rage.

Blood pounded in my ears. *A snake... a lion...* I couldn't visualise it... what if I missed? What if what happened when I'd tried to shoot Metcalfe the first time, happened again? If I didn't get in a clean shot first, he would shoot back at us, and he'd hit one of us at this range.

Holding up my left hand, palm towards him, without breaking eye contact, I reached slowly with my right into my coat pocket. I gripped the handle of the Ruger, my finger finding the trigger. At that instant, I saw not the face of Tweedledee, but the sneering visage of my old boss as the target.

I may be a third-rate scientist, but you are not the master of me!

I pulled out my hand and fired at his head. He went down like a puppet with the strings cut, into the mud, and the gun's report echoed over the rocky headlands. The wind instantly whipped away the smoke and the gunpowder scent the shot gave out, and Tweedledee lay before me, his expression blank yet subtly misshapen and not quite natural, an entry hole dead centre in his forehead.

Tweedledum stared at the body on the ground. He looked at Cam, and then at me. I'd killed Tweedledee. Not self defence, not manslaughter, just cold premeditated murder. He was a scumbag. *So am I.* I'd walked into this insanity with my eyes open that afternoon when I'd decided to go to the bridge club.

I didn't know if Tweedledum had his own gun. If he didn't, Tweedledee's was lying on the ground nearby. I pointed my gun at him, and he looked back at me, his expression oddly childlike. How was it Sage had described him? *Not the sharpest knife...*

Some distance away in the fog-blurred bulk of the land, a blue light flashed, and the wind carried the faint sound of a siren.

Drawn by my change in focus, Tweedledum cast over his shoulder to see the approaching police.

"Walk away," I said. "Take your chances with the police, or die here."

Tweedledum looked at Tweedledee's body again. He glanced once at me, and then turned and ran back towards their car, abandoning his dead comrade. An engine started, revved, and faded away.

"We need to get off here," said Cam. "I've abseiled on these cliffs." He pointed along the rocky edge of land. "There's a couple of places down there, though you wouldn't know it from up here. There are parts of the cliff where it's hard to see what's below from the top."

I looked down at the sea boiling in the chasms between the rocks far below. I looked up into the grey of the sky. "We've still got the blood. We have to make it look like the Tweedles killed us."

Awkwardly, he struggled out of the backpack. He retrieved the blood bags, the computer, and the plastic wallet with his documents in.

"Hold up the bag," I said, "facing me and away from you."

He did as I asked, and I fired the gun through it. The bags had thawed inside the rucksack. We punctured the first one and squeezed it out over the rucksack on the ground. Then we spilt the other open and scattered it on the ground and in a trail up to the edge. It poured down onto the rocks and the wind caught it and strewed it away in a stream of tiny droplets. Ashes to ashes, dust to dust. These were the last remains of our old lives. Scattered and gone. The empty plastic bags fluttered aimlessly about the cliff face before they caught the wind and sailed out to sea.

Cam held my hand and I followed him along the line of the cliff. "We need to climb down, quickly. Tweedledum probably delayed them a bit, but the police will be here soon."

My foot slid on wet rock, my hip crashed into the hard

ground. The world became a chaotic jumble of rocks and sky. I don't know what would have happened had he not caught my sleeve. "Take your time," he exhorted.

I went backwards down the route he showed me, the sharp edges of rocks digging into my knees and hands. Most of it was clambering down a slope and moving along the side of the rockface, but there was a steep drop to a ledge below, alarming for the sheer fall to the sea beneath it. Once we'd slid down, a depression in the face of the rock sank into a narrow crack of a cave that offered some shelter from the wind. We pressed ourselves together into it, and we waited.

It was really, *really* cold on this exposed cliff, and now the adrenaline had worn off I was breaking out in uncontrollable shivers and starting to feel the bruising where I'd fallen against the rock. I pushed my back in against the hard Atlantic stone, directing my eyes away from the vertigo-inducing scene below, and held on to him.

I used to feel shame and guilt, even anger, when I thought about the person I used to be and what I did. But now it was as though a tsunami had washed over the past, taking all the negative emotions I'd associated with it. History was just things that had happened, decisions that couldn't be undone, no matter how bad they were.

Father, I'm coming after you. Not that he'd recognise me even if we could meet again, not after everything that had happened. I wasn't the daughter I'd been in his time. That girl had grown into someone else, and the world had moved on. The revelation had come upon me when I'd stood for his favourite song, when the curtains had closed over his coffin. My eyes had burned, although every other part of me had been numb, my mother beside me, mascara streaked down her face. I'd realised that all these platitudes about going somewhere else spoken by pious priests to those who listened were just sham and lies, people kidding themselves because they couldn't come to terms with their own mortality. My dad killed himself, and innocence died on the day of his funeral. And he didn't go anywhere, apart from to a cold grave.

The veil that separated the living from the dead seemed frayed and thin in this place, suspended in limbo between the wrath of the ocean below and the world above that sought to destroy us.

There came distant snatches of human voice carried by the wind from the land above. The throb of a helicopter's passing made us press ourselves in tighter to the back of the shallow cave. Still we waited, the cold eating into us. The day began to wane, and the lighthouse above began to once more cast its beam out over the ocean.

"We can't wait any longer," said Cam. "Let's get rid of the evidence and start climbing back up."

I took the gun out of my pocket, and threw it as hard as I could away from me, towards the sea. My pact with it was over. I did the same with my mobile phone, and then with the SatNav. Cam threw his phone and his laptop off the cliff, destroying the trail of bank accounts we'd used to launder the money.

"You got your IDs?"

I nodded.

"Okay. You first."

He pushed from behind as I grasped my way up back the steep rise from the ledge. I was lying on my chest just over by the time his reach ran out of range. I used the rocky surface to haul myself up. I turned around and leant back towards him. "Come on, climb up."

But this seemed easier said than done. When I'd climbed

up, I'd had him pushing and supporting behind me. When he tried to get footholds, the cliff started to disintegrate and pieces fell away under him. I tried to pull him up, but he weighed nearly twice what I did, and the laws of physics were against me. The rock at the top of the cliff was hard and jagged, and it dug into my knees so sharply it made me gasp and brought tears to my eyes whenever I put my weight against it to try to get leverage. I was cold, so cold, and my hands had become feeble and numb, and I couldn't seem to get a firm grip on him.

He looked up at me, eyes fierce, exhorting. "Go and look for a rope, or get help. Or just leave and let the police have me. You have a chance at everything we talked about. Go to New Zealand and see your aunt and uncle. Save yourself."

"You know I can't do that." Because I knew he wouldn't let the police have him. I knew that if I turned away from this ledge for one moment, I'd return to find the narrow space below empty. My vision blurred. Why was I stuck here? Why couldn't I save this situation? Why was this like my dad, all over again?

I remembered him sitting in the living room, a glass of whisky or something in his hand, and he looked like a zombie, like he'd stopped living. An American action film was on the telly, with car chases and guns and helicopters, him staring at it, not watching it, like the images were going in his eyes but his brain wasn't processing them.

I'd gone up to him, and I'd said, *I love you Dad*. And he put down his glass and put his hand on my shoulder, and said, *I love you too, kid*. And he looked at me, but he didn't *see* me.

I've asked myself a thousand times what I should have said instead that night to make that morning right. If he'd loved me, he wouldn't have done it.

If I'd loved him better, he wouldn't have done it.

My cousin used to say if you failed at something, it was because it was meant to be that way. It was fate, she used to say, and the Universe had other plans for you. It probably goes some way to explain why she only got four GCSEs, and one of them was in Food Technology. I'd thought it was stupid back then, and I still think it's stupid now. There's not some great cosmic conspiracy that says we can't have what we want. What happens to us depends on our actions and our choices. There's a parallel universe where wind and tide eroded the cliff face differently and either the police caught us or we both plunged to our deaths. There's a parallel universe where I stand up here and I walk away. I can see all these separate outcomes, these different futures of myself, like I'm standing in a hall of mirrors at an amusement park, and they're all distant and untouchable.

I looked down on the churning waves below the rocks, and at this moment I never want to see the sea again for as long as I live. There's a parallel universe where my grip fails and he falls.

But it will not be this one, and it will not be me!

I leaned forward and took hold of his belt, and pulled with all my strength. The rocks dug in to my kneecaps as I struggled against his weight. The pain was unbearable. For a moment the hideous noise of waves and wind became distorted and my view of the world turned to static.

And then Cam's hand was up on the rocks and he was hauling himself away from it, and I realised that somehow I'd made myself more than human for those few seconds when it mattered. I opened my eyes and saw the sky, and I put down my hand and felt solid rock. I was still alive and the world was still here. *Dad, you can keep your cold coffin and your afterlife, because I am not going to make your history happen again.*

Cam was saying something, and it seemed like he'd been saying it for a while and I hadn't been hearing it.

"You have to get up."

I was chilled to the bone, but his hand still felt warm, sort of, as he pulled me up. Clinging to each other, we retraced the route back up to the headland.

The Tweedles' car had gone, and so had Tweedledee's body and Cam's bloodstained rucksack, just a muddy crisscross of tyre-tracks on the road that might have been dirty with more than just mud, and a few forgotten coloured plastic markers of the sort forensics use when they take photographs, betrayed that anything had happened here.

We hobbled together back towards the lighthouse. My bad knee hurt like hell. A car was coming, but it was growing dark and they wouldn't see us unless the headlamps chanced upon us, or we stood up against the empty sky. We managed to get behind the wall around the garden, away from the road, before I collapsed again.

Cam held me to him, and in the warmth of his embrace my head gradually stopped swimming and my grasp on reality pulled together.

"We're getting cold," he said. "We can't stay here any longer. Let's go back to the village and find a B&B."

"Do you think the police think we're dead?"

Cam breathed out as he helped me to my feet. "I hope so. There's only one road out of here, so hopefully they've got Tweedledum and they won't believe him if he tells them what really happened."

Every step on that darkening moor was agony. I was sure if I fell over again I would just fall asleep and never wake, but Cam was there, holding me up. The only thing that kept me going that night was him being there, and the image in my head of us going into an airport with our good fake IDs and leaving the country, never to be pursued by the law again. And that thought was real. I could reach out and touch it. In a few days we would be there, doing that.

At last we found ourselves in a street, although I didn't remember clearly how we got there, and everything was numb, like in a dream. I remember the light in the window, and there was a sign there, but I couldn't read it.

Inside, I remember Cam speaking, and it sounded like his voice was coming from somewhere distant underground. *My wife's taken a funny turn while we were walking. I wondered if we might have a room for the night.*

Then there was a woman's voice, sounding concerned, but I didn't understand the words.

No, it's nothing serious. Just a medical condition she suffers with from time to time. It's under control.

My feet stumbled on stairs, Cam still beside me. Then, a door, and a light.

As soon as I was inside the room, the strength that had carried me all this way, across the cold and empty moor through boundaries I'd never known existed, left me. I fell on my face on the bed and just lay there. Every part of me ached with cold and exhaustion. My hands felt callused and grotesque against the fabric of the duvet, the rough skin snaring on the weave.

Cam sat in a chair and tried to pull his shoes off. He was so weak and uncoordinated he looked as though he was drunk. I stared at the brown pattern on the coffee-coloured wallpaper, and it struck me as kind of profound and simultaneously silly that I was probably legally dead now, and yet I was lying here staring at this banal wallpaper and doing the same stupid little things that every person alive does.

There came a knock on the door. "Come in!" Cam called out.

The handle jerked down and the bottom of the door rubbed on the carpet. The old lady entered, carrying a teapot and cups on a tray.

She looked at me on the bed, and at Cam collapsed in the chair, and it was only then that revelation started to dawn on her face. The crockery began to rattle uncontrollably on the tray. "Oh, God, it's you," she began. "They say that you're a maniac," the pitch of her voice was beginning to rise, "and a child molester!"

I didn't have the strength to get up. If she called the police and they came for me, they'd have to handcuff me here and drag me off the bed and outside to the car. All I could manage right now was to turn my head to face her. I managed to say, "The media is not the whole truth."

Cam heaved himself up to take hold of her tray; it was threatening to tip its contents over the carpet. He set it down on the table and stepped back, watching the woman warily, as though she held a loaded gun. For an instant, the thought of killing her crossed my mind. Perhaps I shouldn't have thrown away the Ruger.

"Please sit down," he said. "If you will listen, we can try to explain to you what it is we did and why we did it. But please don't call the police. The police think we're dead, and it's very unlikely they're going to come looking for us. You're not risking anyone by letting us stay here."

Shaking, the old lady reached behind her, groping for the arms of a chair. She sat in it and spread her fingers over her face.

"I'm not a child molester," Cam began.

"Shut up!" she shouted at him, taking her hands away from her face. "I don't want to hear it!"

The air in that room weighed down, suffocating me against the mattress, as I watched the woman force out a shudder of a sigh, her fingers twining with the forelock of silver hair overhanging her face.

After what seemed like a long time, she spoke in a low voice. "My son used to be a... a physiotherapist. Until one day a customer of his decided to tell the police he sexually assaulted her while he was trying to show her exercises to help her, and I knew he wouldn't do that. And the police arrested him and he got taken to court, and even though they cleared him of the charges, his name was ruined and he ended up bankrupt and homeless."

I stared at the woman from where I lay crushed. This was not what I had expected.

She ran her fingers through her hair again. "I have read all manner of things in the papers. Some of them make you out to be a tragic romance story, starving people who turned to crime to survive. Others call you murderers and deviants."

The woman took her hands away from her face and gripped the arms of the chair. "I have had enough with the law. I think — I think if you pay your bills and do not go causing trouble — I think I shall not say anything about you having been here to anyone."

As she left the room, the only response I was able to give was a weak gasp of, "Thanks."

Cam reached his hand onto the bed feebly, and then he was lying next to me. It was all I could do to lay my hand on his and let sleep and the warmth of the room heal our exhausted bodies.

20

YELLOW PRESS

THE BLUE MOON SEVEN, AN OBITUARY

by Donna Besman

For the past few weeks, one story has made the headlines every day. Now, that story is finally over. It's time to reflect on what really happened out there, and who the real people behind the Blue Moon heist were, rather than the demonised and, in turn, angelised versions of them the media presented.

One of the reasons it took the police so long to discover the identities of the Seven is that they didn't actually know each others' identities. They identified each other using code-names, never asking or offering their real ones. Which is why, in this article, I've used the names they came to be known by to the police; the names they became notorious for; the names that, for a short while, caused the public to see the Seven as the romantic modern equivalent of Robin Hood or Alfred Noyes *The Highwayman*. If you want their real names, you'll find them on the front page of any broadsheet.

GENGHIS

Genghis's mother arrived in England in 1953, a refugee from the Korean War. She became pregnant by an Englishman and in 1954 gave birth to a son. This was possibly a failed attempt to gain British citizenship. Subsequently, Genghis was taken into care and his mother deported. Genghis never had a consistent home or loving people around him as a child. He left school with no qualifications and turned first to shoplifting and burglary, which eventually led to organised crime. Genghis was convicted and sent to jail twice, once for his involvement in an organised burglary of several shops in Birmingham's Jewellery Quarter, and on another occasion for fraud. He considered these two brief stints in the penal system as 'good networking opportunities' and they allowed him to make further contacts in the criminal underworld

Genghis was found guilty of numerous crimes and sentenced to twelve years in jail. We have been unable to trace his deported mother. He produced at least five children, and possibly more, from casual relationships in his early adulthood.

SAGE

Sage worked for most of his life as a clerk at an accountancy firm. At the age of 51, he lost his wife to cancer. Aged 65, he unwillingly retired from the job he loved. Soon after, he began to be affected by both arthritis and Parkinson's Disease. Finding conventional drugs only partly alleviated his condition, he began to self-medicate using cannabis, and this is how he came to be introduced to the world of crime and gained his involvement with the Seven. Sage's wish to feel useful and necessary, along with his desire for something to do in the retired life he felt was purposeless, drove him deeper into crime, and he became the mastermind behind many minor acts of fraud and deception, managing to evade detection for many years.

On the morning of the Blue Moon heist, Sage was involved with the handling of the money in the Seven's robbery. He suffered a heart attack in the getaway car, possibly brought on by the shock of seeing Tweedledee shoot a police constable who had attempted to intervene. His comrades took him to University Hospital in Birmingham, and three of them even risked arrest by accompanying him into A&E. Sage received treatment, but suffered another heart attack and died in hospital. He was 79 at the time of his death and is survived by one daughter, living in Australia at the time of writing.

ACE

A young black man with a foul mouth, Ace tended to intimidate older people with his language and his dress sense. He spent his youth in and out of school, rotating through a constant cycle of being suspended or expelled for swearing at teachers or what was seen as 'aggressive gesticulation'. He left school at sixteen, having never sat a single GCSE exam. This was despite a natural ability with figures and computers and an interest in science.

It was not realised until after he was arrested that Ace has Tourette's syndrome. Tourette's causes tics (involuntary movements) that can manifest as uncontrollable inappropriate language as well as limb and whole-body movements, of which Ace suffered both. Unemployable because of his condition, Ace wandered into petty crime. It was his ability with computers that drew attention to him from Genghis and how he came to become one of the Blue Moon Seven.

Ace was captured on the day of the Blue Moon heist when he and his fellow felons abandoned their getaway car in order to get Sage to hospital. While in disguise in purloined medical clothing, the police noticed something suspicious about him, resulting in his capture in the hospital gardens.

Ace was given a lenient sentence, taking into account his history and his undiagnosed condition, and the assertion that he had not been aware of Tweedledee's shooting of the police officer, which the judge believed. He is to spend two years in an open prison for young offenders with disabilities. We learned that Ace will be taking GCSEs later this year on the advice of staff at his detention unit, and hopes to do A-Levels in Maths and Computing should he be successful.

TWEEDLEDEE

Although he was the son of Genghis and the two were known to each other, neither Genghis nor Tweedledum's father had much involvement in the rearing of the two brothers. This was mainly because their mother didn't want a spousal living arrangement because this would reduce the amount of benefits she was entitled to. Indeed, Tweedledee was the penultimate of nine children in whose interests their mother spared little attention. She spent her time gambling and chatting to friends online, and seemed to view reproduction and the state funding it received as a means to an end.

Tweedledee was a violent boy who grew up to be a violent man. Although this could in part be blamed on his upbringing, it was also discovered on his postmortem that Tweedledee has the chromosomal abnormality XYY, a condition where a boy accidentally inherits two of the male y-chromosomes. This is thought by some specialists to lower IQ slightly and increase violent and aggressive behaviour in some people affected by the condition.

Tweedledee constantly brutalised his younger brother. He also tortured and eventually killed his mother's pet cat, along with a number of gerbils the family owned at one time, and a pet turtle which Tweedledee sadistically attempted to extract from the shell. His first experience of the legal system was at the age of twelve, after a 'crusade of terror' as the judge described it, against an elderly neighbour, culminating in the discovery by the neighbour of the mutilated corpse of her Yorkshire Terrier on her own doorstep, having had a firework inserted into a bodily orifice and lit. The police never ascertained whether the dog had been dead already at this point.

After serving his sentence at a young offenders' institute, Tweedledee spent much of his remaining teenage years in and out of jail. This ceased when he was seventeen, as he began to spend more time with his father. This was not, however, because Genghis was providing a good influence, but because he was teaching Tweedledee how not to be caught.

Tweedledee's contacts in the more violent, gang-dominated side of new criminality made him a valuable addition to the Seven, and Genghis must have felt a sense of familial responsibility towards the younger man.

Tweedledee was shot dead on the Butt of Lewis during an altercation with his half-brother Tweedledum and Doc and Cam.

TWEEDLEDUM

Tweedledum grew up a special needs child. At the age of eighteen, he had and IQ of sixty, putting him in the 'mentally retarded' or 'imbecile' bracket, and the mental age of a seven-year-old. From the day his mother brought him home from the hospital, Tweedledum's life was made a misery by his half-brother. Rather than growing to loathe and detest him, Tweedledum idolised his abusive elder brother, a condition specialists refer to as Stockholm syndrome.

Despite mitigating factors, Tweedledum was found to be guilty of Doc and Cam's murder by the court, with evidence suggesting both suffered gunshot wounds and died falling from the cliff if not from these outright. He will serve a life sentence. The judge recorded an open verdict as to the death of Tweedledee. Tweedledum denied that either he or Tweedledee fired any shots, and swore that Doc shot his half-brother, but it could be that in a heated disagreement about the spoils from the heist, Tweedledum finally chose to take revenge against his abusive older sibling.

CHAMELEON

Cam, as his partners in crime called him, was 32 at the time of his death. Of all of the Seven, his true identity was the one that took the longest for police to track down.

As a child attending school in Edinburgh, Cam was bullied incessantly and suffered with low self-confidence in his teenage years, which persisted into his early twenties. He was a socially awkward boy of reasonably good academic ability, who had a notable ability to do vocal impersonations and mannerisms of various famous individuals. At Leeds University, where he studied Law, he was academically successful and joined the local stand-up comedy club, but his romantic endeavours were met with derision and ridicule when he attempted to approach female students.

While celebrating his graduation and his recent success in obtaining a graduate post at a solicitor's firm, Cam had a sexual encounter while in an inebriated state with a fifteen-year-old girl. The girl later reported the incident to the police. Cam was found guilty of rape and sent to jail for three years, with his name added to the sex offenders' register.

In jail, word got around the other inmates that Cam's name was on the register, and that he was there for sexually assaulting a girl. Without knowing the full circumstances, his peers jumped to conclusions. He was assaulted several times during his time in jail on the grounds that 'paedophiles deserve it'. One of the assaults occurred while he was working in the prison kitchens, and necessitated skin grafts over a ten-square-inch area of his back. He left jail an emotionally and physically damaged man, unable to find employment because of his criminal record, his qualifications wasted.

Soon after his release, members of the public identified him as a sex offender and he was targeted, again by people unaware of the full circumstances. What began as graffiti escalated into bricks through the windows and petrol bombs. Fearing for his life, the police gave Cam a new identity and moved him elsewhere. His family had to sever all contact with him so as to avoid risk to themselves.

Soon after he disappeared. His training in law and his time in jail had given Cam insights into how the legal system worked. He'd become a master forger. He'd turned his talent for acting and voices to disguising himself from the unforgiving eye of the public. For years he sustained himself on fraud managed through a large number of bogus identities, never once being caught, and never trusting anyone. At some point in his dealings with the criminal world he met Genghis, and Genghis, somehow, over a period of time, managed to gain his trust. Cam was vital to the Seven in the way the money was laundered as soon as it was stolen, and in the planning and execution of the heist.

We do know that Cam never revealed his past to any of the surviving members of the Seven, although he was known to have friendships with Sage and particularly Ace. Whether or not he revealed it to Doc is a secret they both take to their graves.

DOC

Doc died aged 30, falling from the cliffs at the Butt of Lewis. Tweedledum denied either he or Tweedledee had shot her, but the identification of her blood on the cliff suggests otherwise, and since her body was never found, the truth will probably never be known for sure.

Born to middle-class parents in a picturesque locale in Solihull, Doc was an only child. Her father, with whom she is believed to have had a strong relationship, sadly took his own life when Doc was twelve, after his relationship with his wife became strained and he lost his job at an accounting firm. This early trauma was to have a profound effect on a girl who would grow up to be a woman who herself struggled with depression and unemployment.

Doc studied Chemistry at Bristol University, gaining both a BSc and a PhD. She went on to work for a drugs design firm in Birmingham. During this time, Doc's mother was diagnosed with Alzheimer's disease and her paternal aunt and uncle, with whom she also had strong ties, emigrated to New Zealand following a traumatic house burglary.

Investigations into Doc's previous work uncovered several complaints made over a number of years by her of bullying from her line manager. All of these allegations appear to have been dropped or otherwise concealed by the company's directors. Towards the end of her term of employment there, NHS records show Doc had been diagnosed with stress-related illness and was also suffering from regular panic attacks at her workplace. Following such an attack and while on sick leave as recommended by her GP, Doc was made redundant from her job, with the reason given being a funding cutback and a necessary staff reduction.

Due to a combination of the recession at the time and being unable to obtain a good reference from her previous line manager, Doc was unable to find employment subsequent to this. Her medical records show she developed depression and received treatment for it for some time. A year after losing her job, Doc had exhausted her savings.

She could not afford to heat her house, or to feed herself, and she lived in fear of her mortgage going into arrears and her home being repossessed due to a recent cut on mortgage interest assistance for those on benefits.

When she met Genghis in the Jobcentre, and he offered her the chance to earn the money she so desperately needed doing the work she knew and loved, it seems quite understandable that she was prepared to overlook the fact the drugs he asked her to synthesise were illegal. As she became more deeply embroiled in the Seven's felony, she and Cam became lovers.

In the Blue Moon Casino heist, Doc acted as getaway driver and provided forensics advice to the Seven. Her quick thinking was no doubt at least in part responsible for the successful escape from the hospital by her and Cam when the plan went wrong. That she and Cam survived so long without being captured when the case became so public and so significant is a testament to both of their wit, their courage, and their faith in each other.

Doc is survived by her mother, who lives in a nursing home in Solihull.

AFTERMATH

There is something about the Blue Moon Seven, and about Doc and Cam in particular, that has captivated the British public. Though forensic evidence says even if Doc and Cam survived the gunshot wounds, they could not possibly have survived the fall into the sea below, where they undeniably did fall due to the volume of their blood that was found on the cliff, crackpot theories abound about how they might still live; how they might, as you read this, be lying on some tropical beach and living off their ill-gotten gains. We almost wish these felons had lived and had escaped with their freedom. Perhaps it's nothing more than the perceived glamour of their lifestyle compared to the humdrum repetition of reality that forms most of our day-to-day living. Perhaps it's that they died together in strife, rather than be captured and live without each other — the 'Bonnie and Clyde Factor' as some reporters have been calling it over the past few weeks.

On the other hand, perhaps we sympathise with these people because this case says something about our legal system and the world we live in that resonates with us. Each of these seven individuals has been wronged by society. Each of them has had something that was a part of them stolen by some faceless entity, be that entity corporate management, the school system, the government, or any other unaccountable bureaucracy. The things that were stolen from them were nothing less than their freedom, their future, their family, perhaps even their sanity in some cases, and other pieces of our selves and lives we might otherwise consider fundamental entitlements. When we read that Doc and Cam had evaded capture again and that Tweedledum and Tweedledee were still at large, did a part of us deep inside feel they had a right to what they had taken, that they were only stealing back what was correctly theirs? When we read that Doc and Cam had been killed and that Tweedledum and Tweedledee had finally been arrested, was there anyone amongst us who did not feel regret; who did not know in the depths of his or her soul that a great injustice had been done?

The case is finally closed. While the money was unfortunately not recovered due to the complicated method Cam and Doc used to launder it, it is presumably still scattered throughout various accounts, and most of it will, we presume, be recovered by either the government or members of the public when those accounts eventually go unclaimed for a long enough time. Everything returns to normal, and as the hype dies down and analysis articles (such as this one) disappear from our newsstands, the Blue Moon Casino Heist and its band of merry men will fade from the media spotlight. It will, however, live on in the hearts of the people touched by its perpetrators' struggles and strife.

And, if you happen to receive a statement from a bank where you are sure you don't have an account telling you have ten grand in savings, one might be forgiven for spending the money quietly on something nice, and raising a drink with your mates to the Blue Moon Casino.

21

GOLDEN DAYS

"You finished reading it?" I set down my glass on the rough surface of the table.

A warm breeze tumbled locks of salt-and-pepper over Cam's forehead and ruffled the pages of the newspaper he held as he raised his grey eyes to me.

"Shall we keep this?" he said.

I smiled at him. Cam discreetly tore the page away from the central crease and folded it up behind the shelter of the paper. He put the folded square into his pocket as he stood up, and shoved the remainder of the newspaper into the litter bin as we walked together away from the patio and onto the beach.

"I'm glad Ace got off lightly," I said.

"Yes," Cam agreed. "I hope he gets his qualifications, and when he gets out he'll get a job he likes, and that he'll have a life to be happy about."

"It wasn't too late for him, like it was for the rest of us."

We walked steadily along the beach, away from the hotel with its thatched roofs and the straw parasols over the wood tables. I breathed deep the clean air and watched how the slight breeze moved the fronds of the palms ever so gently. It stirred Cam's hair and his loose Hawaiian shirt and fluttered my sarong around my shins.

"When Ace gets out, I want us to work out a way of

getting some money to him. Let's invent a dead great aunt or someone, and set up a trust fund, or something like that. Can you do that?"

Cam nodded. "Yes, that can be done."

"Perhaps we ought to try to give Genghis some too?" I suggested.

"Screw Genghis. He doesn't care about anybody apart from himself. He's probably plotting his next heist in jail as we speak. I expect he's already found some other group of mugs to help him."

Networking. That had been something my old boss was into.

Two surgically enhanced young women in bikinis threw derisive scowls in our direction as they headed up the beach.

"They probably go to some stinking night club and get pissed, and have crap sex with a stranger on the beach," Cam suggested.

"And get sand up their unmentionables."

"And not be able to remember it in the morning."

"Youth is wasted on the young," I said.

He frowned. "Did we always sound this middle aged?"

I laughed and pressed in close to Cam as we walked, slipping my arm around his waist and taking comfort from the feel of his flesh under the fresh cotton of his shirt. In the evening, we would turn the air conditioning right up as far as it would go, so we could snuggle together, almost like being back in the Hebrides in the winter, or in Birmingham on the dole and unable to afford to run the central heating.

"What if it doesn't work out?" I said. "What if our cover gets blown?"

Cam glanced at me sideways. "Or you might get bored of this fool's paradise, and being in it with this old fool."

I stopped walking momentarily to dig my toes into the wet sand. I smeared my foot down the side of his calf. "I don't think I'm going to get bored of you. I don't think I have the energy to get bored these days."

"Well, if ever you do, we can always both be someone else, somewhere else, together." He shrugged, settling me more firmly under his arm with the motion.

THE END

Also by Manda Benson

PILGRENNON'S CHILDREN

Pilgrennon's Beacon

Dana Provine is an autistic girl with a secret ability to mentally control computers, who runs away from bullies at her school in Coventry after a hospital scan reveals an object lodged in her brain. A compelling signal leads her north to the Outer Hebrides and an abandoned military facility on the remote and supposedly haunted Flannan Isles, where she hopes to untangle the mystery shrouding her birth and her missing parents. But as the lies of the past unfold, Dana unwittingly finds herself the focus of events that will change the future for everyone.

The Emerald Forge

Following the Information Terrorism attack on London, a radical new government has risen to power. The world is changing, but so far as it concerns Dana Provine, an unusual autistic girl growing up in an unforgiving society, everyday life is much the same. When Dana is troubled by disturbing dreams about a hospital, and a boy from school who seems to know far too much about the past starts following her, it's just two more problems on top of many. But when she encounters a bizarre construct, half beast, half machine, she realises something dangerous is going on that could affect everyone. The answer she seeks could confirm both her greatest hope and her deepest fear: that Ivor Pilgrennon still lives.

TANGENTRINE

Milton Keynes UK
Ingram Content Group UK Ltd.
UKHW041037110224
437582UK00005B/330